Like a Man

Also by David Chacko

Price
Gage
Brick Alley
The Black Chamber
White Gamma
Red Bishop One
The Shadow Master
A Long Way from Eden
Less Than a Shadow
The Peacock Angel
Graveyard Eyes
Martyr's Creek

Like a Man

David Chacko

Foremost Press
Cedarburg, Wisconsin

David can be reached at his website at
http://www.davidchacko.com
or by email at david@davidchacko.com

Second Edition
First Edition published 2003.

Published by Foremost Press

ISBN-10: 0-9723737-4-8
ISBN-13: 978-0-9723737-4-6

Cover Design by Betul Aydiner

This is a work of fiction. Any similarity of characters or events to real persons or actual events is coincidental.

For Chuck Byler

If future generations ask us
what we were fighting for in this war,
we shall tell them the story of Lidice.

Frank Knox
U.S. Secretary of the Navy
Washington, 1942

I survived, and today
there is an emptiness around me.
All my friends, those who worked with me,
are dead. . . . My hair is gray.
Once again I teach chemistry and
walk between the school benches.

Ladislav Vanek
alias Jindra
Prague, 1965

Part One:

Falcons

CHAPTER 1

Churchill was pleased when he inspected the Czechoslovak troops at Edgehill and found them in the semblance of British uniform. That task had consumed the better part of six months, but since the Czech Brigade had little to do, and nowhere to go, speed did not seem of the first consequence.

For all that time, Hitler sat with his armies in France as if he liked the long view. With his air fleet badly damaged, and his sea-going fleet stillborn, the middle-class Anti-Christ had postponed his Operation Sea Lion indefinitely. For that long was England safe.

Churchill hoped that he would be apprised of any change in the mind of the monster. SIS had made progress in deciphering the product of the Enigma machines that encoded German military communications. When Sea Lion was put off, he knew of the decision within six weeks.

Six days would have been better. Six hours, of course, was the purview of God—and President Benes.

The little man walked at Churchill's side with his hand at his breast under his topcoat. In many ways, Benes seemed to mirror the land that he had been elected to govern—compact, industrious, efficient. When the Allies handed Czechoslovakia to Hitler, they had given a madman the means to conduct an intercontinental war, and prolong it endlessly.

The Hun had it all—the Skoda Works, the arms factories in Brno, the rolling stock that made Prague the turnstile of Europe, the tanks and aircraft of their well-equipped army—everything but the inner workings of the Czech intelligence service, which had been transferred intact to England. Its networks were what made Benes no mere ally, but the oracle of this war to date.

"Impressive." Churchill gestured with his walking stick. "Look at that fellow. He's seven feet from the ground."

Benes began to move closer to the sergeant in the front rank, but stopped when he noticed the photographer ahead. Conscious of his image, the little man would never allow himself to be trapped in the same frame with a giant. It was part of the wartime fiction: that Old Winnie was usually sober; that Roosevelt could walk.

"Almost all these troops saw action in France," said Benes in the soft voice made softer by the silvery mustache at his lip. "To a man, they're anxious for another chance."

"They will have it," said Churchill. "The question is when and where."

"That is no longer the question," said Benes. "It is doubtful that it will be here. And certainly it will not be soon."

His quiet words thumped like horse-apples onto the spring grass as he continued up the line. The little man was being coy. Benes was well aware that his sources were not simply the best available to the Allies, but at times the only ones.

Still, Churchill waited to enquire of the Sibyl until the end of the formation had been reached; until the voices of the squad leaders began to sound up and down the line; until the Humber staff-cars were in sight, and he had lit a cigar.

"I take it, sir, that you have word."

"Yes," said Benes. "From Three Kings."

That was how Benes always referred to the information that came from on high and so far in advance. Although MI6 held the opinion that Three Kings was only one man well-placed in Nazi intelligence, that did not detract from his infallibility.

"And what do the wise men say?"

"That Hitler will invade Russia," said Benes in a whisper. "Operation Barbarossa, so-called, commences in June."

"But are you sure? We've been told this before."

"The plan has been in circulation for a year or more," said Benes. "It was presented as a contingency, but it's the same plan, and it will be enacted soon. I'm told the campaign would have begun already if Hitler had not diverted his resources to Yugoslavia and Greece."

Diverted his resources. That was too coy for the rhetoric that lay in Churchill's breast like a heart. Belgrade had been bombed into rubble. The Yugoslav and Greek armies were destroyed within a month. Four British divisions sent in relief had been overwhelmed and withdrawn in an action no less remarkable than Dunkirk. It seemed impossible that any good could come of catastrophes of that magnitude unless—

"If Hitler attacks Russia in June, he could be caught by the oncoming winter."

Benes shrugged. "The German General Staff is predicting a six week campaign."

"Are they as mad as he?"

"Perhaps," said Benes. "Their aim is to smash the Russian Army. At a minimum, they think they will be able to control enough territory so Russian bombers cannot reach important industrial areas in Germany. They will succeed, I think."

A very correct, very dry assessment. It reminded Churchill, as he consulted his flask, that Benes did not drink either.

"That degenerate will succeed until he fails. He took a backward step when he attacked England and lost so much of his air force. If he commits his armies to Russia, they will be lost in that immensity."

"It seems unlikely that he can conduct a two-front war."

"Yes," said Churchill. "But it's the myth that matters. To this point he's been invulnerable. The Wehrmacht invincible. A crack in the facade is precisely what we need."

"Let's hope we have it soon," said Benes. "The Russian officer corps is in disarray due to Stalin's purges. And taking the Baltic lands has stretched their lines of defense much too far."

All true. But Churchill was thinking again of myth. It was the most abused and powerful force on earth. Any man who knew history knew that first.

"Adolf Hitler will not conquer Russia," said Churchill, liking the sound of it. "If what Three Kings says is true, what the Hitler gang has done is present us with an ally. A formidable ally."

Benes nodded as if he had found the means to express the things he wanted most. "The nature of this war will change in an instant. The role of the occupied countries, too. With Russia under attack, we would be obliged to mount actions of our own."

"What sort?"

"Clandestine actions."

"These would be—" Churchill paused for the word that best fit the moment, and his inclinations. "Spectacular."

Benes nodded with the single most vigorous action that he had ever shown. "I guarantee it."

"We must have the world's full attention, and its help," said Churchill. "This war will be won by all, or it will not be won at all."

"I promise you the complete dedication of my men," said Benes. "They will require special training, of course."

"They will most certainly have it."

"And the government of Czechoslovakia in exile must be recognized as the unified voice of the land."

"Agreed."

CHAPTER 2

Mallaig, Scotland
September, 1941

"Sergeant-Major Josef Gabcik, sir."

Franta looked over the battered table in the borrowed office of the Scottish castle where his paras were being trained. The man he saw was of middle height and an extremely compact build. He might be said to be of pleasing compact looks—brown hair parted so far back that it seemed hardly parted at all, bright and quick blue eyes under sleepy lids, a mouth that smiled easily. All these things were good. Excellent.

"Call me Franta," he said. "It's good practice to dispense with rank."

"Yes, Franta."

"Do you know why we do it?"

"I imagine I'll find out," he said, smiling.

Czech NCOs understood how to handle their officers. They ran the army, and they knew it. This one had run considerably more. He held the Czechoslovak War Cross and French Croix de Guerre. By one account, he had been the last man to give up the Battle of the Marne.

"Perhaps it would interest you to know that you're the best man here at Cammus Darrah," he said. "Your English instructors think they've never seen a better soldier pass through commando school."

Gabcik smiled again. "I doubt that's true. What impresses Englishmen is someone who speaks their language. I do it better than most."

"That says a great deal about your intelligence. English is a difficult language."

"Not for me," he said. "I was born in the homeland, but my father lived many years in America. I would have grown up an American if the Depression hadn't forced him to return home."

The rest of his life was as interesting. Several years in the Home Army. After the German occupation, he sabotaged a magazine of poison gas and escaped to Poland. Later, he enlisted in the Foreign Legion, which took him to France for the fighting and to England for the long wait. Only one point of his dossier demanded clarification.

"I understand that you were born near Zilina."

"Yes, Franta."

"At the foothills of the mountains," he said. "Are there still bear in those hills?"

"Not many, I think."

"It's quite beautiful. In the mountains. In all Slovakia."

Gabcik did not react quickly to the statement, although he understood what lay behind it: the Germans had split Slovakia into a separate fascist state. Many Slovaks no longer saw themselves as citizens of a united nation. And that mattered.

"I believe in free Czechoslovakia," Gabcik said finally. "That was Tomas Masaryk's dream, and mine, too."

"You've proven that," said Franta. "But some people require assurance of a man who will operate behind enemy lines. There must be no doubt as to any part of your allegiance."

"There is none."

Franta understood why the English thought so highly of this man. Though not quite thirty, he conveyed an impression of calm that was nerveless. Nothing hesitant. Nothing backward. His skill in every aspect of clandestine warfare was awesome.

"What if you were asked—" Franta hesitated for the right word. "What if you were ordered to do something that most people, even most soldiers, would think of as . . . unacceptable?"

"I can't imagine what that would be," said Gabcik quickly. "We're at war with Nazis. It's total war."

"So you will do anything you're told?"

"Without hesitation."

This is the man, thought Franta. This is the one who will do the unthinkable, and do it very well.

* * *

London
December 28, 1941

This should be classified, thought Benes, as another descending rhythm. In late spring, the Gestapo arrested the first of the Three Kings in Prague. Less than one month later, a direction-finding van tracked a radio signal that led the Germans to Colonel Masin and Leon.

Masin had fought the SS troops, wounding several before he was captured. Leon escaped into the underground. He was still at large, still in Prague, but hard-pressed to maintain contact with his primary source in German Army intelligence.

The information that had come like crown jewels now arrived seldom if at all. Benes had lost influence with Churchill and the Russians, who demanded every scrap of intelligence throughout the long autumn of Barbarossa. They had already accused him of withholding information in their hour of need.

The only answer Benes had were his paras. Six months training had put them at a peak of readiness. Tonight, a three-man team—Silver A—would drop into Bohemia with a transmitter. Their mission was to reestablish the link between the Last King and London. Silver B, a two-man team dropped at the same time, would provide backup.

One more team was to jump with the group—Anthropoid. Benes had chosen the name from his store of the macabre. It meant to describe a creature that resembled what it was supposed to be, but lacked just the thing that made it so.

Benes remembered the two sergeants chosen for the mission. One Czech. One Slovak. Good balance—and hardly cynical. Impressive biographies and skills. Both would have been officers if the army had not been so top-heavy. Both spoke English, but the Slovak did it better than Benes.

"Tell me, Franta, will the radio teams maintain contact with Anthropoid?"

"No, sir. If Anthropoid is successful, we'll know instantly."

"But what if they encounter difficulties? Shouldn't they have some way of communicating with the others?"

"It would be dangerous for anyone to have knowledge of them, sir. The Anthropoid team must remain in isolation."

"Won't that make the job more complex?"

"In these matters, the easiest way is never a consideration," said Franta. "Every person who knows of their presence increases the danger of discovery by a factor of five. That's especially true in the beginning, when capture is most likely."

"Do you think our paras would talk?"

"The Gestapo are unsubtle, sir. A man who falls into their hands is asked one question. 'Who are your collaborators'? The torture continues until the names are given—or the victim dies."

"And this is always so?"

"Always," said Franta kindly.

Benes accepted the word of his closest advisor. Franta had long ago proven himself far-sighted. When it became clear that the West would award their country to Hitler to satisfy his claims of race, Franta evacuated Prague, taking his files and staff to a waiting plane for England. Was he ever wrong?

"What are the chances for this mission? Realistically."

Franta's face swayed to and fro in the shadows of the lamp. His dark eyes moved toward the light and became strangely polar. "If they survive the drop, and the first forty-eight hours, I'd say reasonably good."

"Good?"

"Fifty-fifty."

The odds suddenly seemed high. Those two NCOs appeared in Benes' mind as if they would never die.

"Perhaps I should have asked the chances for failure," he said. "There's no way to calculate the aftereffects of this. That makes it very risky."

"The aircraft's not yet over the drop-zone," said Franta quickly but with little conviction. "I'll phone Tangmere Field. They'll radio ahead. The mission could be aborted."

A tempting offer. What could Anthropoid really do except light a torch?

But it would certainly do that. The flames would be seen all the way to America. The attack on Pearl Harbor three weeks ago had brought them into the war. What they needed—what all the allies needed—was a symbol of resistance to terror.

"No, Franta. This is a chance we must take. If our men are successful, the whole world will know Anthropoid. And they'll know us for what we are."

CHAPTER 3

After two hours in a plane with no soundproofing and the engines hammering, Josef Gabcik found that he was hardly nervous, hardly capable of thought. The telepathic farewells that he might have made with the living had been shaken from his mind. The deep vibrations had entered his bones and exchanged meaning, as if he were bonded by rivets and struts, a creation in steel, something new and composite.

And that was true. He knew that he must respond to the name Zdenek from now on; that he must think of himself as Zdenek; that he must rehearse and even dream the new life.

For how long? Days? A week or a fortnight? Setting up the mission would probably take that long, but once they were in position to close out Anthropoid, he did not see how it could be more than a matter of hours to the end.

Zdenek was the best small-arms marksman in the Czech Brigade. The man sitting beside him on the canvas webbing, Jan Kubis—code-named Ota—was as good with explosives. In training, Ota had tossed a grenade fifty yards on a trajectory with little arc to a target the size of a bushel basket. His gray eyes were twenty-ten, as bright as alloy. His hands were the size of two men's. His only vices were cigarettes and poor card tricks.

They had left Brigade together and stayed together in the same string of volunteers for months. First, at the commando in Scotland, where they honed necessary skills; then to England for training in special means. It was October when they finally came to the estate that was called STS 2 by the English and Shithouse Manor by everyone else. There, they were put on ice with a small number of men who awaited orders.

Sitting on the canvas bench seats in the bay of the Halifax with Zdenek, sweating in the superheated cold, were six men who had also been with him at STS 2. To a man they were communications specialists.

He knew what they would do on the ground—reestablish the radio link with London—but he did not know the details. If these men had absorbed any of their training, they would not tell him anything—not even Valcik, his best friend. Even if they had wanted to speak, Zdenek would not have heard their words through the noise of the engines and the rubber helmet strapped to his head.

Zdenek had not seen any of the comm specialists for weeks—not since the day the colonel called Franta picked up Josef and Jan from STS 2 and delivered them as Zdenek and Ota to a safe house in London.

Things were well there. They had the first floor of a private dwelling to themselves, separate rooms, a kitchen of the English sort and a garden of the same. Women—whores but nice ones—twice a week. A library of books that more than anything made him feel rich for having read nothing but the covers.

In some ways, the new space was strangely disruptive to Zdenek. He had to admit there was something in him that missed the barracks, the everlasting noise, the bets on everything, the feeling of the hive. He had lived so long with elbows in his face—in the home army before the war, on the run in Poland, and in the village near Shakespeare's birthplace where they were billeted at brigade—that he found it hard to remember another way of living.

They saw no countrymen for three weeks except of course, Franta. Although they knew that they had been chosen for something important, they were surprised when one day a staff car picked them up and brought to the office of the president of the Republic, Doctor Benes, who gave them their mission.

Do this thing, he said. Change the world.

* * *

They were deep over German territory when the fighters began to dog them. Zdenek had no idea what had happened in the first few moments because his stomach had taken control of his body when the aircraft began to pitch and roll wildly. It took long moments to realize that the maneuvers were deliberate and that they were not looping out of control.

No one said anything—your ass had to be on fire before a pilot would tell you to put it out—but Ota had a bad time when he understood what was happening. He swallowed the toothpick that he usually carried in his mouth when he could not smoke. Carefully, like a man counting his money, he took off his helmet and began to puke in it as the noise of the fighters grew to be a roar within a roar.

Loud. So damned loud. One of the fighters came so close in the night that the sound of its engine overwhelmed the sound of the Halifax's engines.

A fighter. An ME-109.

Zdenek was sure because he had heard that wretched crank all over the backroads of France as the Messerschmidts pounded their line of retreat with strafing runs so low on the deck that they seemed to come screaming out of the ground, putting down death in perfect rows.

It was a miracle they hadn't been rammed. Whose nightmare was that? How many people dreamed of a mid-air collision, counting the seconds before the earth rose up to meet them? Slowly, Zdenek felt the Halifax swing around, lumbering like a river barge until suddenly, in one-and-a-half terrifying seconds, they dropped and bottomed, as if it they hit stone.

They bounced. Zdenek's stomach spasmed but did not release its contents. He would be sick if he did not die, and he would die unless this thing ended soon.

With another thump like a crash, they leveled out. Cruised. Zdenek waited, counting the seconds again. It was one thing to be safe, another to be safe and not know it. He could see nothing in the interior of the aircraft except metallic darkness and eyes drugged with tension.

Had the pilot found cloud cover? Were the fighters gone?

Ota, sitting next to him, gave the thumbs up. That was encouraging. He didn't know they were clear—he couldn't—but Ota never thought the worst.

He would need to keep that attitude. Last spring the British meant to drop a man in Czechoslovakia, but kicked him out into Austria, where it was a short walk to his death.

That could happen to Anthropoid, but the Halifax was a better plane with better instruments, and the four Rolls-Royce engines had better range. Slowly, Zdenek felt the shift as the plane angled to correct course, getting back on its heading.

It was going to be all right.

* * *

About two o'clock they began to descend from high altitude. Shortly afterward, Anthropoid was told that they would be first to drop, and at almost the same time anti-aircraft guns fired on the plane.

The fire meant that the aircraft had passed over the center of Pilzn. They were supposed to drop several kilometers east of the city, so the flak probably came from positions near the Skoda Works—the most important factories in Central Europe.

On hand signals, Zdenek and Ota stepped up to the hole that had been cut in the belly of the Halifax. The dispatcher for the mission, a Czech captain named Sustr, stood by the bay. Zdenek thought it was right that he should be the last man they would see. When they had arrived at the airfield early in the day, the captain told them with a gold fountain pen and a smile to be sure to make out their wills.

Now Sustr's mouth was moving; he shouted, but slowly, so Zdenek could read his lips. "We've got some fog on the ground!" he said. "But you'll be put in on target!"

Zdenek nodded with a long movement, like a man in a silent film, but thought: they don't know where in hell we are. They got us this far, which is as far as they ever got anyone.

"We'll drop just as in training!" said Sustr. "Eight hundred feet—or less!"

When Zdenek nodded again, Sustr extended his hand, in gloves, to be taken. What did he want?

"Good luck!"

"You'll have word of us!" said Zdenek, speaking loud. "We'll do everything that can be done!"

Sustr might have said something in return, but Zdenek would never know. Just then the red bulb above the bay flashed: STANDBY.

Sustr and an RAF corporal opened the hole. The sudden draft was chilling, though the aircraft had cut its speed to a hundred miles per hour. That was approximately what they were used to and had practiced. Everything was approximately familiar to this point.

Sustr released the static lines from their back-chutes and hooked the catches onto the steel wire that ran above their heads. Ota stepped down into the well and sat like a boy on a high wall, his legs dangling free. When the bulb flashed green, Sustr gave the go-ahead, and Ota squeezed through the hole with his pack.

Zdenek watched the thick tensile wire snag, grow taut, then jerk and sag back. Gone. Ota was gone.

Zdenek stepped up to the hole, braced himself against the cold and crouched like an animal. It was blue down there, dark but glowing with a core, like some strange mineral generated in a cave. The cold sucked at his body; it pulled at his ankles.

He pushed off, felt the blast of frigid air all over him, and followed his friend down.

CHAPTER 4

Ota landed knowing that he had been lucky. He hit on level ground, toes-first, but even so his boots were nearly ripped apart when they tore through the top layer of snow. It was deep on the ground as far to the horizon as he could see, a blue-white completeness that looked deceptively smooth.

The first moments on the surface of the planet were always strange and incredibly new. It had something to do with being jerked from a plane on a horizontal stream of air, punched upright by the blast of silk, always falling faster than could be imagined, unable to steer even if power lines were reaching for your feet.

Then bang. Down.

Collapsing the chute and sighting.

Where was Zdenek?

He should have been down too, and unless he had drifted far, easy enough to spot. The terrain was level all around. Fields. Empty fields.

But Ota saw no movement anywhere. The winter moon was up, glowing through a gap in the clouds. The light came on in a weird haze that seemed to put thickness—a depth and distortion—over the white fields. Off to his right a thin line of scrub bristled with a halo, as if were about to move. A small patch of low ground ahead seemed to bog. Then suddenly, fifty meters to the left, Ota saw real motion.

Zdenek. He stood but seemed unsteady, gathering his chute not far from a group of snow-covered mounds. They looked weird in the moonscape, too. Muddled.

Ota waved and gave the OK signal. Zdenek did not return it. He beckoned instead: come to me.

A para would never do that unless he was getting a blowjob—or had been injured. Ota bunched his chute in his arms and began to move across the snow toward Zdenek, thinking with dread that came from a long way off: how bad?

It could happen anywhere at any time and luck was most of it, but how bad was the damage? Anthropoid had been planned as a two-man operation. Its thinking was based on that. Support. Physical and mental. And in the end, knowing that if the first thrust failed, a second would follow.

But was that still true when he looked across the dark whiteness and saw his partner slumped down in the snow, sitting in it like a child?

"Are you all right?"

"It's my foot," he said. "I jammed it."

"Broken?"

"I don't know. I can move, but there's pain."

"Did you see the supply chute land?"

"It's over that way," said Zdenek. "Toward those two sheds about a hundred meters off."

Ota looked but couldn't see much. Two tall dark shapes that seemed to arise from nothing, and a third on the ground, smaller, that might have been nothing.

"Can you walk?"

"Let's find out," said Zdenek. "It'll be light soon."

"Get your boot off. I'll look at your foot after I get rid of the chutes."

While Zdenek struggled silently against the pain, and more, the awkwardness of pain, Ota scrambled to bury his chute in the snow close to a pile of forage that had laid down for game.

That was not the best thing to do, but it was the only one. He would have liked to sink the chute far down but for the depth of the snowfall and the dark earth that would be thrown up like dye. If they were very lucky, no one would notice the disturbance for a while, thinking that animals had made those tracks in the snow. That animals had piled the snow in a fatal heap. That they could, with the assistance of a contraption in black silk, fly.

"I'm going to keep your chute out," he said to Zdenek. "We might need it for warmth."

"But if they find us with it—"

"If they find us now, it won't matter. We'll find a better hiding place. There are no worse."

Zdenek grumbled, trying to cover the sounds he made as he slipped the stocking off his foot. When Ota arrived and put his penlight on the wound, he was sorry that he had been so quick.

"Jesus Christ."

"It's not that bad. It feels better now that it's freed."

"Better than what?"

The big toe on Zdenek's left foot was already swollen as big as a foot. Probably broken. The damage elsewhere did not seem great, but Ota could not be sure. The swelling seemed to spread visibly, making a ruddy mess of everything—the toes, the instep, even the arch.

"Why couldn't you have broken your arm?"

"I meant to," said Zdenek. "Sorry."

"You should have reckoned the impact off those bushes."

"I didn't misjudge the height," said Zdenek. "I thought the ground was clear. I landed with my right foot solid, but my left struck something harder and threw me this way."

Ota traced the landing back toward the source. Yes, he saw the bounce. Zdenek had come down near the edge of those snow-covered mounds that had been visible at a distance. Closer up, they seemed even stranger. Taller and more definite. Out here where there was nothing, they seemed like clues left by men in a more ancient time.

"I must have hit one of the headstones."

Of course it was a cemetery. And Zdenek, swinging down from Mars, had ruined himself on the dead.

* * *

After Zdenek got his boot back on with some difficulty, they walked with more difficulty beyond the cemetery toward the huts on the outskirts of a village. What they saw in the darkness told them next to nothing. It was a small place with no name and no signs of life under the heavy burden of snow on the red roofs. It could have been anywhere in the country, or even in another.

They had luck getting into the huts, though. The first was filled with hay, but they found the second empty except for some gardening tools, wooden trays, and sacking. Locked, but just barely.

Ota forced the door with his field-knife. Once inside, they rested and opened a tin of biscuit, eating with the hunger of animals that had been on edge for hours inside a loud machine that now found themselves breathing ice crystals. The cold was less cutting within the timber walls, but it was no less clear.

The air should not be so clean in these parts, Ota thought. Not with Pilzn close and the Skoda Works at full shifts.

It wasn't the only thing that seemed wrong. The drop zone should have been near a wooded area, but there were almost no trees in sight. The land should have been hilly. It was flat as far as the eye could see and probably beyond.

"We can take a chance in the village," said Ota. "We'll find someone to look at your foot."

"If you pulled that idea from your ass, it wouldn't smell as bad," said Zdenek. "We'll walk up to the first door, knock, and hope the Gestapo don't answer."

"The Gestapo wouldn't waste themselves in a place like this. There might be a police post in the area. But nothing more."

"And the villagers won't talk."

"We'd be away quickly."

"We'll be doing nothing quickly, Ota. You should go on alone."

Ota was glad Zdenek had said that first. A wounded man had no chance far behind enemy lines. He was an impediment that would destroy any chance of the mission's success. Zdenek would have to be left behind. Although he had a pistol, that chance could not be taken. Ota would have to do it, wrapping his own weapon in dark silk as he held the barrel to his friend's head.

"There's a copse of trees on the other side of that field," he said. "I saw them clearly as I was coming down."

"I saw them, too," said Zdenek. "But they're probably a mile away."

"We've got an hour until daybreak. An hour and a half if we're lucky."

"It won't work, Ota. I can't make it."

"The hell you can't."

And that was all there was to it. Ota would not listen to the rest, which was a lot, and totally stupid. All Slovaks were like Zdenek if they were worth anything. As boys, they played the usual games of Cowboys and Indians, but the winner was always the redskin who died as he drew his bow one last time, cut down by the white man's rifle from an obscene and unfair distance.

Ota went back to retrieve the supply chute, which had come down less than thirty meters from the sheds. It was intact, and seemed undamaged by the landing. He knew that he would be unable to carry the gear and Zdenek too, so he manhandled the chute and supplies back to the shed. He hid the heaviest things under the trays, and body-packed the lightest and most important—the pistols, the torches, the Sten gun, the plastic explosive, but not the canisters.

He would have to come back later for the weight. That would be dangerous, but Ota saw no choice. Once they got away from the village, he would have the time to think this through again.

They began to walk toward the trees that gradually became visible on a rise across the open field. Looking at a distance like the dark demonic woods of myth, lifted on a crust of ice like a frozen mirage, they would provide cover if nothing else. There was also the chance that the land might drop off some point beyond if this were a plateau, or rise and become more as it should be in the minds of headquarters.

Zdenek labored badly through the snow, putting no weight on the injured foot, leaning on Ota all the way. The soles of their boots felt like tarpaper, crunching to depth with each step. The hard glaze at the surface cut into their calves and the cold cut deeper. No more than two hundred yards into the field, Zdenek called for a rest to ease the pain.

Ota did not mind the pause, because he was almost spent. The problem with injury was not just the thing itself but the way it put strain on the good parts. One leg doing the work of two became half a leg. A team became a worthless thing channeling all its energy into maintenance.

And making itself a target. Ota felt sick when he looked back and saw the tracks they had left in the snow. The smooth glittering surface was marked by deep indentations, as if someone had trailed behind them, filling each footstep with a black liquid of shadow. Theirs was the only trail on line-of-sight. Any tracker—any child—would be able to follow them.

It was too late either for turning back or cutting losses with a bullet. They were not going to make it. And the half-man who had turned their country and most of Europe into a slaughterhouse would escape with his putrid life.

CHAPTER 5

Zdenek could not believe his luck. It had all been bad from the moment he dropped into space from the Halifax, a world of darkness cloaked in the strangeness of white. From the debris that they found in the huts, they knew they had come to earth in the homeland, but where was unknown. It seemed certain that the names they had been given of people to contact in the drop zone were worthless. Attempting blind contact in the village was guaranteed to end their mission and their lives.

He wished that he could have been thinking better—more positively—but the pain had worsened with the cold and the need for quick movement. For an hour and more they lurched across the frozen plain with snow pulling them down, gathering dead weight with the wetness, losing the last of the stamina that they had gained in six months of training. They were physically and mentally exhausted before they reached the copse of trees at the top of the rise.

What kept them going the last three hundred yards were the boulders that slowly appeared within the trees. They loomed like shadows out of the darkness of false dawn, then receded but did not disappear as the light failed before its return. Zdenek felt a mysterious allure in those rocks. They seemed to offer the possibility that somehow, hedged by stone, two men could fort up and wait out the bad time.

They entered the woods while it was still dark, hobbling through the trees and around the boulders and over the brush. Every maneuver demanded incredible effort for two men on three legs in snow. Overhanging branches required major shifts of attitude and the smallest saplings were man-traps. The only thing that gave them hope was the sun that came first at the margin of vision and afterward in a soft blaze. Slowly, the near distance began to open up. Something ahead was unobstructed.

As they cleared the last trees, the sight that came precisely with the dawn took back the hours of continuous panic and replaced them with something like peace. They found themselves atop a ravine that fell into a small valley where a pond was shelved with ice. To the left stood an old stone hut, and beyond that a small wood. Big rocks—some so big that the snow did not cover them—rose on the hillside above.

"God exists," said Zdenek. "He spent some time here if I'm not mistaken."

"It's perfect," said Ota. "We might not know where we are, but we landed in the right place."

It became more perfect when the light began to spread in the tops of the trees, filtering through the winter spaces in the small valley. Things separated from the darkness. The snow changed color; it dazzled.

That would be a quarry beyond the hut—where the snow was shaped like big blocks falling off in giant steps. They seemed to lead directly and suddenly into the earth.

On the hillside beyond the hut, Zdenek saw something that looked odd and promising in the way the snow drifted and draped, as if pinned. He was sure the sweep of it hid something.

"I'll bet that's a cave," he said. "The mouth's right there."

"Our luck hasn't changed that much."

"I say it has."

"A thousand crowns," said Ota, tapping the billfold in his pocket.

"You're covered."

Ota was free with the mission stash that he couldn't spend, which was the only way he ever let loose of anything but pussy money. Leaving Zdenek atop the ravine, he walked down the slope to check the site and reconnoiter the area.

It was always good to be cautious, although it seemed obvious by the undisturbed snow that no one had been around here for days. Or longer. In the oblique winter sunlight, this place among the rocks gave the feeling of never having been shared for long by tame men.

Zdenek did not wait for his partner to return and fetch the cripple. He sat in the snow. Cradling his bad leg in his arm, he slid down the embankment.

* * *

That queer swirl of snow and ice among the rocks turned out to be a cave and more: a cave with two exits. It was as if they had ordered it.

The first mouth was in the place behind the hut, but the other reached back among the rocks for a way until it came out on the far side of the valley. The cave was big enough to be passable at a good pace, and dark enough to hinder anyone who did not know the way.

It seemed that not many did. The only marks on the walls were left by primitive people—boys from the village who played in the cave and carved stick-figures and sexual parts into the rocks. Who burnt small wood fires in offering to their gods.

Zdenek was happy with every new thing. The thousand crowns were never mentioned because this was the place he would stay for healing or forever. If they were found out or betrayed, there would be no more arguments about who was left behind. Even Ota could see that a wounded man fought best as a rear-guard. He also knew that this man was bound to find a way to get his partner clear of the cave because he was one of the few people on this earth capable of doing it.

For the time being they were still a team. They had shelter and food. They brought the gear into the cave, and while Zdenek set things up, working around the pain like a booby trap, Ota went into the woods to cut pine branches for kindling and bedding.

With the chute tented around him, and a fire going, Zdenek felt something more than pain in his body for the first time since the drop. They ate more biscuit and some tinned beef. It was tough going, the haunch and probably the hock of a bull that had died with a hard-on, but nothing ever tasted better than meat in the open air on a morning that they should not have survived.

When they were done eating and congratulating themselves, Ota took out the map to see if there was some way to figure out their location. Zdenek felt good enough to go with him into the better light at the mouth of the cave. That might have been a mistake, but it was one with clean air to it.

The problem with the map was that it needed a reference point to be useful—a beginning. They had none. The stretch of flat land around them—even if it extended for miles—was too small to match any region of the country, especially if they had dropped somewhere south or central.

Even that was a guess. What seemed precise in technology had gonc wrong in human error. The Halifax probably had fallen off its heading during the fighter attack and never regained it. If so, near which concentration of anti-aircraft fire had they dropped? If that was not Pilzn they had overflown, what was it? Which city or important installation was close by?

"My guess is that they mistook Brno for Pilzn," said Ota, tracing his finger on a line directly east. "There'd be German anti-aircraft around the munitions factories there."

"That's a long mistake."

Ota shrugged. "At a couple hundred miles an hour?"

"So you think we're in Moravia."

"I can't say," he said, looking off Zdenek's left shoulder toward the village. "But I'd be able to tell. When the first man opens his mouth, I'll know within fifty miles of where we are. My family's from Trebic."

"You're not thinking of knocking on doors again?"

"I won't have to," he said in a voice that was too calm. "If you look over your shoulder, standing beside the first row of trees, you'll see a man."

Zdenek did not look. "Is he alone?"

"Appears to be."

"Armed?"

"Not that I can see."

"Let him make the move," said Zdenek. "I can still handle a pistol."

Zdenek turned slowly toward the figure in the trees. He was a tall heavily padded man of middle age dressed for outdoor work—boots, leggings, a rowdy cap. Nor was he inattentive. As soon as Zdenek catalogued him, the man moved his head and called out.

"Good morning."

They returned his greeting as if it were the normal thing. Ota, as always, smiled like a salesman.

The fellow did not come toward them. With deliberate movements, he lit a cigarette, shaking out the match and dousing the head in the snow.

"What are you two doing here?"

"We want to start working this quarry again," said Ota, as he looked around the old ruin. "It shows promise."

The man blew smoke as if it meant something. "If you mean the stone in that pit, why, you couldn't pave Hitler's asshole with it." He gave a smile that could be seen clearly. "But don't worry about a thing. I've come to help."

"The town drunk," said Ota softly. "He strays this way when his wife runs him off."

"Moravian?"

"Not on your life."

"Can we take the chance of letting him go?"

"I don't know."

Zdenek eased the safety off the pistol in his pocket. He tried to call out with the same ease. "All right, friend. Come on down."

The man maneuvered down the slope of the ravine carefully, his hands held out for balance, but also meaning to show that he had nothing in them. He seemed to know where to step without looking at his feet, and to be agile for his age. Not the town drunk, it seemed.

"My name is Antonin Sedlacek," he said as he drew near enough for the pistol. "But I'm called Lojza."

"What brings you out here so early in the morning?"

"I'm the gamekeeper hereabout," he said, taking another step closer. "Back in '38 a group of factory owners rented a hunting lodge up the way, and they needed someone to improve the stock.

So I took the job. It's not a bad one even in winter. A lot of it's just being outdoors and looking around."

"How did you find your way here?"

"I was out checking my forage by the graveyard this morning," he said. "That's how I tripped over the parachute you buried in the snow."

Just like that. Your parachute, sir. It was the one thing that guaranteed a man's bloody end from the Gestapo.

Zdenek turned to Ota half-face, speaking softly. "Will I be sorry if I kill him?"

"Don't do it yet. We've got to know what he knows." Ota turned back to the game-keeper, closing the distance between them by a step. "Tell me, where did we land when we came down from the sky?"

"You're outside the village of Nehvizdy."

"And where would that be?"

"Very close to Prague."

Prague? Could they have fallen off course that much? Not east, but northeast. A feat of incompetence like that did not seem beyond the technical capabilities of English pilots. At least they had dropped in a part of the country that was in many ways a better place to close out their mission.

"Which way is Prague?"

"Due west," said the gamekeeper. "About twenty kilometers by the road."

The correct drop zone had been a few kilometers east of Pilzn. It seemed logical that the pilot had taken the lights of Prague for Pilzn's, dropping them in the same direction sixty-five miles away.

"I can tell you don't believe me," said Lojza, as he reached slowly, carefully, into his back pocket. "But here's my keeper's card. See for yourself."

He handed over a ragged piece of paper that looked bland, and official. The document had been signed by Antonin Sedlacek and countersigned by the representative of the government of the district of Brandys on the Elbe in the Protectorate of Bohemia and Moravia. This was what most of the country of Czechoslovakia was called now. Zdenek found that he could not hold the thing for long in his hand. He wanted to burn it.

"You seem to be what you say you are," said Zdenek. "That's healthy."

"I plan to stay this way, too."

"That might be difficult, if you want to help us."

The gamekeeper understood that he had been caught in an inconsistency. A hunter and a survivor, he did not need to be told the situation was dangerous. His eyes had never roamed for long from the hand that Zdenek kept inside his coat pocket.

"It won't be hard," he said. "Poachers are around all the time. The authorities know I'm out in every kind of weather, doing my job."

"Authorities," said Ota. "Are there police in the village?"

"Two of them."

"Are they diligent in their work?"

"They're Czech," he said, as if that answered the question. "But the Gestapo are as close as the nearest phone."

"Would the police call the Gestapo if they saw something suspicious in the area?"

Lojza's thin lips seemed to taste something sharp and very bitter. "Where in the hell do you live?" he said angrily. "Don't you know what it's like here? They keep a card on every human being in the Protectorate. Written on it is our fate—when the Nazis get around to gathering us up. A blue card says you can be trusted as a slave. A yellow card says you're to be watched. A red one means you'll be arrested and deported. To a concentration camp. It's strange how nobody comes back from those places. Even Czech policemen who don't do their jobs well enough are sent to KZs. It's like death but more uncertain."

Zdenek was impressed by the gamekeeper's speech. In it was a passion that did not reside naturally in any soul.

"Let's say I trust you, Lojza."

The gamekeeper smiled. He seemed to want to sit and share the outdoor life. "Do you have a choice, my friend?"

Zdenek looked pointedly at his pocket. "Yes," he said. "I could have you quarry your own gravestone before I blow out your brains. That's what the Nazis would do."

Lojza blanched. He seemed not to want to sit any longer. "It's unnecessary, these threats."

"A matter of opinion," said Zdenek. "We want you to know that betraying us is not an option, Lojza. We'd like you to return to the village. Look around, act naturally, but be sure to find out if the police know of unusual activity in the area. Maybe they've heard of other paras landing in the Protectorate. Or heard a low-flying aircraft."

He nodded. "I did. Late last night. It woke me."

"Maybe others heard it, too. And maybe they'll come into the woods to enquire."

"I'll cover your tracks, don't worry," said Lojza. "I've got good reason to go around in the fields and plenty of forage to scatter around. No one will suspect anything."

"Good," said Ota. "But don't think of changing your mind, and don't use your mouth too much. Understand that we'll radio your name to our friends. If we're discovered, our deaths will not be the last in this village."

The gamekeeper took a look in his eye like something he had found on a shelf. "How you boys talk!" he said. "It isn't a damned bit polite. I'd bet we share the same friends."

"That's hard to believe," said Ota.

"I'll just give one word," said Lojza with a quick wink that changed his looks for the better. "Falcon."

In Czech that was Sokol. The word also meant freedom. It stood for the athletic clubs that had been in every town in the nation before the war. Outlawed by the Nazis, they were now the heart of the resistance.

CHAPTER 6

They spent a tense day and night and the greater part of another day in the cave. The team had been trained to survive on its wits—there was no other strategy—but so far the mission had consisted more of error than thinking. A wrong drop, a bad landing, a worse foot, and now held prisoner to the promises of a half-wit.

Lojza was not as stupid as he seemed, though. Part of his act was an act, an instinct that had become a reflex for staying alive. Zdenek noted it because he could see how well it worked. Pride had to be eaten, chewed and swallowed with every word, but hell, regular army was used to that.

Zdenek knew he would have to live the idea, too. As long as his foot was bad—and it could not have been much worse—Anthropoid was powerless to act as a unit. It had no mobility, no eyes. To correct that condition, Ota set out from the cave twenty minutes before dusk on the second day to reconnoiter the area. He said he would return in an hour or less, whistling "Boleraz, Boleraz," as his signal.

Zdenek spent the time close to the fire examining the map for the hundredth time. The village of Nehvizdy appeared as one of the smallest dots on it. A road to Prague ran through it, and more than a kilometer distant was another road going the same way. And a railway line.

They could make for the railway station, and Prague, at any time, but it was better to wait for the foot to heal so Zdenek would not attract attention. It was also better—necessary—that they have somewhere they could go in the city. The addresses of the safe-places that they had been given were in Pilzn. As a last chance, they could take the train south to that city, make contact, and work their way back to Prague.

Either way was feasible, or could be soon. They had plenty of money—more than fifty thousand crowns—and their papers should be good enough to pass inspection. If Ota found the train schedule, and a way of approaching the station, that time could be moved up.

So when the whistle came from just outside the mouth of the cave, Zdenek smiled to himself. Ota had done his work quickly—only forty-five minutes had passed—but why was he not whistling Boleraz?

Zdenek threw his parachute over the fire and sat on it. He felt more warmth than he had since leaving England, and he felt better, more alive, because for the first time he had the chance to do what he was meant to do. His right hand found the Colt pistol that he kept under the second chute, and his left hand found the shaft of the flashlight.

"Come in," he said. "I'm right here."

He saw a thick shadow move until it nearly filled the mouth of the cave. The light was bad, barely making an outline, but Zdenek could see that the shape did not have Ota's dimensions. This one was more squat and ominous. Nor was he the deliberately retarded gamekeeper, Lojza.

"Hello," said the man in a high voice. "I'm over here. Can you show yourself?"

Zdenek was not about to do that, or switch on the flashlight that would make him a target for another pistol and a kill for a submachine gun.

"Put your hands high," he said. "Move two steps forward."

The man did as he was told. His hands rose above his flat cap, and he took the steps. He spoke again in that very high voice, "Listen, now—"

"Don't speak," said Zdenek. "Don't move until you're told."

Zdenek was sure the man could hear him as he left the fire, dragging his foot by the heel, until he reached the cover of the sentinel rock. When he was behind it, Zdenek put the flashlight atop it and switched it on.

The man moved one hand to shield his face but otherwise did not react stupidly. He did not look like much of a Gestapo, or a legitimate policeman. Beneath a dark beret, a pair of big glasses sat atop a bulbous nose that had turned shiny in the glare.

His breathing was bad and his smile chattered, as if he were about to faint.

"Who are you?"

"My name is Baumann."

"You come alone?"

"Yes," he said. "I'm a friend."

Another friend. Either Ota and Zdenek were the luckiest men in Czechoslovakia, or the whole district knew they were here.

"How many gamekeepers do you know?"

"Only one," said Baumann. "There used to be more, and a lot smarter, but they're all dead now. Everyone who knows how to shoot is either enlisted for the duration or dead."

"Not quite," said Zdenek. "The Home Army is alive and well. A little late, but well."

"Thank God."

* * *

It turned out that Baumann was the miller hereabout. When he got rid of his nerves, he seemed like a reasonably collected man who was important enough for the Nazis to keep alive but not too prominent to draw attention to himself or his movements. After he sat down at the rekindled fire, nothing seemed to shake him, not even the sight of Ota, who appeared twenty minutes later with a second pistol.

The miller had interesting things to say. Everyone in the village knew that an aircraft with engines louder than anything they had ever heard came in low over the village the night before last. Some thought the plane must be crashing to earth, while others said they had seen parachutes in the sky, and one fellow put a ladder to his roof, where he climbed to watch the show.

"Tell him to come down," said Ota. "He'll freeze his ass off."

"He came down quickly," said Baumann. With his hat off, he had red hair and a face that was slightly less in color. "I think you should know that when I saw him, he was in the tavern talking about three men who dropped from heaven."

The third man would have been the supply chute, but Zdenek did not want to tell the miller any more than he already knew, which was more than enough to see them dead.

"If they're talking in public, it won't be long before the police find out. And the Gestapo."

Baumann blinked, as if that struck him too close. "I told them to keep their mouths shut. I appealed to their patriotism, saying that the Nazis would kill everyone in the district if they found out that paras had landed and weren't reported."

"Did they believe you?"

"Oh, yes," said Baumann. "The Nazis always do what they say. I've even heard they want to send guillotines our way. They think a beheading is better than a common hanging."

"It seems like their methods might be effective."

"They are," said Baumann. "Everyone's cowed. If you'd shown your faces in the village, the Gestapo would have you already."

"And if they knew you were here?"

"I'd be killed," he said. "For helping an unregistered person in any way the penalty is death. Since you're parachutists, they'd kill my family, too. Sometimes, when they feel generous, they stop at second cousins."

"You must have a small family."

"I'm a Falcon," he said. "If you want to get out of this place, I'm your man."

So they were faced with the same choice again: kill him or trust him. Would it be this way every time? If the man was sincere, he was a hero. If not, they were finished.

"Of course we want to get out of here," said Zdenek. "We have things to do."

Baumann smiled behind the huge lenses of his glasses like light in a frosted window. "We need a resistance," he said. "A real resistance that acts. Something that will make these pigs sit back in their slops and squeal."

"We're going to do that, I promise."

Baumann put his hand out to shake theirs, and in his grip lay the best evidence that he was a strong man, an athlete, a Falcon.

* * *

So they had hope to go along with their home in the rocks. That was good, because home quickly began to seem like a frigid prison.

Zdenek had once read that the people who had given the world the religions of one god took their ideas of hell from the desert heat that surrounded them. Others, which meant most of mankind, should have gone the other way and imagined the worst to be the bone-breaking cold that seeped from the earth, always wet, always dripping and pooling in the worst places, always, in spite of the fire that they tried to keep going, thickening their blood.

Ota was better off because he could move around. Twice he went back to the village at night to retrieve supplies that had been left in the gardener's shed. He continued to scout the area in bad light and stand watch in the better. He did the chores, complaining all the while about goldbrickers.

Zdenek's work was trying to walk. He did it several times a day, hobbling over to the stone hut and back. He probably would have been better off staying still, but the foot stiffened when he lay too long in the cold. It was mostly black now, but who knew, that could have been frostbite.

He did not think he could stand one more day in the cave. Then he spent another. And another. When he was sure that he could stand it no longer, the miller who looked like a German and talked like a German and most certainly had a German name put his face among them again. Zdenek heard his voice outside the entrance to the cave about noon of the sixth day.

"Hello, my friend."

"Come in," said Ota. "Come in."

Zdenek watched Ota and the miller enter the cave, stooping less from the height of the ceiling than from the waning light. Zdenek said hello and smiled, but thought: I wonder how much it would take to turn him around. Or what? If he were a patriot one day and a traitor the next, how would you know until they found you and took you alive and fed the best parts of your body back to you?

"I'm sorry I was so long getting back," he said. "But these things take time."

"What things?"

"Travel arrangements."

"We understand," said Ota. "Do you have good word for us now?"

Baumann smiled. It was not really a bad smile. "How quickly can you be ready to leave?"

"For Prague?"

"Yes."

"Ten minutes."

It took longer, almost half an hour, because neither of them was much at shaving in icy water, and Zdenek was not much at the movements that should have been so simple. Because Baumann said they could not take anything with them but portable items, they had to cache most of the supplies and police the cave thoroughly. And beg luck again.

By the time they got underway, Baumann was frantic. Zdenek thought that he was doing well, forcing his body through the pain, but as they made their way from the wood that ringed the rocks, he had trouble keeping to the slow pace that was set. He dropped back even more as they crossed the field to the road that led to the railway station. Baumann kept looking over his shoulder, saying, "I didn't know your foot was so bad."

Not bad. Wretched. And it seemed to worsen with every step in the open as they moved along the side of the road rutted with the tracks of oxcarts.

Zdenek had the strangest feeling as they walked the road that stretched as flat and almost as far as the horizon. Twinges. Nerves. He never wanted to find himself in a cave again, but he missed the sensation of having stone between the body that performed badly and the enemy who could be anywhere with a shot from distance, or closing in a rush of fast vehicles.

He could not run. Never. Ota, in spite of what his mouth said, would stand by him. They might die with incredible ease without striking their blow.

But Baumann did not waver. They neared the station at a quick country pace. Zdenek saw it clearly—a small red-roofed building set off from the village a couple hundred yards. That was very good.

The pain in his foot began to numb as they got within fifty meters of the station. He didn't know if that was good or deadly but it was welcome. He managed to curb his limp as they came up to the building with the sign on top—the first thing he had seen written in Czech—and a wooden bench that ran along the platform.

He sat. That felt better than he could say, or would admit. While Ota went to the ticket window, the miller came and sat on the bench, too. He seemed less nervous now.

"You arrive at Prague in an hour," he said. "There you'll be safe."

That might be true. Zdenek wished he could warm to the man who had saved their life, and their mission, but he knew that he would not be able to do that with real feeling until they were on the train pulling away.

"Will someone meet us at the station in Prague?"

"Someone's here to meet you now," said Baumann. "You'll be taken directly to the next Falcon."

Zdenek thought that Baumann had misspoken. Only two people stood on the platform—a pair of young women, one quite young, perhaps still in her teens. The younger and fairer was pretty. She looked at them with a curiosity that was heartening.

"Where are they?"

"I did my best for two parachutists," said Baumann with a quiet laugh. He beckoned to the girls with an almost unnoticeable movement of his hand, and they approached the bench at once. "I hope you don't mind, but we've found that women make the best couriers and guides. No one sees them at all—except as the thing they're not."

"You're serious."

"Very," said Baumann, getting to his feet. "You'll be two young couples on your way to the city for an outing. No one will trouble you."

The girls stopped before the bench, smiling from almost identical, very alluring, heights. "Hello," said the prettiest one. "My name is Libena. This is my friend, Anna."

Zdenek rose, forgot his foot, and nearly fell to the platform. He reached for support and found Libena's hand.

"Sorry," he said. "I'm unstable."

Libena smiled again. With her lips parted, she was not pretty: she was perfect. Her skin seemed to take its color from the opalescent pin on the breast of her cloth coat. Her bright brown eyes were large, changeable to hazel, and friendly.

"Is it your leg?"

"Yes," he said. "I hurt it in a fall."

She moved closer, put her arm through his, and accepted his weight against her body. He was looking down at her hair—long light brown hair bound by an amber barrette—when she raised her face to him.

"We'll take you to a place where you'll recover," she said. "It's never any good to come down from great heights without a soft spot to land."

So she knew that he was a para—that he was a walking death sentence—and she wasn't afraid.

"My name's Zdenek," he said. "That fellow at the ticket window is Ota."

Ota left the window and moved back toward the bench. Zdenek could tell that he was surprised but willing to understand when Anna stepped up and slipped her hand into his, speaking like an old friend—and more.

"Look, Ota, there's the train now. It might be the same one we took to Metuje for the skiing."

Ota smiled. He rarely showed any other expression of his mood to strangers, but this one was different. That might have had something to do with Anna's deep black hair, or her blue eyes. Not a usual combination, and not the worst.

"Yes," he said quickly. "I believe it's the same one. I'll never forget that time in the mountains."

The train was far out—several hundred yards. There was a point where it got bigger, looming suddenly, preceded by a high-shouldered locomotive with dual spotlights and an iron swastika mounted on its nose.

It was the first sign Zdenek had seen that his homeland did not belong to its people. The swastika rode into view like a cold brand that hurtled across the country, searching out flesh.

"Look, Ota's bought first class tickets."

"The compartment car's the third from the end," said Libena. "The train must have come from Hradec-Kralove."

"No," said Anna with fire rising in her blue eyes. "Not Hradec-Kralove. Koniggratz. Don't forget."

In a way, it was good to hear that the names of the places they had known all their lives had been made ugly. Germanized. Those people who could not construct a toilet that did not stink of merciless Teutonic shit now had the best railway system, the best arms plants, and the most productive farms in Central Europe. And it had cost them nothing. Yet.

"Come," said Anna. "Let's move toward the front."

They passed beyond the ticket window to where the car would come to rest. It seemed as if the noise of the locomotive would destroy their conversation, but the women shouted over the engine and the brakes. By the time they reached the coach, it seemed as if they had known these girls for years.

Anna did not reveal her age, but Libena made it known that she was nineteen. She made it seem as if she had been stuck there a long time. Life had stopped, she said, forward-looking ended, the day the Germans entered Prague.

The conversation stopped, too, as they boarded the train and moved down the passage to their compartment. It was an old Pullman car that could have predated the Republic. The wood was mahogany glazed with the filth of ages, the upholstery was plush in every place except where passengers put themselves, and the floor was carpeted in Oriental designs but as bald in the center as a footpath. Near the end of the passage where they stopped, one of the plaster cornices was still inscribed with a coat of arms—a Bohemian lion, a German eagle—entangled as if they would always be fraternal, always at war.

As if. Strike that. The Germans had taken Czech land, Czech women, and cheapest of all, Czech lives. The only thing new about the Nazis was that they did not bother to apologize.

For the time being, Baumann was right: no one paid four young lovers any attention. Most of the passengers on the train were Czech; the railway workers were Czech; the two army officers in the compartment across the passageway were German, but they seemed to be on leave, with their minds, so-called, on other things.

The two couples settled down in shabby comfort as the train left the station. The scene that began to pass from the windows, accelerating like a sprocket, was white, flat—a farming plain with crusted snow and a snap-to-grid march of utility poles but hardly any woods or much in the way of orchards. He and Ota might have wandered in that chaste wasteland for days without finding shelter. Instead, they were being carried toward a great city in a gently heaving coach with two lovely women at their sides.

"Tickets! Papers!"

The middle-aged conductor put his high-capped head into the compartment as if he were barely concerned with who they were. He spoke Czech, but standing behind him was a short stout man who said nothing intently. His eyes were the same brown as his suit—as muddy and as motionless. He could have been anything, but was not.

"Gestapo," said Libena softly into his ear.

The girls handed over their documents with just the right amount of annoyance, while Zdenek and Ota searched their pockets. Not a big moment. Huge. This would be a test of the skill of the forgers in London. Or where their mission ended.

The conductor gave the girls' papers a quick inspection, then held his hand out to Ota, who filled it. Zdenek, waiting, made the mistake. He looked at the Gestapo as if he were making contact with a human being. The Gestapo looked back at prey.

"Next."

Zdenek surrendered his identity card and work certificate with his ticket. He thought that his smile must be in his face more mechanically than the German's eyes, but it was still his best weapon. Without it, he looked too much like himself.

"Born in Slovakia," said the conductor as if that were a minor crime. "Working in Prague."

"Yes, sir."

The conductor did not look at the certificate, which he had probably memorized. He probably chose one of every group of passengers to harass at random to satisfy the Gestapo.

"I've got a cousin who lives three blocks from you," he said. "His name's Grbac. A steelworker."

Zdenek shrugged. "Don't know him. Sorry. It's a big city."

The conductor turned to the German standing in the doorway. If Zdenek read the look, he guessed it was a shrug on just the wrong side of freedom. Libena, watching closely, seemed to think so, too. She spoke quickly.

"You might like to know, sir, that we're to be married on Tuesday at the Evangelical Chapel in Zizkov. With your permission, of course."

The German and the conductor looked at her with more interest, the first because he did not know the language, the second with surprise.

"Has your father spoken to you about marrying a Slovak?"

"Yes, sir. He told me they think about nothing but sex, and that I should be on guard."

"Sex and wine," he said. "A hideous combination."

"But not fatal."

The conductor laughed. He turned to the German and spoke in German, "Young blood."

"And that one?"

He meant Zdenek. The conductor shrugged without apparent concern. "Take him for questioning if you like."

The Gestapo continued to stare at Zdenek without hatred or feeling. Slowly, one of his nostrils collapsed, like an animal sifting the wind for the smell of blood. A wound. It was as if he knew something, which was nothing except the fear that had been instilled in all of Europe by men like him.

Zdenek was thinking that he could take this one, and the officers across the passage, which would be good, three less of those fuckers to mar this good earth, but that would be only for the satisfaction, a pleasure that would end their mission and their lives and the lives of the women, too. They didn't deserve to die in a worn coach or a frozen field. They should be loved. Yes.

Zdenek let his hand drift off Libena's shoulder until it touched the side of her breast. There, he circled his thumb slowly. She turned to him and smiled as if she recognized the move, and every response, in a long slow sequence.

The Gestapo followed the movement as if it were his own. Blood or sex? The trail had been confused. That one thick nostril collapsed again, and his hand moved from the coat pocket where it nested. Lazily, like something loosed from its mooring, the hand sought the ceiling.

"Heil Hitler!"

Part Two:

Postcards to the Gestapo

CHAPTER 7

SUMMARY: ICE TO FRANTA
January 15, 1942

Subject: Mission Status. Be advised that Team Silver A is on the ground and intact. Radio Libuse is now operational.

Status: Silver B. We have no word of this team, but rumors persist that a group of paras has been taken by the Gestapo. The report cannot be verified at this time.

Status: Team Anthropoid. Unknown.

* * *

FRANTA TO ICE

Our most heartfelt congratulations. Eagerly await your contact with Three Kings. Advise earliest possible moment.

Urgently request status Team Anthropoid, when known.

* * *

"What is that?" she asked. "What happened to you?"

They had never made love in daylight or she would have seen it. Ota was conscious of it always, but when he was with people for a time forgetfulness set in. He never bothered about it with men, because he didn't care what they thought, and there had been few women, most of them paid, to worry about in the past three years.

Anna was different. From the moment she left them at the Piskacek's apartment in Vysocany, Ota had known that he would see her again. Although that had not happened for days that became weeks as Anthropoid moved around the city through the Falcon network, passed from family to family and spare room to spare room, one late afternoon there she suddenly was, standing in the doorway of the Khodl's kitchen, saying hello, how have you been?

Bad, he thought. I've been given a mission like few men ever have and my partner is crippled. I don't wait well, but I've been sitting one day short of forever in the basement and attic spaces of good people hoping the Gestapo don't come through the door. I need to feel unlike a prisoner. I need someone to talk to. Or love.

"It happened before I left the country," he said. "In '39. The army demobilized after the Germans arrived, but some of us got off with our weapons and tried to form a resistance. We did some very fine damage until one day I was caught."

"And they did that to you."

"Yes."

"Seven times?"

"I think the number must be significant in Nazi mysticism."

When she touched him on the highest part of his thigh, where the first dark scar was, Ota was afraid that he would feel the pain again. He often did when he thought of it—the brand that had sunk through his flesh, the stench of himself burning—but that did not happen. Anna's touch was feathery and deft, not something that he could ever regret.

"They have a way, don't they?" she asked, but not as a question. "They know how to destroy."

"They didn't destroy me, Anna. They made me more determined."

"Perhaps you're right," she said, putting her palm over the scar, as if she could blot the mark, or lift it off by contact. "What's left is sometimes stronger. I often think that of myself. But only when I'm alone."

It wasn't just then. No matter who made up the company, Anna seemed to be alone much of the time, as if there was some secret in her life that she thought could not be shared. Ota sensed it even when she was being so cheerful that first day at the train station. It was something that almost hurt to see when she turned her head at odd moments and looked at objects so commonplace that they did not bear a glance. She was not studying them. She was awash in them.

"Your scars are the color of ash," she said. "Seven ashen swastikas."

"They weren't very careful," said Ota. "I think I was last in line."

"Did they take you to a concentration camp?"

"No," he said. "It was a jail on the way to a KZ. Some friends got me out, and I found my way over the Polish border."

"But you were a soldier," she said. "You were not a normal man with a normal job."

"Yes," he said. "I was lucky."

"Is that what you are?"

"I'm with you," he said. "That's the luckiest I've been."

She shied a bit, withdrawing her body from his by inches. He didn't know what that meant.

"My husband was unlucky," she said. "You knew that I was married. A bride at twenty-one, a widow at twenty-three."

"I was told."

"He was involved with the resistance at the place where he worked," she said. "I knew nothing about it, because he didn't see fit to tell me. Perhaps he thought he was protecting me. I know now that's probably true. But I was baffled when one day he didn't come home at six-fifteen. The Gestapo had taken him, it seemed. That was all I knew until two weeks later when I received his ashes in the mail."

Before Ota said something—he didn't know what—Anna rose and walked one step to the window that overlooked the street where the trolleys passed, rhythmically clicking. They left behind a silence that seemed smooth and wanting to be filled.

"Ota, you know that I work for the resistance."

"Of course."

"What would you say if I told you that I came to see you at the Khodl's for only one reason," she asked. "That I brought you here to my home and made love to you for only one reason."

Ota shook his head. He assumed that she watched him for the others. He knew her questions served the purpose for which they were meant as well as the other that might be called love. He didn't care. Ota wanted them to know him so they could help the mission. He wanted her to love him for herself.

"If you said that, you'd be lying. You came because you wanted to, Anna."

"Yes, I did. Perhaps you won't believe it, but I haven't been with a man since my husband died. It was as if I couldn't be with a man who didn't feel the things I did. If he couldn't hate the way I do, he couldn't love the way I do. He couldn't really know me, and I didn't want to know him." She turned back, looking at him without clothes like a much smaller creature with much larger breasts. "Do you understand?"

He answered with a movement that took him off the bed and across the space that separated them. He made his body fit to her body at every opening.

"I understand, Anna. I love you."

"It isn't necessary to say that."

"I did."

"Jenick—"

"Please don't call me that. No one has since my grandmother died."

"Jan."

"Not that either."

"Ota."

"Yes."

She pressed against him. Her hands moved along his back and down to his buttocks, lingering, as if she were trying to locate the marks of the brand by variations in the texture of his skin.

"I know what you're here for."

"Do you?"

"I can feel it in you. You're going to do something great. And I'll help you all I can."

"You know what's necessary," he said. "It's been necessary for the past three weeks. I have to see the leadership. UVOD. The Council."

"They want to see you," she said. "It will be soon, I'm sure. Tonight or perhaps tomorrow."

"Then they think I am who I say."

"I do," she said. "They will."

He turned her back to the bed, scissoring between her legs. She was wet, wetter and more wonderfully soft than any woman he had known. When her legs opened, he slid into her like silk on silk. He did not feel her hand at his chest until he had moved deep, wet and warm and deep.

"Move up," she said, rocking back under him. "Yes. There. I want your wounds in my hands when you come."

* * *

Zdenek was listening to the churchillky—the little crystal set that brought in BBC and nothing more—when he sat up on the sofa as if someone had stepped on his bad toe.

"The Russians have broken through again," he said with a full stop that meant he was still listening to the voice in his head. "The German northern armies have been pushed back a hundred miles from Moscow. It's thirty below zero, and their tanks don't like it."

"The men either," said Ota. "I heard that Hitler refused to give his troops winter clothing. The campaign was to be over by now."

"What if it is?" said Madame Moravcova from the kitchen. "What if this is the beginning of the end?"

Zdenek took the plug from his ear and smiled. "Of course it is, Auntie. With the Americans coming in, the Germans don't stand a chance in hell, which is exactly where they are."

She came into the room, where she sat in the big chair, took the nurse's cap from her head and dropped it into her four-family lap. Auntie had big shoulders and a chest like a man, but her face was as kindly as cream and her dark eyes seemed to call on a flow of energy that was not there for most people. She took care of a household of a husband and a son, while working most of the day at the Red Cross. That was a perfect job to have—mobile and respectable—for someone deeply involved with the resistance.

"I shouldn't be so happy," she said. "A hand that touches metal in that kind of cold leaves skin behind. But I've heard such terrible stories from the East. One from a young German boy. Whole villages have been wiped from the face of the earth. All the people killed. Sometimes, it's said, the SS herd them into pits and turn flame-throwers on them."

"I doubt if the Nazis would waste fuel," said Zdenek. "Not that they care about *untermensch*."

Subhumans. It had taken some time for Ota to get used to the idea that Russians—and Czechs—had the worth of an animal, but less than a German pimp. In fact, he was not used to it.

"What about the meeting, Auntie? When do we get to see the people who make the decisions?"

"You can't ask me about things I don't know," she said. "Those people are still alive after two years of violent repression and five months of Heydrich's hell. That should speak for itself."

"It tells me they're careful," said Ota. "But it doesn't say much for their will."

"Relax," she said. "Anna will be here at any moment. She'll calm you down."

"She does not calm me down, Auntie."

"Nor is she meant to."

The big woman rose from the chair like a light-footed man. Before going back into the kitchen, she gave a wink that was good-natured and lurid. How much did she know? Did Anna tell her some things or everything? How he made love. What he said when like a dying animal he released inside her.

They all worked together for the Red Cross—Anna, Auntie, and Libena, who came to visit Zdenek as often as her father, who also worked for the Red Cross as their secretary, allowed. He probably thought that it was safe letting a young girl do what she did so well—help a wounded man. But Zdenek was not safe. Never once.

He was a great friend—a great man—but Libena was in danger if love was dangerous. Four days ago—while they were still at the Khodl's—Ota came back from Anna's flat in Mala Strana. He saw Vasek, the Khodl's son, in the hall with another boy, so he knew the door was open. He went into the flat and through the main room to the bedroom where he and Zdenek stayed. He pushed open the door, then stopped, shut it, and stood there more shocked than the day the SS put a brand to his ass.

Ota moved away from the door as if he had been clubbed. Why should the sight of a young woman sucking his best friend's cock affect him like that?

He could not forget the way Libena's bare back arched and the length of her bare flank and the long brown hair that fell across Zdenek's belly and the religious concentration that she had given the thing that swelled so big in both hands.

She had not seen him—never—and Zdenek had only glanced at him as the door closed with an unfocused and tilted look. Neither mentioned the incident, but the memory stayed with Ota for the next week, because in all that time he did not see Anna again. He went to see her after two days, traveling across Prague on three trolleys, only to find that she did not answer her door. Was she gone? Was she in there, taunting him with the meeting that would never take place?

When he returned to the Khodl's, Ota went into the bathroom, barely saying hello as he passed. He took down his pants and began to masturbate, seeing Libena's delicate lips around that big thing, pretending it was Anna's on his sucking, sucking it forever, and the next day, when he had gone into the bathroom and taken down his pants again and taken it in his hand again, he stopped.

Is this why they had come to Prague?

Yes, Mister President, that is my dick in my hand. It's all I think about, unfortunately.

Ota left the house at once. He told Zdenek where he was going but no one else. He walked four blocks to the trolley stop and waited ten minutes for a car. A few seconds before it came, two well-built men appeared at each side of the bench and boarded the car with him. They sat with him on either side. They stayed with him all the way to the railway station and the rest of the way on the train to the village of Nehvizdy, where he retrieved with their grudging help most of the supplies that had been left behind.

The trip told Ota how closely they were being watched. Controlled. And how. He did not blame Anna—he could never blame her because she was an honest woman—but he was determined to break their hold. When they got back to Prague, he told the two men what was in the boxes and how to store the volatiles and everything but what they would be used for.

The message got through. The next day he and Zdenek were moved again—this time to Moravcova's. Auntie was very kind and willing to please. She washed their clothes and put them to bed with a smile and the next morning produced two of the rarest things in Prague—pork chops. She also told Ota that Anna—the wonderful girl she worked with—would appear soon. Today she had said, yes, tonight, and here it was late afternoon.

So when the doorbell to the second-floor flat rang, and Auntie called to Ota to answer, he was sure who would be on the other side, because he was still thinking, from time to time, with his prick.

The man who stood in the hallway, smiling, did not resemble Anna, or anyone that Ota had ever known. He seemed to contradict the word that no one had ever escaped from a concentration camp. He had no hair and almost no lips and no meat on him anywhere. Half-circling his head were dark-rimmed glasses as thick as his wrists. If it wasn't for the humor that haunted his face like a memory, Ota would have been appalled.

"Hello," he said. "Are you visiting?"

Ota said, "Yes," but he felt like someone behind him had said it.

"Riha," called Auntie gaily, as she came from the kitchen and stopped, exhausting the space in the doorway. "Come in, old friend. Come in."

He did so, slipping into a space between them that no other person on earth could have found. "I'm sorry I'm late," he said. "But you know how the Gestapo are."

"Riha's our neighbor," said Auntie. "He lives just down the street, but he's constantly wandering around this big city. It's a demanding job, having care of all the submarines in Prague."

"Submarines," said Ota. "Illegals."

He shrugged modestly. "It does keep me busy. If you'd care to get your coat on—"

"My coat?"

"You don't want to be late for the meeting," said Auntie. "It's important, you know."

They were playing with him to show how clever they were. No doubt Riha lived down the street. Ota had never seen him in the neighborhood, but the man looked like he only came out in the dead of night.

"I'll fetch Zdenek."

Riha smiled again. His face was open and friendly, but with so little flesh behind it, every gesture seemed to emerge from the void.

"No," he said. "Just one. The one who can walk."

* * *

They took a trolley to Prague-Smichov and got out two blocks from the boulevard along the Vltava River, where they walked in vectors that seemed random. Several cars passed along the route, creeping behind blackout headlamps like giant phosphorescent insects. That could change instantly, though, and for the worst, because official cars usually had spotlights mounted on the fender.

Ota caught glimpses of the river, which had been frozen since they came to the city. In the moonlight, the surface looked inlaid and highly polished. Luminous. The last time he left Anna's flat, he had watched skaters cascading across the ice. They were—if you looked at it that way—walking on water.

Ota was glad to know it was not impossible. As hard as it had been getting through to the people high in the resistance, he could not fault their security. The Gestapo were everywhere. Strangers in any neighborhood were noticed, and the man who noticed might be a German, or one of the Czechs who had registered as a German for the extra fat ration, or just someone who wanted to get his brother out of a KZ.

That was the reason Ota and Zdenek moved so often and changed identities. They had papers that said who they were not, and others that said what they were so sick with that they could not work. Until tonight those papers had been good for sightseeing in the capital—for acclimation—and little else.

The promise of change excited Ota, moving through his body differently than the tension that came with nicking back the window shade fifty times a day, or the paralyzing excitement of thinking that he would see Anna again. When they turned from a street that ran parallel to the river into a dark courtyard and across it to a flight of stairs, Ota notched the safety off his revolver. This might be UVOD he was meeting, or it might be a group of good men all but one.

He could be the man that stood on the second floor landing, loitering in the cold.

Or the other that Ota had seen standing at the window across the street from the entrance to the courtyard. The lights had been out in the window, but the blackout curtains were lifted and the man had been smoking a cigarette cupped behind his hand that glowed as he inhaled, illuminating his face. It was like that all over Prague—idle people standing at darkened windows in defiance of the rules smoking wartime tobacco so foul that it stunk right through the glass—but they usually did not cup their hand to hide it.

No one was in sight on the third floor, where they turned and passed along the hallway. That might be worse. Thinking someone must be hidden in deep shadow moved the taste of blood into Ota's mouth.

Riha stopped before a dark door with the number 67 and a paper insert that said: Stastny.

A joke. Stastny meant lucky.

Riha rang the bell. It sounded in the hall through the door like something that was failing.

The man who opened the door was as wide as it. He had arms like a chest, and a chest like a horse. Ota supposed he should be used to these sorts by now, because the Falcons had been the best gymnasts in Europe.

This one had been a champion. As he let them into the anteroom of the flat, he seemed not so much to move as throb. His gruff voice throbbed as he spoke to Riha.

"We expected two of them."

"The other is crippled," said Riha. "For this one I can't speak."

"I can speak for myself," said Ota. "For the team."

"I'm impressed," said the gymnast. "As long as your team understands this is not a game."

He stepped back, and they entered a room with several chairs, a table, and another man. He looked like a bandit—a weary one. His hair was dark and his eyebrows dark and his mustache dark and drooping. He had some extra flesh that put a slope in unexpected places, but his skin looked healthy, as if he took care to find the sun in every season.

"Some tea?"

Ota nodded. He would have to drink the stuff, which might be almost anything in wartime, to show that he trusted them.

"Your name?"

"I'm called Ota."

"Jindra," said the bandit.

The gymnast brought the tea, already made and almost hot. Ota sipped his, and waited. Jindra sipped, and the gymnast took a big unfeeling bite of his.

Jindra put the cup down with exaggerated care. "I'm afraid that I never know what to say to a man who keeps one hand in his coat."

"I thought it was the fashion in Prague."

Jindra smiled like a bandit. "In some quarters, guns are the fashion. I think we all have the same heavy pockets tonight."

Ota returned the smile. He pulled the automatic pistol from his pocket and held it out like bread. Slowly, he put it on the table but within easy reach.

"My partner's the specialist with firearms, but I have a liking for these things, too."

"Where did you acquire the habit?"

"Serving my country," said Ota. "Free Czechoslovakia."

"There are many kinds of patriots these days," said Jindra. "Where do you come from?"

"The sky."

"You can't say more?"

"The reason we're here is secret."

"But you've already told other people in the network that you came from England."

"True," said Ota. "It seemed to mean something to them, and perhaps it should to you."

"I'll tell you what it means to me," said Jindra in a tone that seemed to fall off a cliff. "Germans. In the last six months, the Gestapo has sent three men to us with the same story. They were all parachutists landed from England."

So that was the reason for the caution that seemed so near to crazy. The Gestapo must have gotten the idea from the bad drop in October—when the para fell into their hands.

"How did you discover these men?"

"They tripped themselves on questions they should have known the answers to," said the gymnast.

He held out a photograph of a man with his arm around a young girl, passing the picture to Ota. "I asked one of those agents—the one that ended up in the river—who this man was."

"I don't know his name," said Ota quickly. "But I saw him around brigade last spring. In England."

The gymnast took back the photograph. "That's a good answer," he said. "But a German could know it. The Gestapo keeps files on every man who serves abroad. They know more of our boys than their families do."

"Are you related to him?" asked Ota. "Your son perhaps?"

"We ask the questions," said the gymnast. "You answer for your life."

So it went for the next twenty minutes. Ota did not mind the questions. He had undergone mock interrogations at STS 2 that were considerably worse. Practice had taught him everything but patience, it seemed. Ota thought it sinful to be so near his goal only to be grilled by pedants.

Where had he been stationed in England? Company? Platoon? Who was his commanding officer? What is the first name of the president of the Czechoslovak Republic? When did Churchill last review the troops in Warwickshire? Had Ota ever met a man named Franta?

The questions went on and on until Jindra said, "You seem to have a Moravian accent. Tell me, what is extraordinary about the railway station at Vladislav?"

Ota bagged them with that one. At the station was a great bed of roses—a display so magnificent that one of the railwaymen must be mad for anything with petals and a long stem. Perhaps no place in the whole country had anything like it.

"It's a mass of blooms all summer long," he said.

Jindra, who had seized on Ota's accent like a noose, now decided to bring the biography to an end. "Let's pretend I believe you," he said. "Now tell me your real name so I can trace you with our people."

"My name is Ota."

"That's your code name."

"Correct. That's all you'll have from me. The code name of our mission is Anthropoid, which is all you'll have there."

From the corner where he had taken a chair, Riha broke his long silence with an unearthly smile and a strange sort of hum. "Anthropoid," he said, rolling the name until it seemed even longer than it was. "You know, once I was a schoolmaster in the classics. My memory tells me that *anthropos* is the Greek word for man. So anthropoid might mean—like a man."

"Or something not quite a man," said Jindra.

"A half man," said the gymnast. "A piece of shit that walks and talks like a human being."

"A monster," said Riha, smiling as if he had discovered sin. "You know, Leon always said it would be necessary for us to kill a Nazi monster. Then we would truly become a resistance. For months—while we still had communication with London—he begged them to send over men who could accomplish great things. That's exactly what Leon said—great things."

"But which monster does this refer to?" asked Jindra. "Mister Anthropoid."

"You might start with the biggest one," said Riha. "The man who secretly runs the Reich and controls its networks of terror. The Gestapo. The Criminal Police. The Jewish Office. Every branch of Reich Main Security. Who kept all these things for himself after he was appointed to rule this nation of ours."

"Not the Protector," said Jindra warily. "You can't mean Heydrich."

Riha smiled again. "He's right, isn't he, code-name Ota? Or should I say, our giant killer?"

Ota looked at Riha, who seemed to like the idea as much as he liked finding it out. The same reaction, quite obviously, was not true of Jindra.

"We promised the president that we would complete our mission," he said. "We will do that. But the planning must be precise. There are many things we need to know. I came here tonight to ask your help."

"So it's Heydrich," said Jindra.

"Perhaps."

Jindra did not respond. He had heard the near-confirmation and seemed to weigh the possibilities as if his own death had been proposed.

But Riha entered the lull with enthusiasm. He rose from his chair and held out both hands. "We're glad that you have come," he said. "And we're glad that Heydrich will die. As for planning—that's what we do best."

CHAPTER 8

SUMMARY: ICE TO FRANTA

We have received the codes that will enable us to contact Three Kings and Anthropoid. Now we feel it is time to acquaint you with the realities of life in the homeland.

The terror that has been thoroughgoing since the occupation of the homeland by the Germans became complete with Heydrich's appointment as Protector. With the SD and the Gestapo at his personal command, thousands have been murdered or sent to concentration camps. The resistance has been decimated. Little of the intelligentsia exists any longer, and for every man who is or was politically active, a permanent Gestapo agent is in place. Random checks for documentation are pervasive. Searches of permanent records are routine. Police controls on railways and hotels are tight, making travel very difficult.

We are sending a man, but have little hope of carrying out your wishes. Our previous efforts at contacting Three Kings were rebuffed. Of Anthropoid we know nothing.

* * *

Just as everything began to move ahead when UVOZ was finally satisfied that they were authentic and agreed to help with preparations for the assassination of the most powerful man in the Nazi hierarchy, the security of the resistance network was disrupted by a man who appeared in the coffee shop of the Golden Goose Hotel, and later, at a dry goods store in Zizkov, demanding to be put in touch with Anthropoid.

And he knew the code: "Miluska from Station 17 greets Vyskocil."

Station 17 stood for STS 17 in Hertfordshire where they had trained in sabotage, and Vyskocil was Zdenek.

But no one knew Miluska. He appeared first in Pilzn before being shunted to Prague. Although he spoke Czech fluently, he was said to look like a Nazi movie star. At that point, Zdenek began to think that he knew what he was dealing with.

Still, he was cautious in the approach. Because Ota was at Anna's, where he went daily, Zdenek set up a meeting at a tavern three blocks from Auntie's apartment in Zizkov. The walk was nothing, even for a cripple who had begun to move like a man. Zdenek entered the tavern by the back door and slipped into the kitchen, where he could watch most of the taproom.

He saw what he had expected: a homeless angel named Josef Valcik. Perhaps it was the blond hair, or the blue eyes that looked as if they had been jerked from a bed of arctic ice, but no one thought of Valcik as normal. He had dropped with Silver A the same night Anthropoid dropped, and it might as well have been from heaven.

He was too good looking for a para. The barmaid was already fingering the lace at her bodice as if she couldn't wait for an offer. The barkeeper, a grim sort with reasons for it, had already bought him a beer. They couldn't help themselves. They either joined the party, or they missed it.

"Miluska?"

Valcik did not turn when he heard the voice from the doorway behind him. He continued to offer a cigarette to the barkeeper from the pack in his hand, then returned the pack and the hand to the pocket where he would keep his weapon.

"My friends call me worse," he said. "Especially Vyskocil, the locksmith. He has the key to my heart."

"No one has that," said Zdenek, louder. "They can't open a thing they can't find."

Valcik spun around, hands out, smiling. "Zdenek. Older brother."

They embraced like brothers. Zdenek never asked why Valcik called him that, but it didn't stop with the fact that their names were both Josef. The bond was something they recognized from the first day they met at STS 17. Some of the recruits were making noises at playing Russian Roulette to show their balls when Valcik took the revolver, put it to his head, clicked out one round of nothing, then turned and fired the next round, loud and live, into a potted plant by the door. Over the next few days, the plant died. It was Hun Ivy, said Valcik—a lesson. They shouldn't play at suicide until they reached a place where it was more productive.

Well, here they were, sitting in St. Peter's taproom as the barkeeper put fresh steins of creamy beer on the corner table in front of them.

"I knew it was you when they said Miluska made a move on the concierge at the Golden Goose," said Zdenek. "She's seventy-three, you know."

"And horny," said Valcik. "My success with women is good—unbelievable—because I don't discriminate. You never know what you might miss."

"I think it has more to do with those fanatic blue eyes," said Zdenek. "Put an SS uniform around that Nordic face, and we could walk right into Prague Castle."

"Is that what you want to do?"

Zdenek spoke quickly, but with a hitch that almost betrayed him. "Of course that's what we want. At the head of our army."

"Our army's in England, my friend."

"For the moment."

"That could be the longest moment in history," said Valcik. "Is it possible you meant something else?"

"What?"

"C'mon now. You can tell Miluska."

"I don't like that name," said Zdenek. "We'll have to find you a better one."

"Well, I don't know. How about Ice? It's our call-sign at Radio Libuse."

"That's good," said Zdenek. "It fits. All the women who make pilgrimages to your grave will recognize it."

"So I'm going to be famous. Like you and Ota."

Zdenek took that in without smiling. "What makes you think we'll be famous?"

"It's obvious, isn't it?"

"No," he said flatly.

"London's crazy to know where you are. Take all measures, they said. Compromise yourself and everyone else. Now, why would they risk destroying the network they tried so hard to get into the country—for a mere sabotage team?"

Zdenek was thinking of how to contain the damage, though it seemed pointless to deny the purpose of their mission to a man who knew their whereabouts and background.

"We don't need help," he said. "Just good security. Our mission will go ahead as planned."

"You've been on the ground almost two months," said Ice. "It won't be easier the longer you're here."

"That's our problem. You'll be needed at Ice Base."

"No, I won't. I've nothing to do there, and Emil and I are not getting along."

"You mean the lieutenant."

"His Highness," said Ice. "You see, Pardubice is his home. The second day we were there, a man came up to him on the street and said, 'Well hello, old friend. I see you're back from England'."

"Are you serious?"

"Deadly. We had to move to a nearby village where there's not a hell of a lot to amuse us. After we settled down, our leader took a shine to a young woman. He fancied her so ineffectively that she fell into someone else's arms the minute he said hello."

"You're incredible."

"Available," he said. "I've got a high-risk job as a waiter at the Veselka Hotel. All the best-looking women pass in and out. The good thing is that sometimes they come on the arm of the local Gestapo."

"You light their cigarettes, I suppose."

Ice nodded like the actor he had become. "And sell them rubbers, too. Close combat socks, they call them."

"You should be able to get good intelligence that way."

"You mean, who tells me with a hearty laugh that he takes an extra large?"

"Is that all you learned?"

"Practically," he said. "And London cares for nothing but Three Kings. The oracle. They want me to contact him, too." Ice's face lit with inspiration. "Or maybe it's her. A woman."

Zdenek lifted the glass of beer that was not as good as it had been when it was the best in the world. "Three Kings is a man," he said.

"Bad break."

"His code-name is Leon," said Zdenek. "He's in direct contact with a spy in German military intelligence."

Zdenek paused, because he knew that name would mean something to Ice, as it did to nearly everyone. Leon was the man who had carried the resistance single-handedly for years. He was the legend of the movement.

"Leon's network is tightly controlled," said Zdenek. "No one's seen him for months."

"It shouldn't be impossible," said Ice. "The BBC broadcast a message saying that I was on my way. His people should be expecting me. Hell, that's why Silver A is here. Radio Libuse is the only way that Three Kings has of passing information back to London. Will they wait until the war's over to tell what they know?"

"I think they want to live," said Zdenek. "Some people do, even in the middle of a war."

"Well, tell them they're in the wrong damned business. I have to reach Three Kings, Zdenek. I have my mission. We all have our missions."

Zdenek wiped the sweat off his glass with his thumb, as if he could shed a friend as easily. Ice was brave—he was suicidal—but wrong for this situation. He was lucky that he hadn't blundered into the Gestapo already, and luckier that he hadn't met the wrong member of the resistance, who might have shot him on the spot.

"I can help," said Zdenek. "But it'll take time. You'll have to return to Pardubice as soon as possible. We'll contact Leon. If everything's right, he'll set up couriers from this end. You do the same from yours." Zdenek smiled. "Try finding women for the work. They're best."

"You really are trying to get rid of me."

"Let's say I know how."

Ice laughed and moved back in his chair for the duration of the war. "It won't work, Zdenek. I'm staying here until my mission's accomplished." He thumped his empty glass down. "Let's have another drink. Then we'll see Leon."

* * *

It didn't happen like that, of course. Nothing happened in the resistance without six essential consultations. Zdenek put Ice up in one of Riha's safe-places. Two days later, while Ota attended a meeting concerning the meeting with Leon, word came unexpectedly by a secure courier who said that the legend would be available that evening. Zdenek might have waited for Ota to return; but this seemed like an opportunity to get things done.

The Nazis had made the Old Town their own, but the stamp shop on Na Porici lay close to the trolley line from Karlin. It was an old place that seemed folded into the block, overhung with a patch of neon that had been painted bright red for the blackout. The steady flow of trade passing through the doors made it a reasonable place for a contact. Convertible currency was in short supply throughout the Reich, and stamps, particularly valuable ones, were a good currency substitute.

The man behind the counter had a face like the image of Tomas Masaryk that had appeared on many stamps of the old Republic—a wide bald head, pince-nez glasses, neatly trimmed beard. He looked up over the glasses, as if they might be camouflage, too.

"Can I help you?"

"I'd like to see Germany," said Zdenek. "The '36 Olympic series. The one with the gutter."

" '36," said the man. "The Heydrich Games."

Zdenek nodded because they were called that in code and in reality. Heydrich had staged the Games so the world could see the benign face of Nazi Germany. Yes, there were concentration camps, but only for communists and incorrigibles.

"The series with the gutter is rare," said the man. "I keep it in the back."

Zdenek followed him from the front counter through a door and down a short hall to a small room that was kept, perhaps, for private showings. Inside stood a small table and two chairs.

"I'll wait for my party here."

"It would be better to wait inside, sir. I'll bring Mister Gruber to you."

Zdenek said nothing. This thing was going by the book—the one that had not been written yet. The first page said that it was unhealthy to be trapped in a tiny room with no visible exit.

"That's all right, Oldrich."

The voice came from behind—from the end of the hall where Zdenek had seen nothing but shadow. Now something detached from the darkness like an extension of it—a man who was as gaunt as Riha and filled his clothing even less. He wore a dark overcoat that would have had more form on a one-peg rack, and a Tyrolean hat that shaded his face. A tuft of badger hair had been tucked in the brim that was pulled low, almost to the top of his nose, and a nest of worry lines scurried from the corners of his eyes.

Zdenek did not speak until the proprietor turned and left by the opposite way. And until he was sure no one replaced him.

"Gruber?"

The man seemed to smile under the tilted hat. "Call me anything you like, but I was told that you insisted on speaking to Leon."

Zdenek moved down the hall. Was this really Leon—the man who sent postcards to the Gestapo; who had escaped them so many times—the last by sliding from a third-story window on an aerial that severed one of his fingers? Who always wore gloves to hide the fact?

When Zdenek put out his hand for the greeting that was universal except in Greater Germany, the man extended his left hand in a leather glove.

"This is the one you want," he said. "The ring finger of the left hand."

Zdenek took the left hand in his left hand. He felt all the fingers in the glove and the ring finger alone. That space was spongy, as if it had been filled with packing.

"Are you satisfied?"

"I'm glad to meet you, Leon."

"Let's walk a while," he said, tilting his head toward the darkness behind him. "We might have some things in common."

They left by a door that led to an alley. The movement was awkward and nervous as Zdenek tried to maintain pace on his gimpy leg. Leon had evaded the Gestapo for two years, and for the last six months as the most wanted man in the Reich. In the blackout night that had fallen like earth onto the city he moved fast but carefully.

They crossed the street and entered the Old Town. It was a maze that grew darker and narrower until the buildings seemed to overhang the street, but Leon knew every byway, even as they turned, and turned again. When he heard footsteps approaching, he knew exactly how far off. He continued at a normal pace if contact was unavoidable, but fell back if it was distant. And when the footsteps came from behind, Leon lost them with series of maneuvers that left Zdenek confused.

"We must be in the Jewish Quarter by now."

"An empty name," said Leon.

"Are things as bad with them as they say?"

"I'd think they were much worse. Since November, thousands of Prague Jews have been sent to Terezin concentration camp. It's the first phase of a plan that was announced at a conference in Berlin. Heydrich presided. He ordered that a Final Solution to the Jewish Problem be undertaken immediately."

"The Final Solution," said Zdenek. "That sounds very German. Sanitary but for the blood."

"Our Jews will be shipped to new camps in Poland," said Leon. "So will the other Jews from all over Europe. There they will be killed."

It wasn't easy to doubt this man, but Zdenek could not help it. "That can't be," he said. "Not all the Jews. There must be millions in Europe."

"Yes. Millions." Leon slowed his pace, as if stunned by his words. "I wouldn't worry so much if they didn't have Heydrich for the dirty work."

"But will they continue to have him?"

"I suppose that depends on two men called Anthropoid," said Leon. "Are you and your friend as good as they say?"

"I don't know what they say," said Zdenek. "My foot's been bad since we dropped. The local resistance seems to be good at holding meetings, but short on results."

"They're afraid of repercussions," said Leon. "Who can blame them? We've had no decent contact with London. We have no orders, no direction. And we have no way of verifying you—or anyone else."

"That's what we're offering," said Zdenek. "Silver A is operational near Pardubice. They had some trouble with their small receiver, but they've been on the air since mid-January."

"In contact with London?"

"Daily," he said. "Hourly, if necessary."

"No problems with the Germans tracking their signal?"

"Their direction-finders have limited range," said Zdenek. "Unless they know the area where the transmitter's located, they can't pinpoint the signal."

"I'm glad to hear that. I lost two friends and a finger to one of those vans."

"Radio Libuse is secure, Leon. They have a good location and will soon have a better one. London awaits the word of Three Kings."

Leon knew that he had to agree to set up the link between Three Kings and Radio Libuse now—or pass. His face had grown thicker in the darkness, less distinct, and he seemed to speak from a receding core of eyes.

"We call our man Rene. He's a genuine Nazi—one of the early storm troopers—a man with the Gold Party Badge." Leon put his hand on Zdenek's arm. "I'm telling you this because London will need to know. The Gestapo thinks Rene is the man they call Traitor X. They arrested him two weeks ago, but had to release him. They can't use torture, because he has powerful friends. In the old days, he was a comrade of Himmler. That's protected him until now, but perhaps not much longer."

If the skeletal hand on his arm had not stopped Zdenek, those words would have. He stood on the cobblestones, swaying in the loose joins around a sewer.

"London will be sorry to have this news. Rene's the reason Silver A is here."

"I'll see you have all the information he can give for as long as possible."

"You mean he still has access?"

"Himmler's friend has to be a hero or a traitor. He can't be shunted aside. Even Heydrich watches himself there."

"I see."

"Now that you do, promise you'll be there to back me up. I may have to pull Rene out suddenly."

Zdenek tapped his left side twice. "You'll have our guns."

Leon took Zdenek's hand and held it tightly. "I'm happy to have them," he said. "For the first time in a long while I'm beginning to think I can count on someone besides myself. I want you to feel that way, too. Let me know if you need anything."

"I'd like you to set a fire under the local people," said Zdenek. "This man Jindra seems to have lead feet."

"I'll see what I can do," he said as if that might be more than nothing.

They turned and began to walk along the twisting streets again. Zdenek took his bearings when they skirted the Old Town

Square and turned down the Melantrichova. Quickly, they turned right again and left, walking along the block to an old house that seemed about to fall into Michalska Street by its gables. Zdenek told himself that he should not be surprised: Leon had brought him, with the speed of rumor, to the safe-place where Ice had been stashed.

"Would you like to come in and meet him?"

Leon laughed for the first time. "Is he worth it?"

"He's the best," said Zdenek. "Ice would kill his mother if she was German."

"Then by all means."

Inside the cozy first-floor flat, they were welcomed for the night by the lady of the house—and her guest. Ice acted as if he had been born to the place, as he did in every place, and Mrs. Svatos was a fine hostess who wanted most to fill her dangerous guests with food and winter cheer. When she wasn't working with the resistance, she ran a business that made evening dresses for the many German whores of the city. They were rich bizarre creations fashioned from silk and moire, studded with rhinestones, false pearls, and hatred.

CHAPTER 9

"Who is this man?" asked Zdenek. "This Frantisek Safarik."

In the lateral winter sunlight that filtered through Mala Strana Square, Riha's smile spread like a thaw under his broad-brimmed hat. The thin man had a friendly face if he chose to show it, and gentle eyes, if he looked at you without measuring.

"He's an old pupil of mine. When I coached the football team at Liboc School, he was the goalie. Perhaps I should tell you that no one else wanted the job."

A good recommendation nonetheless. Since Zdenek had spoken to Leon, things moved steadily and quickly as Riha took over liaison with the resistance. He had always been resourceful in obtaining documents and housing. In his expanded role, he performed like the master that he was. After Ice left for Pardubice, a string of couriers had been set up between Anthropoid and Silver A. Messages now could be sent to London from Prague in two days.

"Are you sure that Safarik has access to the castle?"

"Yes," said Riha. "He can go almost anywhere he wants. At almost any time."

"Odd for a carpenter."

"That's because he's not just a carpenter. Frantisek is a skilled craftsman. His job is to maintain the furniture in the castle—the modern pieces, and the antiques, of which there are many. The Nazis haven't replaced him, nor can they. He's free to wander the premises to look over the furniture and repair it."

Ota moved a pace from the column of the arcade where he stood lookout. He could still see the four sides of the square, but now he shared their words under the noise of the trolleys that rolled through, wheels grinding, bells ringing.

"How do you know you can trust him, Uncle?"

Riha pursed his match-thin lips. "If he comes today, he'll do what we ask."

"And if he doesn't?"

"Then we'll find someone else."

Always an alternative with the thin man they had come to call Uncle. He seemed to have the patience for the work, as well as the contacts, which were vital. Everything that could be known about Heydrich must be. All his movements, especially the consistent ones, noted. The SS security accounted for.

"Look," he said. "There he is across the street. The man in the smock."

Not a common carpenter. Safarik's smock, which made him look like more of a painter than a woodworker, belled loose in the wind. With a delicacy that belied a broad-shouldered man, he forded the deep slush in the street, holding onto the hat on his head. He jumped to the curb without soiling his shoes.

"Dammit, professor, I wouldn't have come out in this slop for anyone but you."

"For your country, Frantisek. Not for me."

"Don't tell me why I'm risking my life," he said. "It's only because an old friend asked me to." He cast a glance about him that was known all over Europe as the German Look, a slow furtive rotation that asked: who is listening to my words? "I don't feel comfortable here."

They began to walk down Letenska Street, where the sidewalk was clear and soon covered by overpasses where the trolleys went. Safarik took the lead a half-pace ahead, like someone who was not quite attached to the group, gathering ground with the tip of his walking stick. It looked like an antique, too.

"I'd like you to meet my friends," said Uncle. "Ota and Zdenek."

Safarik turned sidelong, nodded. "Good people, I'm sure."

"They are the best at what they do," said Uncle. "Much like yourself."

"Not antiques, I'd bet."

"They're more specialized, it's true."

"I wouldn't have dreamed this scene," said Safarik. "Not with my schoolmaster. You couldn't have made me believe that Jan Zelenka would be involved in this kind of business."

Uncle grimaced when his identity was revealed so casually as his old pupil went on. "What would Master Petr say about this?" asked Safarik. "Or Master Fiala?"

"Master Petr was shot last fall for being a member of the Falcon committee in Liboc," said Uncle. "As for Master Fiala, no one's heard from him in some time. He went on an unexpected trip, along with most of the intellectuals of Central Europe."

Safarik maintained his lead of eighteen inches on the pack, as if that made a difference to the Gestapo. "You don't have to sell me the idea that the Germans have ruined our lives. What you can do is show me how I'll keep mine. For God's sake, I have a wife and small child. Every man's first duty is to his family."

Zdenek moved into the slot that had been created by Safarik's hectic reach. "I promise that nothing will be required of you but information. When the time comes to turn it to some account, you'll not be involved at all."

"To some account? Is that what we're talking about—a bank deposit?"

"An investment in the future, yes."

"And you think there is one?"

"I know it," said Zdenek. "One day our children will talk of the heroes of the resistance. They'll remember the late winter day when four men walked along this street planning the overthrow of Nazi tyranny."

Safarik turned aggressively to Uncle. "Did you teach him to talk like that? In unanswerable phrases?"

"No," said Uncle. "I believe he learned them abroad. In England."

Safarik stopped instantly. Zdenek almost stepped on his heels and Ota ran by him.

"England," he said.

"We're professional soldiers of the Home Army," said Zdenek. "We've been trained to strike targets, and with careful planning, succeed."

Safarik put his hand to his wide forehead and ran it down his wide jowly face. "I didn't know. Are there many of you?"

"More every day," said Zdenek, who was sure there would be. "Each with a mission."

"And yours?"

"We'd like to know the time each day when Heydrich arrives at the castle. And when he leaves."

Safarik began to walk again slowly, his stick tapping not the pavement but his leg. It made Zdenek wince. He was able to walk now without much discomfort, but there were problems that seemed to have more to do with memory than muscle and bone. He still could not run. Soon, perhaps.

"I knew you'd ask this," said Safarik when they had gone half a block. "Or something like it. And I told myself I'd refuse to help with anything that stinks of the graveyard."

Zdenek said nothing but smiled. When a Czech gave his reasons for refusal, he was about to accept without reservation.

"How would I get this information to you?"

"You'd deliver it to your schoolmaster's home."

"Why, he lives in Zizkov," said Safarik. "That's way across town."

"Then you can bring it here."

"Here?" Safarik looked at the pavement of Letenska Street as if it might spring a genie. "You want me to leave it beneath the curbstone?"

The timing could have been better, but not much. Ota did not answer Safarik. He continued up Letenska a few steps until he came to a window that overlooked the street. It had many small panes, but in one on the lower left corner was a snowflake—more of an ice crystal—in decorative paint.

"You'll knock on this window."

Ota knocked. The window opened several seconds later. A woman with long brown hair stood framed in it, looking out as if she saw nothing but pale March light. It was Anna's flat, but this was the night that Libena and Zdenek had it. Every third night through the kindness of friends.

"It may be this woman who answers," said Zdenek. "Or another with darker hair. You'll give the message to one of the girls if you think it's safe, and walk on."

Safarik seemed stunned. He stared at Libena until she returned his look, smiled, and closed the window quietly. "She's like a Vermeer," he said. "We used to have one in the Master's Room at the castle, you know."

"That's next," said Zdenek. "Let's take a look."

* * *

It would have been shorter to climb the backstairs, but they wanted to scan every angle of approach in the street that Heydrich's vehicle might take if he came down the hill from the castle. They walked slowly up the street known as The Royal Way. All conquerors—including the last and most barbaric—had ascended to Prague Castle by the same perpendicular route, mounting to the city's bastion.

But no place along the steep street offered a good point of vantage. Heydrich's machine, hurtling down the hill, or moving up as quick, would never have to slow. The shortage of cars, and gasoline rationing, meant that reduced traffic moved even in daylight. Except for the sharp bend toward Mala Strana Square at the bottom, the rest of the long street was a straight shot to the ramp near the top.

But there it might be possible. The sweeping turn into the ramp was approximately one hundred and forty degrees. No vehicle would be able to take the angle anywhere near full speed, and from the corner building across the street, an ambush might be set.

"What do you think?"

Ota shook his head. "The problem is being sure. If security cars are in front or behind, they'll close up fast. You might get one quick burst."

"Explosives?"

"The same. If we got lucky and blew the fuel tank, there'd be a nice fire. But it wouldn't be certain."

Nor were the chances for escape. The castle grounds were filled with troops able to fire from above. That was to say nothing about additional security on the fly.

"Frantisek," said Ota. "What of the escort cars?"

"They're almost always filled with SS."

"Almost always?"

"Yes."

"You can't be more specific?"

"Do I have to be precise about suicide?"

"We'll try to avoid that," said Ota. "But our job will be easier if we know exactly what we're facing."

"Exactly," said Safarik, tapping his stick against his leg again. "Follow me if you want to see precision. The Protector should be leaving the castle soon."

They walked up the ramp to Hradcany Square, a huge expanse of open ground that stood to the west. To the east, overlooking the river, the Old Town, and much of the city, lay Prague Castle, a sprawling complex of buildings from which the government of the nation had been conducted for centuries. It ran for hundreds of yards, mirroring the natural fortification of the hill in a unbroken cliff-like formation.

The castle could be entered in several ways, but Heydrich, the showman, always came and went by the main gate, where the guard was. Two SS stood outside the gate, and four more occupied the inner courtyard. They were on duty at all times.

"We should keep moving," said Safarik nervously. "The guards will notice us."

They peeled away, acting like tourists, of which there were a few in the square on a sunny day. Germans mostly, being lectured by guides. What did they think when they saw a city more beautiful than any in their own country?

They didn't think. They obeyed, or were destroyed by their own creation—the Gestapo empire ruled by SS Obergruppenfuhrer Heydrich.

"How does he keep all of Reich Security under his control while he's in Prague?"

"The answer is he's not here a lot of the time," said Safarik. "He has an aircraft. He flies to Berlin—and other places—when he wants. There's a special train at his disposal, too."

Having Heydrich out of the country for extended periods that might occur any time created a problem that they had not anticipated. But he would return, and the movements he made coming and going could provide opportunity.

"We'll need an idea of his unscheduled movements as well as the day to day," said Zdenek. "When he leaves and returns."

"I can't give you that," said Safarik. "Only someone in his office would have the information."

Another job for Uncle. Zdenek wondered if the thin man was up to a second penetration inside the castle. A deeper one.

"Where's Heydrich's office?"

"You can't see it from here. He's more intelligent than to show himself at the windows." Safarik pointed above the titans. "It's in the west wing. Over there."

When he raised his arm, the courtyard began to function in its moveable parts. Two cars appeared and wheeled across the broad cobblestones to the entrance. The first carried SS heavily armed; the second was more interesting, an open-top Mercedes-Benz with one occupant—a huge SS sergeant.

"Heydrich's touring car," said Safarik. "That's his driver—Oberscharfuhrer Klein."

"Klein?"

"Sergeant Small," said Safarik. "A perfect example of Nazi humor. Black is always white, except when it's also black."

The courtyard filled with uniforms as the guard fanned out into a double column and clattered to attention. Suddenly, there he was, striding by twin columns into the courtyard—Anthropoid. General Heydrich moved briskly in jackboots and a long black leather coat. He carried black gloves in his right hand, shifting them to the left as he returned the Nazi salute.

Heydrich rose higher, like a frantic war-toy, as he stepped into the car by the door held by Klein. The top was down. He stood for that second in the clear. It could be done now by any man who was a good shot and did not value his life.

"Does he always ride in front with the driver?"

"Sometimes," said Safarik.

"Is the car always open?"

"In good weather."

On any clear day. Zdenek could feel his pulse accelerating like the engines in the courtyard. Heydrich sat down in the front seat, and as if that were a signal, the four SS moved off into the second car. Klein heaved his enormous bulk behind the wheel.

The driver's side was now the left, like all the occupied countries, opposite what it had been. That was something to remember, an instinct that had to be reversed. It would make a difference in the kill.

The green Mercedes with the license plate SS-4 pulled out first, engine roaring. In snug formation, drafting its mate, the security car followed.

Zdenek watched as the Nazi Protector passed within twenty meters of their position. He saw an arrogant face, a misshapen thing near the Teutonic ideal but far from any. The blue eyes were too close together, the long nose wandered off-center, and the skin was so mealy that it meshed in joins like a cheap mask.

Heydrich looked toward the three men who stood near the Sternberg Palace, but seemed to sense nothing. The ice-blue eyes did not recognize his fate. The long-stemmed neck did not adjust. He tugged his peaked cap once to settle it in the rising speed-wind as the cars moved in tandem toward the end of the square and disappeared into the street that led down the hill.

"Does he leave in that direction every time?"

"Unless he has business in the town, yes."

So it would be difficult to intercept Heydrich if he were going into the center of Prague unless some function had been planned in advance. And unless they knew the time exactly.

"Does more than one security car ever accompany him?"

"Rarely," he said. "Sometimes none."

That was the best news Zdenek had heard. If security was light, the odds for success would increase dramatically.

"When you write the times of his arrival and departure," said Zdenek, "tell us if the security car accompanies him. Just say with. Or without."

“Five twenty-nine,” said Safarik. “With. My first report, and it’s easy.”

“It should be, always. As often as you can make it.”

“You can depend on me. In time, I should develop into a first-rate agent.”

“It’s more certain that Heydrich will die,” said Ota, as soon as the furniture-master had gone.

CHAPTER 10

SUMMARY: ICE TO FRANTA

This is to alert you to a possible loss of function at this station. One of our team was betrayed, and we do not know the extent of the penetration. He is on the run and will contact Anthropoid for new identity papers—as well as his own safety.

* * *

At four o'clock in the afternoon on the first day of spring, Zdenek found himself in Mala Strana at the bottom of the Old Castle Stairs, which were newer than the New Castle Stairs. That was the way of Prague, and the way of Leon.

Everything funneled through him like the long line of steps enclosed by walls rising steeply to the castle. Leon was the conduit between scattered resistance groups that sometimes worked at cross-purposes, and he was ghostly at the business. Zdenek had watched the steps for almost half an hour when a voice behind him, too close behind, said, "Guernica."

He turned and followed the man toward the Waldstein Palace. Leon wore a baggy coat, but the same shabby alpine hat sat above his eyes like a roof with a feather. In his left and bad hand, he carried a briefcase.

When Zdenek drew alongside, Leon turned as if continuing a conversation that lapsed three weeks ago at the Svatos flat. "I understand that you have trouble."

"Everything blew up in Pardubice. The Gestapo got onto Ice. He was lucky that the manager of the hotel where he worked warned him. He was a dead man until he found his way here."

"I knew something was wrong. Yesterday, I received a radio request from the lieutenant in Pardubice. He wants new identity cards made up for his team."

"Yes. I have their photographs."

Zdenek reached into his pocket for the envelope and passed it to Leon, who palmed it out of sight deftly.

"By the way, the request that you received was from the captain in Pardubice. London promoted him for his work in reestablishing contact with you. Another daring exploit like that, and he'll be the ranking underground officer."

Leon shook his head, an abrupt gesture for a man who kept his eyes so still. "Rank means nothing here. What matters is that you can convince ordinary people that you're worth their lives. I hope London keeps sending men who understand that."

"Not if it's up to the captain," said Zdenek. "He thinks too many men will create problems for the ones who are already here. He's recommended against more parachute drops."

Leon stopped. His drawn face took character from his anger, and for the first time Zdenek sensed the discipline that kept him under control. "What did you say?"

"London won't listen," said Zdenek. "They've already told him that they plan more missions."

"When?"

"I don't know. Probably soon."

"It has to be," said Leon, as he began to walk again. "Heydrich's kept up production. It looks like we're helping Hitler. When he loses this war, we'll be seen as collaborators. Czechoslovakia will be lost."

Lost again. For five hundred years the Czechs had been ruled by Austrians. For a thousand years the Slovaks had been ruled by Austro-Hungarians. For even longer, they had been attacked by Germans who demanded living space at their expense. Then there were the Russians, Slavic brothers to be sure.

"Is Stalin doing as well as BBC says?"

"He has held," said Leon. "But the Germans will begin a new campaign soon. Rene thinks Hitler will attack the Russian south, aiming for the oil fields in the Caucasus. If he succeeds, the Russians will only be able to fight stationary battles."

"Have you been in contact with Rene?"

"I saw him two nights ago," said Leon. "He was under close surveillance, but he managed to slip out to meet me."

"Will he be passing information much longer?"

"I doubt it," said Leon. "He's under pressure to bring me into the open. That's the Gestapo's whole plan. I believe Superintendent von Pannwitz let him go this time to get at me. And I've only one way to be sure. I'm going to meet Rene tonight."

"That's dangerous, Leon."

"I have to know," he said. "I've survived these last two years by following one principle: I see everything with my own eyes. I take no one's word for anything."

"Let me come with you."

"No," he said. "If something goes wrong, I want you clear. Anthropoid has to be protected. And augmented. Now that Ice is in Prague, he should be made a member of the team."

"He works best alone. Like you."

"Yes," said Leon. "He's more like me than you know and he's exactly what you'll need." Leon waited until a trolley swooped by before he spoke again. "We can never be sure until the time comes. Some men—some of the bravest men I've known—couldn't put a gun to their heads and pull the trigger. That moment of hesitation has sometimes cost us a great deal."

What was so true could not be argued. Zdenek had practiced the movements of death as if they were dance movements. Every day he took time to imagine the Gestapo coming through the door and the sequence of his response. Cyanide. .45 caliber. But not a fall from a high place or anything uncertain. Repetition and discipline. That would carry him home.

"We have poison, Leon."

"Quick acting?"

"Yes."

"I'd like a small batch that would kill in an hour or two. If I'm taken by the Gestapo, I'd like to laugh in their faces. I'll show them the notches on my gun and what they stand for."

"You mean that."

"More than you think," he said. "My time's growing short, but yours is young. Tell Ice that I'll have a new identity card for him by the day after tomorrow. When he gets it, he's to go to a firm called Topic in the New Town. They'll find him work so he can move about the city. Take him on the team and I'll give you a present in return. His name is Joseph Novotny, a watchmaker with a shop on Uvoz under the castle. He knows more about Heydrich than anyone in Prague. I've worked with him for several months, but never shared him. He'll cooperate if you say you come from me. Use the word Chicago."

"I'd rather go with you," said Zdenek. "Thirty meters back. No one will see me."

Leon stopped as if he would consider the offer. He looked across the street to the building with a blood-red drainpipe that snaked from the gutter to the ground. Then he smiled and put out the five fingers of his good right hand.

"I wish you well in your mission."

Zdenek took his hand, meaning to feel something in it. What? This was a man who had become a legend. The fascination was in the making.

He watched Leon walk back up the street toward the castle stairs. They had almost made a circle to reach this place on the trolley line. Zdenek tried to shake his bad feelings about the meeting that Leon was bound to make, knowing it could be a trap. He crossed the street and began to walk toward the flat on Letenska, telling himself that legends did not die on schedule.

What did it really mean anyway, the Ides of March?

* * *

It was not far to Prague-Dejvice, and the trolley car at six forty-five was hardly crowded. Leon often found he did his best thinking within the rails, but today it did not work. The stops seemed to grind like teeth. The acceleration was not steady but uneven, as if the slick steel surfaces were slipping.

Slipping away. The contest was too uneven. Every day the Gestapo broke some man or woman in the basement of the Pecek Palace, and the names they gave to drive away the pain often led to the destruction of whole networks built up over time by the resistance.

The only revenge was a second-hand defiance. From his briefcase, Leon took up the postcard he had bought at the drop on Na Porici. He wrote on top the case while the movement of the trolley swayed his hand, making the letters jittery, childlike.

> Superintendent von Pannwitz
> Staatspolizeileitstelle
> 20 Bredovska Street
> Prague II
>
> Dear Heinz,
>
> I hope you found the pile of shit I
> left on your desk. I assure you that
> it's genuine. Czech. Don't ask how I
> managed to get into your office. Enjoy
> this gift of love while you can.
>
> Ever yours,
> Leon

The stamp on the postcard was curious. In all venues of the Reich, Hitler's image appeared as a dictator. But Protectorate stamps were different. The Austrian filth stood at a podium as if he were about to orate, or wet himself.

The Germans knew their Czechs. Nothing threatening or insane to speed the mail. Death, which was what Hitler represented, took the form of a bureaucrat.

It was the job of the resistance to make that image revert. When Heydrich died, the face that Hitler turned to Czechoslovakia would be the real one.

As he got off the trolley at the stop three blocks from the park, Leon slipped his hand in his pocket to check his pistol. He did that a hundred times a day. This one was a Czech-made CZ38.

Nine-rounds. He liked the weapon because it had no safety but could be packed safely. In a bad situation, it could be junked safely, because the Luftwaffe and the SS used it, too.

He checked the backup pistol also. The Luger. Caliber the same. Action dissimilar, but also reliable.

At the next block, just before he turned, Leon stopped to mail the postcard at the box. Addendum. My Dearest Heinz. I forgot to mention that I saw you last week with that woman at the Dutch Mill, the one with the hips that begin at the top of her boots. She's the most expensive woman in town, Heinz, and the most popular with Germans, because she'll take it up the ass.

You're an ass-fucker, Heinz, and I'll bet you can't get that at home. What's it like, hearing "No, not tonight, darling," for the last ten years?

You're a dangerous man, Heinz. An unrepentant ass-fucker is the most dangerous man in this world because he doesn't want to put it where it could make more of him.

There are so many of you in Prague now. Once it was easy to know the Gestapo in the city. They could be counted as they climbed into their BMWs after work at the torture mill on Bredovska. Now more appeared every week, following their subhuman leader like maggots on garbage. Forty new SD men had come to Prague with Heydrich simply to track down Traitor X, which is Rene.

That might be one standing in front of the drugstore. He had the look. They all observed the progress of the universe with that queer sidelong curiosity. A primitive thing. Teutonic and unapologetic. A simple yearning for blood.

Leon was unconvinced when the man shifted his eyes and moved off, walking into the drugstore with the wide window. Good enough to see to the end of the block and pass him on?

He had to decide to go ahead and meet with Dandy, or abort. Withdrawing was easy, but nothing was more important than getting Rene out. And Dandy was the way to him.

Leon walked on. As he passed the drugstore, he did not see the man in the porkpie hat standing near the window. Did not see him at all.

Good or bad? Uncertain.

One more thing that was not quite right and Leon would make up his mind by the count. The instincts that had kept him alive for the last two years began to settle in the missing finger of his left hand. An ache. It wrapped itself around the handle of the briefcase like a second glove.

Inconclusive. The finger sometimes throbbed when he did sudden things with the hand, or when he thought of a woman in a sudden way.

At the corner, Leon stopped. How important was the meeting? If it turned up the worst—if Rene had finally been taken—what was the result?

Leon's primary reason for being was gone. That was all. The third king was defunct.

He walked quickly up the side street toward the avenue that bordered the park. It was ten after seven. Ten minutes late. Dandy would wait five minutes more, then leave by the walk.

Leon veered that way to intercept. He saw no further signs of surveillance, but darkness had fallen to within a shade of full blackout night. He could see shapes if they moved quickly or in light clothing, and there were still some people on the street coming home late or going out early.

There were four dark shapes coming down the walk.

Four men.

Make that three men and their prisoner. Leon did not know how he knew that. It might have been the way the man in the middle sagged at the shoulders, as if he had taken on the weight of the world. Or if he was handcuffed.

Dandy. It looked like Dandy and then it was, his fair hair rising from his head, wisping off like dust.

Just as Leon asked himself what would happen next, he felt his body turn to give the enemy the least target, felt the pistol rising in his hand, and heard himself scream, "RUN! RUN!" as he fired.

The first shot surprised him with its noise. He hesitated to fire again, thinking: what if I hit Dandy?

Then: what if I don't?

Leon emptied the magazine at the four shapes that scattered across the walk, one to the right, one to the left, and the two who were joined going flat and unwillingly onto the ground.

It was all noise. He had no idea if he had hit anything until the flash of two muzzles told him he had not hit them well enough. The fire seemed low, badly directed, but heavy.

Leon was already moving, jamming in a new magazine. The pistol was quick and easy to reload yet not quite one-handed. He would have done better to dump the briefcase, but that would mean disaster for others.

He fired again as he moved along the curb behind a parked car. Three answers now, perhaps more, and they were low, skimming the pavement around him. Some glass broke behind him. More broke to the left. A small spike of something struck Leon on his cheek.

Farewell, Dandy. I needed a good gangster weapon, a Tommy gun, to give you a good death.

Head down, running low, Leon broke from the curb toward the side street, hoping that he was as invisible as his enemy but knowing the dim light from the west gave some definition to his shape. The big sounds that followed the little sounds, skimming the sides of the buildings, told him that he was seen.

He did not know how well until he was hit, hit hard, just as he reached the head of the street. Something pulled his shoulder away from his body and punched it into space.

Leon hit the side of a building hard. No. He hit the pavement.

Where was the pain? When he had lost his finger, the pain traveled down that wire as if it were attached to the part of his brain that amplified it.

Where was the briefcase? God, where was the briefcase?

He patted the pavement around him, searching for the dark thing he could not see, and that simple movement told him how complex all motion was, driving a hot deep ache from inside out along the left side of his body.

Leaving the briefcase, Leon got to his feet like an ape. If he could stand, he could run—and he did. If he could run, he could fire—and he began to. They had left the park now and were moving down the center of the street. They were firing.

He was hit again. He felt himself spun by the shoe, bouncing high onto the hood of a parked car as if he had come down from the sky. The calf. Left calf. He felt it at once, the long branding, the burning. Could he still move?

Yes. He steadied the pistol on the side mirror, emptying the second magazine into the middle of the street and ejecting almost within the burst. He felt that he knew what he was doing.

He reloaded and fired three more rounds at something that might have been nothing before he began to run again. It seemed that was possible. The leg was bad and the shoulder very bad but they were on opposite sides of the body and seemed to give a kind of balance. A symmetry.

How many times could a man be hit and still be mobile? In how many places?

He was going to find out. When Leon reached the top of the street a half block from the trolley line, he turned. This is miraculous, he thought. Those bursts of flame, seven now, three on the left, two on the right, two still in the middle, couldn't bring him down.

The magazine was empty again. Leon shuffled from the side of the building—a tobacco shop—loading another clip as he moved. He had taken six steps when he was hit and blown to the ground again.

The right leg this time. The bastards were trying to bring him down but not kill yet. They knew who they were chasing, and how badly he was wanted alive.

Dandy, I forgive you.

But can I get up?

He did it, but felt greasy. The right leg from the thigh down felt pasted to him. Blood. Lots of it. No one ever thought he had that much, did he?

But he was moving. Eighteen inches from the ground, using the barrel of the gun for a cane, but he moved.

There were hot weights on his feet and more on his shoulder, but he moved along nicely. The firing continued. Yes, they were looking, cruising, thinking he was down. The head of Leon would fetch a reward, but the live body would mean medals and luxuries and Miss Tatana Figarova's three meter asshole, too.

Ahead, just ahead, the street widened. He was almost there when he heard a smooth sound within the bark of the pistols. It was a rolling, oncoming sound, a strange hymn in steel.

A trolley. Leon could not see the number. He could not tell what was behind him, but just in front was all that glass and steel and steps. Three cars. Could he make it?

A Number 20. The steps stopped slowly in front of him. The driver had seen him. Someone would be along to collect the fare if only he had the strength to pull himself up by the rail.

He threw the pistol to the ground and jerked himself up by both hands. Amazing. What could be done when it was necessary was infinitely amazing. He pulled again until he sat on the top step, looking back toward the street.

The trolley moved from the stop, accelerating as smoothly as falling snow. What was top speed? Could a man outrun a good machine? Would he try?

Oh yes, if he was German. Leon saw the first shape twenty meters away. He looked like he was being pulled along by the white shirt-front that poked from his coat.

With more effort that he had ever imagined, Leon squirmed the second pistol, the Luger, from his coat pocket. Clicking off the safety, with two hands,he drew on the shirt-front. And fired.

He thought he had hit him, but the white blaze did not stop. And now there was another, a better, who was gaining. He was all in black, but closer. Much closer.

Leon fired at the dark thing. He fired several times. It seemed not to stop. It seemed to increase speed. A muzzle flashed as it returned fire.

Leon screamed when he was hit. He hadn't done that before. Why? Because he hadn't seen it actually happen? Hadn't watched the knee implode, the chips chasing the meat, the wetness on his face, the burst of blood that came back excitedly to cover the bone?

It hurt like nothing else, as if he had never been hit at all. Leon wanted to return fire. He wanted to be sure to kill just one more German, but he had lost count of the rounds expended and he did not have the strength to load the last magazine.

And he was dizzy. Very disoriented.

This could end badly, Zdenek. It could end as the worst.

Leon put the pistol to the side of his head. His hat fell off. That was absurd. How could his hat have remained on his head through it all?

The hat tumbled down the first step, then jumped down to the second like a man. On a gust of wind, it suddenly flew, landing on the ground, flopping, skittering, hesitating, before continuing on in darkness.

Goodbye, little alpine.

Goodbye, Heinz. I'm sorry that we'll never have the chance to know each other. I'm afraid you'll just have to be satisfied with our shit on your dick.

CHAPTER 11

SUMMARY: ICE TO FRANTA

It is with sadness that we report the death of the partisan hero Captain Vaclav Moravek, who was also known as Leon. He died two days ago near Dusty Bridge in Prague, taking his life with his own weapon to avoid capture by the Gestapo.

We have also heard through reliable sources that the agent known as A-54, or Rene, has been arrested by the Germans and placed in Pankrac Prison. Thus the primary reason for this station's being has been eradicated. We are at pains to imagine our future role and trust that you will advise us soon.

* * *

"Why won't you talk about Leon?"

"There's nothing to talk about," said Zdenek. "He lived by what he did. Not by words."

"Like you."

"No. I'm just a soldier with orders."

"You're not just a soldier," she said as if offended. "They didn't choose you from all those men in England without a good reason. What's special about you, Zdenek?"

"You can't tell?"

"Besides a bad foot and a small penis."

"It isn't."

"It is now."

"There's a reason."

She laughed. "You know, I thought it was enormous, because every time I saw you, it was so big. I was almost frightened, and I thought: Is it too big for me? That's why I always took you in my mouth. Of course your foot was bad, and we were always hurried, quick while they're out, scrambling like children before someone banged on the door and said: Come Zdenek, it's time to go out and kill. So I really didn't see it like this—small—until we came here. It's such a nice cozy place. And Anna's so wonderful, don't you think?"

"Yes."

"You still won't answer my question."

He did not want to. Zdenek had known since the age when he was aware of more than his mother that he would do something of importance. Most of it was physical of course. How many men had the vision to pick out, let alone strike, a moving target with a handgun at a hundred yards?

It was accidental. Numbers. Every young boy thought that he would do something of importance in this world. It was only when he stopped thinking it that he stopped being a creature of God. And became just a man.

"There's nothing special about me," he said. "Except that I'm good with guns and I believe in what I'm doing."

"Stalking Heydrich."

"Yes."

"Killing him."

"When we can be sure."

"And you believe in nothing else?"

"I believe in my mission. It's what I was born to do."

"You say that as if you're certain of the end."

"I'm more certain every day."

She picked her head up and put it in her palm, looking at him. "And what if you succeed? What will become of us?"

The answer could be found at the end of every fairy tale: We will live happily ever after. Could he lie like that? How could he lie like that?

"If everything goes well, Libena, we can be married."

"Are you proposing, Zdenek?"

"Josef's proposing," he said. "Zdenek's not sure where he'll be tomorrow."

"Do I have time to consider the offer?"

"Not much, I'm afraid."

She put her fingers to his lips. No question that she meant to still him and everything in the room. The clock on the bookshelf that ticked between heartbeats. The ancient bed that creaked with almost every breath. The sound of the trolley that rolled down from the square on worn countersunk rails.

"I insist on a condition."

"Name it."

"It doesn't have a name," she said softly. "But if we're together when the Gestapo come, promise you won't let them take me."

He felt her fingers leave his lips as if they had passed into a vacuum. To truly have this woman, Zdenek must agree to kill her. Was that the highest form of love in the Protectorate?

"They won't take you alive as long as I'm alive," he said. "I promise that."

* * *

Superintendent von Pannwitz
Staatspolizeileitstelle
20 Bredovska Street
Prague II

Dear Heinz,

Just a line to let you know that the resistance is back in town. You'll be hearing from us in steel jackets very soon.

Forever yours,
Ice

* * *

"Where did you get that dog?"

"From the foremost breeder in Central Europe," said Ice, as he brushed crumbs of sugar cake from the postcard onto the silvery mane of the largest shepherd that Ota had ever seen. "I bought him at Zdenek's suggestion. He wants me to find the man who chased down Leon."

"That animal will have your monthly meat ration before he tracks a Gestapo."

"His name's Moula," said Ice. "A fine rogue, isn't he? We could call him a police dog if he was stupider."

"Speaking of which," said Ota. "Anna saw your picture on the desperado board outside police headquarters."

Ice smiled across the cafe table. "A good likeness?"

"Three women swooned from looking. Even Anna was impressed. She said that you were once quite handsome with blond hair and a clean lip."

Ice turned in his chair to admire his reflection in the window behind them. Seen full-face, the new look—dyed black hair that seemed painted, a cut-and-pasted black mustache—was shocking, as if a comrade had become a mannequin.

"I like what it does for me," he said. "You have no idea the trouble I had keeping women off. Now I can be more selective."

"It must have been a burden."

"I think you'll find that out," he said, finishing the last of the ersatz coffee. "That woman will not let you go. Even when the time comes."

"Her name is Anna."

"No," said Ice. "Her name is Woman. Home. Hearth. Liaison work. They have no place in an operation of this kind."

Ota tried not to respond at once or violently. He knew that he was being goaded. Ice had almost succeeded in getting himself onto the team by promises, much as he made to women, and he would soon try to take over the team with the same kind of bullshit.

"So you think you can tell me my job."

"Someone should," he said. "You're both in trouble. I don't worry about Zdenek. He'd fall in love with Frau Hitler if she had a twat. He's a soldier with a stiff prick. A para. But you've got the look of a husband, and she knows it."

"It doesn't bother you that Anna's the best street-agent we have?" Ota pointed through the window to the shop across the street on Uvoz. "You know that she's already contacted Novotny and sounded him out."

"I could have if I hadn't been sitting for the past week in a hut in Branik," said Ice. "Jindra put me there so you two could enjoy your women. They want you fat and happy, so you won't get on with your work."

"You're the only patriot in Prague, Ice. That's clear."

"Since Leon died, yes. It's quite clear."

Ota didn't understand why he put up with this, but he decided not to encourage it. He looked past Ice down the street to the first floor of the old house. What lay inside was Anthropoid's gift from Leon, the shop of a watchmaker. Supposedly, Joseph Novotny was a man with good contacts at the castle who could provide the kind of information they could not get from Safarik.

That should have been enough to put Ota in the shop immediately, but for the last week the repression had been fierce. Every day the Gestapo penetrated deeper into the resistance. The only thing that saved Anthropoid in the terror following Leon's death was the fact that his network and Uncle's were separate. Having so many scattered groups made coordination difficult, but it created a welcome buffer in bad times.

That Novotny still enjoyed his freedom was a sign that Leon had kept his contact secure. But the sign could be wrong. The Gestapo liked to feed broken people back into the resistance. Usually, a relative or two was kept aside to ensure good conduct.

But nothing unusual had happened to Novotny. Ota had been watching the shop for three days and seen little worth remarking. Anna, who knew the watchmaker slightly, had enquired among his friends and relatives. As far as they knew, there were no unexplained absences, or changes in his habits.

When Anna visited the shop yesterday, Novotny reacted warily but discreetly to the code, though he knew Leon was no longer alive to share it. He expected to see her again, he said.

So when Ota saw Anna walking along Uvoz with her smooth long-legged stride, he put money on the table, patted Ice on his makeshift head, and moved into the sun to join her. They met a step before the wide door with wooden birds carved above it.

The bell rang them into a shallow room crowded with Novotny's wares. Along the walls were timepieces of every sort, antique and modern, pocket-sized and for the mantel. One tall grandfather clock stood by the counter. The window was filled with cuckoo clocks to entice the German tourist.

"I'll be right there."

The high voice seemed to leak through the walls of the shop, but probably came from behind the thick curtain hung like a tapestry across a doorway. Ota saw a flash behind the curtain. Shifting left, he saw a mirror near the ceiling molding. A man, looking small and lopsided in reflection, watched them. He had a jeweler's glass in one eye.

"It's Anna, Mister Novotny."

"What a surprise," he said, appearing full-size in the folds of the curtain that trailed him like a cape. "I didn't expect to see you so soon."

"I came for my traveling alarm," she said. "Is it ready?"

Novotny popped the eyepiece into his hand and smiled with a wide latch-movement of his mouth. "You may speak freely, Anna. There's no one about."

Ota stepped forward to the curtain. "Do you mind?"

Ota moved into the back room but saw no Gestapo there. A workbench ran around three-quarters of the small space. On it sat the remains of every unworkable clock in Central Europe—screws, springs and gears, glass faces, bits of gold and silver, slices of phosphorescent numbers, as if glowing fragments of time itself had come to rest, or an end.

"Are you satisfied?"

Ota nodded as he came back into the room. The gesture indicated satisfaction, and also told Anna to move silently to the front window where she could watch the street.

"We've been under pressure lately."

"More than you think," said Novotny. "The Gestapo are using microphones and recording devices these days. If this was a trap, you wouldn't know it until the door burst open."

"You seem to understand their methods."

"I go to the castle almost every day," he said with quiet confidence. "I hear many things. I can tell you to be careful when using any telephone. They have all suspicious numbers monitored, and many of the public phones, too. And they keep a record of the conversations."

"Every word?"

"Remarked and recorded," said Novotny. "They once asked me if I could repair their Dictaphones at the Castle. I told them that was beyond my limited Czech competence."

"Have you ever been to the Protector's rooms?"

"They're all the Protector's rooms," said Novotny. "But if you mean his office, yes, I've been there several times. It's tightly guarded. The whole castle is."

"How many people have knowledge of his movements?"

Novotny tapped the eyepiece three times. "His adjutant, a schedule secretary, and the chief of the security guard."

"No one else?"

"Not on a steady basis," said Novotny. "But these things do become known at the castle. When everything hinges on one man's will, people make it their business to know what that is."

"Can you make it your business?"

"I might be able to learn his broad movements," said Novotny. "But to know where he's going with split-second timing—that would be luck." Novotny put the eyepiece in a box with others that seemed identical. "Isn't that what you want to know?"

Ota nodded.

"I shouldn't ask why?"

"No," said Ota.

Novotny looked at Ota closely. He understood.

"You could have more luck with your questions at Panenske Brezany," he said. "Heydrich's manor house is there."

"Can you tell me about it?"

"It's the old Bloch-Blauer estate," said Novotny. "He was a millionaire sugar merchant. Unfortunately, he was also a Jew. The first Protector, von Neurath, requisitioned the place for the betterment of the Reich. He'd just begun to make it over in his image when Heydrich took over his job and his house."

"Can the estate be approached?"

"Not easily," he said. "There are two main buildings. Call them castles. Heydrich and his family live in the lower one, surrounded by a large park. Between the castles are the village and a small forest."

"What about security?"

"We were stopped going in at the gate," he said. "The guards knew the driver. They didn't examine the car."

"Patrols?"

"I saw one group of SS about," he said. "Armed. With dogs."

None of what Ota was hearing seemed good, though he had not expected less than excellent security from the head of Reich Security. There were always gaps in any system, however, and those had to be probed.

"I need to know more about the arrangements," said Ota. "Can you go to the estate again?"

"I'll do better," said Novotny with a smile. "I know the cook there. He's a good man. Reliable. He used to work at one of the best hotels in the city before he was requisitioned into the Protector's service. I'm sure he'd be willing to help."

CHAPTER 12

The Mercedes passed at tremendous speed. One hundred and forty kilometers an hour. Possibly more. Estimating the velocity of an object from a stationary position was difficult, but Zdenek had gotten better at it in the last few years. War was all about fast-moving metal.

He was glad that he had seen Heydrich's face that day in the castle square, because he got nothing this time. A pale blur above the black coat, like fungus sprouting from rot.

The Protector had seen less: two men in work clothes standing at the roadside with their caps in their hands. Good peasants. Respectful. Knowing that only a German would be driving a shiny three-and-a-half liter car. Only an important German would have SS flags rippling from his front fenders.

The escort car came along twenty-five seconds later, filled with the usual complement of SS guards. The vehicle could not match the Mercedes' speed with less of an engine and the extra weight in bodies. That was good, but not good enough.

It was twenty kilometers from Prague Castle to Heydrich's estate, and once the road left the suburbs, the countryside was relatively flat with little cover. Except for the pear trees that flanked the road, and the shallow ditches along the sides, it was another Bohemian farming plain.

Zdenek wished for the hills of Slovakia. The Fatra Mountains surrounded his village, and ran until they reached the higher peaks of the Tatras. Three steps off the road into the forest a partisan was born. And he was safe.

No soldier liked to think of suicide in the line of duty. Although Zdenek had not exchanged ten words with Ota in the last five kilometers, he knew his partner felt the same. Unless they could locate an ambush site close to Heydrich's manor house, they would to have to find another way to do the job.

They got on their bicycles again and set off for the town of Libeznice. At this hour—just before dusk—there were no workers in the fields, and few animals that had not been taken into barns for the night. It was a hushed world, serenely beautiful in alternating fields of green grasses deepening in the twilight and mustard that glowed like golden phosphorescence.

As they came into Libeznice, the road rose gently, lined on both sides by chestnut trees with branches that met far above their heads. A right turn brought them into cobbled streets, where they saw the church spire high above the other buildings.

They left their bicycles at the side of the church. They had been told to sit in the back pews and wait for a man to appear in a blue checked shirt. Hopefully, he had the only one for miles. Giving the password to someone in Heydrich's household had been thought too risky.

Except for one man kneeling at the side of the altar before banks of flickering Lenten candles, the building was empty. Wearing a light jacket, his back was turned and his shirt unseen. He seemed not to notice Zdenek and Ota. Crossing himself, he passed the center aisle and genuflected before turning toward them.

He still did not look their way as he came toward their pew, but beneath his coat he wore a blue checked shirt. He stopped and slipped into the row ahead, speaking quietly without turning around.

"Friends of Mister Novotny?"

"Yes," said Ota. "Are you Jiri Kuthan?"

"Until recently," he said. "You should call me by my slave name—Georg."

Zdenek had been in Prague long enough to recognize the accent, which the man had in plenty. He was not a country boy and his attitude showed the right kind of directed hostility.

"My name is Zdenek. This is Ota."

Georg turned slightly, favoring Zdenek. "You're Slovak."

"I am. This country was once one, and it will be again."

"When?"

"If everything goes well—a year," said Ota. "The Germans made their mistake in attacking Russia. The Japanese when they attacked the Americans."

"That's not the way they see things at the estate," said Georg. "The thousand year Reich, they call it."

"A thousand days," said Zdenek. "Less, if we light a fire at their back."

"Is that what you want to do?"

When neither Zdenek nor Ota responded, Georg turned to them, laying his arm over the back of the pew. His face, fleshy and strongly lined, clenched like a fist.

"I'll do anything you ask, but I don't know if I can poison him for you. They have my brother, you see. They're holding him at Terezin concentration camp to guarantee my good behavior. And reasonably decent food."

"I'm sorry to hear that."

"It's not as bad as it might be," said Georg. "He's in the small fortress with the prisoners they want to keep alive. I go to see him once a month. In fact, I was there yesterday."

"I hope he was well."

"Not well," said Georg. "Alive. He told me, if you're interested, that the Nazis had just brought an important prisoner into the maximum-security block. A German said to be a spy."

That might be Rene, the man Leon died for, but Terezin was as secure as every KZ, though it was said to be the mildest.

"Thanks for the news," said Zdenek. "That's the kind of thing we need from you concerning the Protector. Specifically, the security at the estate."

"It's complete," said Georg. "Heydrich scorns protection, but the SS take their job seriously. He's their leader, you know. They treat him like a god. He looks like they say they all want to look. The blond beast. They actually call him that in the service. You won't be able to truly understand Germans until you realize they mean it as a compliment."

"Are there many troops in the village?"

"The troops are the village," he said with emphasis that would have been too loud if anyone else had been in the church. "A dozen stay in the house near the entrance to the park. They patrol the area with those damned shepherd dogs."

"What are the chances of slipping into the park unnoticed?"

"It's possible," he said. "But you might be seen by the servants. Most of them are so frightened they'd turn you in as a reflex. And the Protector's children, too. They're worse than the guards. Klaus and Heider like to stick their SS daggers into anything that comes along. They play Aryan and Jew. With real Jews. The oldest one sometimes carries a revolver. Loaded. You haven't lived until you've had a ten-year-old point his pistol at you for the fun of it."

Zdenek tried to imagine that. It sounded like a carnival booth where the prize was death.

"I understand there's a wife, too."

"A witch," said Georg, who seemed happy to find the right word. "She beats the Czech servants with her riding crop. For Jews, she has a whip. We thought it would be better once she was pregnant, but it's worse. She's bitchier, more brutal. When Heydrich doesn't return home, she hits us with her fists."

"Is he free with the discipline, too?"

Georg hesitated as the church door opened and an old woman with a black scarf around her head moved slowly up the aisle to the altar rail, where she knelt before the figure of Christ mutilated on the cross. Georg followed her progress, staring at the object of her veneration as if his own plight had been mirrored with precision.

"It's a real SS household," he said. "Nazi salutes to and from the bathroom, Aryan runes on the tablecloth. But Heydrich never beats the servants. He's more bloodless. If they aren't to his liking, they disappear. Poof. Gone. No one hears from them again. It's as if he's the void, and people fall into it."

Georg drew closer, reaching to tap Zdenek's hand. "I don't know how to describe him. He's the most frightening human being on earth. The most divided. His face is that way—like halves that don't fit. As if they took him apart and put back him back together wrong. He talks like a recording machine, quick and high-pitched in a tone so cold it should be warmed before serving. It's as if he is that mechanical device the Nazis are trying to make from common clay. He'd be that way even if he didn't have such terrible power."

"Don't worry," said Zdenek. "He's human. There's one way to prove that."

Georg grasped Zdenek's hand and held it tight. "I don't want to see you die proving it. You must be very careful. Don't ever let him see your face. He remembers everything and everyone. Most Germans see us as Goebbels tells them to—as subhumans. As nothing. Heydrich knows we're as good as he is. He always says that he likes us, and perhaps he does. As working parts."

"Thanks for the advice," said Ota. "It would be helpful if you could tell us where we could find him, possibly alone, somewhere outside the estate."

"He's building a racecourse in the forest," said Georg. "But it's unfinished. He doesn't ride there much and he never rides alone."

"The forest," said Zdenek. "Is it well-wooded?"

"Yes. But the SS are close by. It's a question of how much you like suicide. If you had a car . . ."

That would help, but so far the best efforts of the networks had come to nothing. Few things seemed as hard to come by in the Nazi Protectorate as an automobile.

"Does he always drive so fast?" asked Ota. "When he passed us on the road, he was going like a demon."

Georg nodded. "He's obsessed with speed. It's another kind of power. He sometimes drives the car with Klein sitting beside him like a tree. He pilots his own plane, too, a Junkers 52 that he keeps at the airport."

"If you should hear anything about his leaving, we'd like to know," said Zdenek. "We'll arrange a way for you to get word out of the estate safely."

"The charwoman would help," said Georg. "When she finishes her chores, she often goes to visit her daughter in the next village. Klicany."

"Excellent," said Zdenek.

"Can you keep track of the time that Heydrich leaves the estate every day?" asked Ota. "And pass the information."

"So a monster can be killed on schedule."

Ota said nothing. Zdenek said nothing. Georg looked down at the rack in the pew that held the songbooks. "You know, he loves music. Here we are in a church discussing the death of a man whose only link to humanity is that love. I saw him one night in the drawing room playing second violin in a quartet with one of his adjutants and their wives. He's good. They played Schubert—Death and the Maiden. When the piece ended—even before it was done—Heydrich began to weep. Like a child. He'd been reached by the beauty of the music. The perfection."

Ota smiled and placed his hand gently on the cook's arm. "We have to be perfect, too," he said. "We're depending on you to make it so."

* * *

They were flying high by the time they arrived at the Dutch Mill. Into the booth Ice ushered Tatana, whom he had met just that morning, followed by Dieter, whom he had met just that evening at Tatana's apartment carrying a bottle of champagne from the rape of France. Tatana was the finest whore in Prague, and a dog-lover, while Dieter was a high party official with the Winterhilfe—a Nazi charity for widows and orphans.

Ice had been nervous when they entered the club, but he soon found that it was pleasant to be among people who had probably looked at his picture on a wall, but did not recognize the genuine item. Dieter had no clue, and the tables filled with SS looked their way only to dream on Tatana, whose ass sung the Horst Wessel song with every movement.

Germans sat on every side, but the radios set into the partitions between the tables kept their conversations private. Those devises were what made the Dutch Mill a popular spot. With adjustments in volume, the Master Race could say almost anything they wanted about the morons who ran their lives. They had little to fear but a weak signal.

"I was saying . . ."

"What were you saying, Dieter?"

"That Prague's not interesting any more. When von Neurath ran things, this was a civilized place. The Czechs didn't scowl all the time. You could order a salad that didn't come to the table dressed in machine oil."

"It's those damned Russians," said Ice. "If Stalin hadn't provoked the Fuhrer into invading . . ."

"You *are* an innocent boy," said Dieter, as he ran his hand along Ice's thigh. "Are all Czechs so misinformed?"

"I told you I was German," said Ice. "Born in this country of racially mixed parents."

"That shouldn't make you stupid," said Dieter, moving his hand between Ice's legs. "There's only one reason for our trouble—the lack of communications between people."

"Who do you think is responsible for that, Dieter?"

He looked around, in a reflex action, although the radio was loud. "It begins in Prague Castle," he said. "The suspicion. The evil talk. It moves down the hill like fog. By the time it reaches here, it's a fact. Why even Dr. Steinberg has been arrested. A great fellow. You could find him in this place every night."

Ice grew attentive, because Steinberg was another alias for Rene, the agent who had fed Leon information from the Abwehr for years. He and Leon had met in this place many times.

"What will happen to the poor man?"

"He's in a KZ," said Dieter, his hand drawing back when he mentioned the place where every homosexual in the Reich ended his days unless he was a high official. "Heydrich is keeping him there to blackmail military intelligence."

"That sounds like a dangerous game. High stakes."

"Our Protector's a great one for games," said Dieter. "Ask Tatana about that."

Ice leaned across the table, noting that Dieter had his other hand on her dirigible ass. It was that kind of double duty that kept Dieter off the degenerate list and free to swindle babies.

"What about the Protector and his games, *liebchen*?"

"You shouldn't ask me," she said. "I only saw him once."

What did that signify? This woman, a top performer with all the animal kingdom, shrank from contact with the chief one.

"You wouldn't want to talk about it?"

"There's nothing to tell," she said as if there were plenty. "He didn't even want sex as it's commonly known. When I arrived, two other girls were there already. He stood in the bedroom in front of a mirror with his boots on. Just his boots. In his hand he had a bag of marks in coins. He threw them on the floor and told us to fight for them. The winner got the money. The losers got him."

"How did you do?"

"I became rich," she said. "And I think very lucky."

"Did our friend call for you again?"

"He tried," she said. "But I have another friend—with the Gestapo. He made it seem as if I had left Prague forever."

"A friend with the Gestapo? That must be convenient."

"Police are never convenient," said Tatana. "Necessary for business, of course. If you want to meet them, all you have to do is turn around."

Ice turned around. Yes, that might be Gestapo at the table behind. Their radio boomed at the threshold of pain.

"Which is your man?" asked Dieter. "Herr Doctor Geschke or Superintendent von Pannwitz?"

Tatana laughed. "What if I said both?"

"I wouldn't call you a liar."

"If you must know, I've set my sights on that fellow with the sloe eyes," she said. "Do you see him with his back turned? He's the Gestapo hero for the past several weeks."

"What did he do to earn the honor?" asked Ice. "Fuck by the front door?"

"He killed one of the resistance leaders," said Tatana with no relish. "There are two versions of the story. The first says the fellow committed suicide on a trolley. The second holds that August, braving a hail of machinegun fire, brought him down in a bloody pile on the street. Perhaps with a slingshot."

Ice liked Tatana's attitude better every minute. He thought that not much effort would be needed to tap the resentment in her heart. She occupied such a pivotal place in German Prague. Knew everyone, even the killers and their lies.

"That sounds like an interesting story," he said. "Would it be possible to meet this brave officer?"

"Would you like me to wink?" she asked with a smile entwined in the strains of Lili Marlene. "Or crook my little finger?"

CHAPTER 13

SUMMARY: FRANTA TO ICE

Shortly, we will drop two parachute teams. ZINC will provide communications support and liaison with the Moravian resistance. OUT DISTANCE has a special mission of great importance of which you will be informed at the proper time.

Please advise us at once of their disposition. Remember that you are the hope of our nation. There is no other.

* * *

When Sergeant Miks saw Josef Valcik, he knew that something was wrong besides the color of his hair. They had known each other under different names, but that was fond and familiar compared to the off-center way that Valcik walked and the voice that carried across Auntie's living room like a lopsided Victoria.

"Max! Great to see you!"

They shook hands. Max did not bother to give his cover name because he had been using one for years. Everyone called him Max because he looked like and was built like the German Schmeling before Joe Louis fought him the second time and beat him to spaetzle. Max Miks. It was supposed to be funny.

"It's good to see a familiar face. Even yours, Josef."

"Call me Ice."

"Why?"

"To save us from the Bowling Alley. It's the latest Gestapo trick. They hang their guests upside down from the ceiling with their hands and feet tied. Then they swing them back and forth, bashing them together, until the brains run from the pins."

Max laughed, but wasn't sure he should have. Something kept passing through Ice's blue eyes that seemed to feed on a source that was unstable.

"You're telling me this to make me feel better."

"Absolutely," he said, boosting Max by the arm toward the door. "Have you seen much of Prague?"

"Mostly from train windows."

"Get your coat," said Ice with a smile that seemed to happen twice. "And don't forget your weapon."

Max already had his coat on, a jacket suitable for the light rain that they found outside the door. It was the same one he had dropped in, but no one could find a replacement that fit him through the shoulders, especially with a pistol under his arm.

"We'll get you fixed up later," said Ice. "When the rest of your team arrives. Your mission is to back up Radio Libuse."

"That *was* our mission. We dropped with a transmitter and a ton of money, but all that's left is the fucking money."

"I take it things haven't gone smoothly."

They hadn't gone at all. Max filled Ice in as they walked to the bottom of the hill and caught the trolley for the New Town. The car was less than half full, which meant they had no trouble finding seats alone near the back, but the few glum faces made it seem more crowded. That was the first thing Max noticed about the occupation: no one smiled. The first night in Slovakia after they dropped miles off their DZ, Zinc Team went from house to house begging help only to be told by utterly serious people that there was none for them.

"We dropped close to the Protectorate border and walked up to it without realizing there would be customs posts with guards. That it was a different country. So first thing, we ran into a patrol. They chased us all over hell. We got away, but with the police looking for three men, we thought we should split up. The lieutenant went one way, Gerik and me the other."

"Where's Gerik now?"

"I don't know," he said. "We took separate trains for Prague after we hit Brno."

"No one's heard from him," said Ice like an accusation. "Or your lieutenant."

"I'm not worried about the lieutenant," said Max. "But Gerik's nineteen years old, and he couldn't get into a house on a cold night in his own country. It seemed to get to his mind."

"So you think he's a risk."

"Possibly."

Ice smiled again as he rose from his seat to stand in the aisle. "Let's say he is. Could you kill him?"

Max pulled himself upright, wondering if he had really heard the question. He put his hand on the seat that Ice had occupied and almost pulled it back. The seat was hot. Not warm. Hot.

"We went through a lot together," he said, as they banged down the steps off the platform to the street. "Gerik's confused. Maybe he decided to sit the war out. I might have done the same thing if I hadn't found my girl at home and still faithful in our village. She knew some people in the resistance, and they moved me along the line."

"Still faithful," said Ice, as they passed along the street that was crowded around the stop and dark. "That has a nice old-fashioned sound. I have a girl here in Prague, you know. She's not quite that way."

Max slowed his pace along the wide boulevard to avoid the people who appeared suddenly from the dark, looming like trains in a tunnel, moving off-track with the peculiar sideways etiquette of the blackout. Although he had seen little of this nightly ballet, Max found a startled romance in it.

"A city girl," said Max. "You better be careful."

"Oh, but I am," said Ice. "When I leave her, I always say, 'Now I don't want you sucking off anyone less than a Standartenfuhrer. And don't take it up the ass for less than a Gestapo superintendent'. I lay it on the line."

Max felt disoriented in the darkness that changed in whiffs of smoke and cologne to became human at the last careening moment. He bumped against a woman with a heavy sack at her knees; but he did not stop walking because Ice had not.

"Your girl is a . . . businesswoman?"

"Good word," said Ice. "Her business is pleasure, and what could be better for knowing the right men?" Ice stopped on the corner and pointed across the street. "Look," he said. "The German Theater."

Max looked but could not see much—a gross building that gained strength from the lighter darkness of the night sky. Two stories. Classical columns, perhaps.

"An example of Winterhilfswerk," said Ice, strolling through the German word. "You know the Winterhilfe. It's a charity for widows, orphans, historical works—the symbol of all that's dull in Nazi life."

"Not all. A beginning."

"Very good, Max. And you haven't seen what's going on."

Max heard himself laugh but asked: when was the last time I heard my own laughter? Could it have been the last time I was scared to death by what I was laughing at? Because they were walking through the misty rain toward the greatest gathering of Nazis this side of the Russian Front.

Already they were close enough to see the front of the building. A wide staircase led to an entrance flanked with double columns. One bright object, a gigantic Nazi eagle suspended from the gallery on the second floor.

"If shit could fly," said Ice, stopping near the entrance as if he had taken up station. "Look, they're coming now."

The Master Race. They were passing out the open door into the street. The peeps of light that filtered from the interior and the flash of matches and the glowing cigarettes made them the brightest thing in the night. Long shimmering dresses and jewels for the women. Evening clothes and uniforms for the men. All along the curb the Horches and Mercedes began to whine.

"You know, these glittering pigs are planning to kill all the Jews in Europe."

"What?"

"Every Jew," said Ice. "Dead."

"That's insane."

"Yes. You see now."

He wasn't making sense. Nervously, Max felt that he knew what this man would do, but couldn't accept the idea. Not here. Not now.

"Ice, I think we should leave."

He laughed. "What kind of pistol do you have?"

"CZ38."

"The caliber's too small," he said. "I should have found you a nine millimeter."

"What are you talking about?"

"Stand at my back," he said. "There. By the little bush. You shouldn't have to do anything but watch."

Max did as he was told. He could do nothing else but run and he could do that to a friend from Scotland, where they had learned to kill by every means but always in silence. The way Ice's hands moved beneath his coat could mean several things but Max thought he was fitting a suppressor to his pistol.

Ice stopped completely still as he watched a group of four people descend from the stairs toward a Horch with a six-foot hood. The door, held by a chauffeur, opened and lit the interior of the car brilliantly. Black curtains at the windows, black leather upholstery with tilt-down tables and a sparkle of glassware. A bottle.

The two men stepped aside as they reached the car and began to feed the ladies in. Big glossy hips, a lovely flash of leg, an even more lovely slice of thigh, the first man climbing in, and then the second, a young man with a mustache and a clump of hair oozing down his forehead like Hitler's, stooping to slide onto the seats when someone called a name—his name.

"August."

The man turned, half in, half out. A dark shape passed between Max and the back seat, made two sounds like a cough underwater, made another, then moved away quickly.

The dark shape came his way, taking Max by the arm, leaving him with the image of a well-lit back seat and a man going down among gilded women, his hand flapping at his chest as if he were trying to swat away the blood that appeared instantly on his light gray tunic.

Now that was gone, too. Ice and Max walked down the street fast, entering the deeper darkness that began five paces off. They glided past the things that did not glitter, counting on luck to screen the rest. When they were ten paces away, and turning toward the central square, they heard a woman's voice. No, a woman's scream.

"What would you say to a nightcap, Max? I know a place where there'll be an empty table."

"I'd say you're crazy."

* * *

Superintendent von Pannwitz
Staatspolizeileitstelle
20 Bredovska Street
Prague II

Dear Heinz,

August sends you greetings from hell.
Says it's worse than the English spring.

Affectionately yours,
Ice

* * *

It was raining when Zdenek and Ota got off the Number 21 trolley. They met Ice at Bulhar Circle by the post box and continued to the top of the hill together. Zdenek thought the meeting they were to attend would be a disaster, but he was surprised when they arrived at Auntie's, for Emil did not seem to mind Ice's presence. Having been at each other's throats for weeks in Pardubice—and having fought over a woman—that seemed odd.

But everyone was happy that revenge had been taken on Leon's killer, and they knew who had done it. Emil was also happy being promoted to captain over the radio. He wasn't the worst officer that Zdenek had known, and probably would have been good in the field, but the pressure of surviving underground had worked for the worst. The color in his broad face was bad, his brown eyes seemed unable to hold a mark, and he spoke as if he were in some pain.

"Good to see you boys," he said, shaking hands. "I'd like you to meet Kral. No rank here, of course, but he's an officer, too."

Zdenek knew him from training in Scotland. Kral had been a quiet man there, too, but he usually rose from his chair to greet the men. He had an understated presence, dark hair and complexion, a deep voice that resonated, and predaceous blue eyes that reminded Zdenek of his own.

"You'll have to excuse me," he said. "I hurt my leg when we dropped."

"Nothing serious, I hope."

"No," he said. "Not with me."

What Kral left unsaid was enough to sober the group. While Emil kept himself upright stiffly, the team took seats in Auntie's kitchen on the sofa surrounding Kral.

"I suppose you know that two teams jumped last week," said Emil in a tone that fell just short of self-importance. "Kral's team, Out Distance. And Zinc. I'll let Kral fill you in on his, but let me say this about Zinc. Max found his way to us, but their lieutenant was killed in a gunfight outside Buchlovice. Their corporal, Gerik, nineteen years old, made his way to Prague, but never contacted us. He went over to the Nazis."

Zdenek looked around the small circle of eyes as if seeing faces at the bottom of a pond. This was the worst. A para who turned could bring them all down if he knew enough.

"What the hell does London think they're doing," said Ice. "Sending children."

"The Gestapo have had him for several days," said Emil. "From what we've heard, he's cooperating with them fully."

"What can he tell them?" asked Zdenek.

"Everything about his own mission," said Emil. "And that another team dropped on the same night. But of our networks he should know nothing."

"He'll know that we exist," said Ice. "Passwords and procedures should be changed immediately."

"No reason to panic," said Emil, beginning to dig back into his relations with Ice by small changes. "I'm sure he was told nothing in London."

"You're dreaming," said Ice. "Everyone talks among themselves. I knew the missions of the other teams before we dropped. I guessed Anthropoid's target with common sense."

"I don't think he knows enough to hurt us," said Kral in a voice that wanted to smooth over differences. "We heard in England that parachute groups had landed safely and were operating in the country. But that's all. The Germans know as much from interrogations."

"Interrogations," said Ice. "You are new to this."

"But willing to learn," said Kral. "It's a process. We knew when we were over the Protectorate that we were off our drop zones, but we wanted to take our chance. Zinc jumped first, badly, but Out-Distance landed in decent order near Telc." Kral's pause allowed room for the worst again. "It wasn't long before we realized we'd never get anywhere together. We split up to make our way to Pardubice, but I'm the only one who arrived."

Two more dead, captured, or missing. Zdenek made himself ask the question. "Nothing on the others?"

"Unfortunately, yes," said Kral. "Corporal Ivan Kolarik was taken in Zlin. He committed suicide."

No one said anything, but they were thinking: Kolarik is the first. They had all known him and understood that what happened to one could happen to them all.

"Did he compromise your mission?"

"Not Kolarik. I know him too well."

"What about the third man?"

"No word yet," said Kral. "He may show in Pardubice. When he does, he'll join the mission."

"If he doesn't?"

"That's why I'm here," he said. "To talk to you."

Kral's answer was so leading that it moved Ota from his usual silence. "Are you saying you want us for your mission?"

Kral nodded. "I want you to know this has already been cleared with London. They'd very much like you to help."

Ota looked at Zdenek, who read his thoughts. Why would London jeopardize Anthropoid's mission? What target could be as important?

"We'll be glad to lend a hand," said Zdenek. "After we finish our job."

It was Kral's turn to look uncomfortable. He seemed not to want to beg or to order. "I'm afraid there's a time limit on Out-Distance. The work has to be done while the nights are long enough for the bombers to make a run successfully. That means very soon."

"So we put our work aside and do yours," said Zdenek. "Even though the Gestapo might know what it is."

"I wouldn't do it if I thought they knew," said Kral. "And I certainly wouldn't want you to do it."

"This must be an important mission."

"London wouldn't ask for you otherwise," said Kral. "Can I count on your help?"

"It's not a bad time to be getting out of the city," said Ice. "What's the job?"

"We're going to lay down radio signals at Pilzn," said Kral. "RAF bombers will home in on them and level the Skoda Works."

CHAPTER 14

When Out-Distance began to go wrong, Zdenek could find no one to blame but Cyril. He was the last member of the Out-Distance team, and the least. The mission had already been set up from Prague. They had detailed plans of the Skoda Works, the cooperation of key people at the plant, and they were waiting for the weather to clear, when Cyril appeared in Pardubice, saying that he was glad to have finally found his way.

It had taken him more than two weeks to travel the few miles from his drop zone to contact Emil, and the miracle was that he had arrived at all. The first time Zdenek saw Cyril, he thought: this man is to blame.

For what? Zdenek did not know, but he had seldom been close to anyone who was so nervous. Cyril's eyes, which were set far to the side of his head, seemed incapable of meeting others frankly. His thick lips were unnaturally twisted, as if he were about to curse himself, or the world that badly abided him.

And he stuttered. The mumbling that mangled a perfectly good word could go on for seconds, or forever. How Cyril had passed the most casual inspection of his papers was unknown.

But here he was enlisted in the most important land-air mission of the war. When Out-Distance landed, they cached their equipment in a field near the DZ, including the most vital item, a Rebecca beacon. Preset to a frequency on which the RAF would home, and implanted near the Skoda Works, the beacon would lead the bombers to their target.

But when they revisited the cache before going on to Pilzn, the beacon was gone. Dug up. A farmer, probably. Whether he had turned over his find to the Gestapo was a mystery that they could not afford to solve.

So the team continued to Pilzn, where Ice had gone ahead to set up liaison with the Skoda workers for sabotage on the ground. London had no intention of giving up on the mission even if the means of achieving it no longer existed. The Skoda Works were the second biggest arms center under Nazi control. With Germany being bombed by Allied planes, more production had been shifted to the factories in Pilzn. Tanks, planes, trains, armored cars, and every mechanized component rolled off the assembly lines. Not only were current systems manufactured, but advanced prototypes, too.

The new orders that Out-Distance received from London by radio were simple but very dangerous. Prior to the raid, the team would travel to each side of the city to light fires that could be seen from the air on line-of-sight from the night sky. The pilots would zero between the fires, where the Skoda Works must be.

It was not Zdenek's place to argue the feasibility of the plan. He went along with Kral to rooms that belonged to a warder at Bory Prison, where they met Ice. What happened when that man saw Cyril was one of the wonders of the war.

Ice wanted to kill him outright, one shot to the head, dump the body in the river with the rest of the garbage.

It didn't take long to learn the reason for his anger. Zdenek had not known Cyril at Brigade, because the Czech troops were billeted all over Warwickshire, but Ice had been in the same company. He said that Cyril had been a heavy drinker, a card sharp, and an anti-Semite who openly praised Hitler. He was so personally and politically unreliable that a petition was sent to the general staff, signed by most of the battalion, asking that Cyril be separated from the service.

Even after discounting half of Ice's claims, Zdenek had to conclude that London had no idea of what they were doing. Almost everyone who volunteered for special training was accepted if he had the physical skills. Their psychological fitness seemed to carry no weight.

In fact, Cyril's nerves seemed exactly those of a man who drank too much but did not have access to his poison; who lived to cheat but found himself in a situation where cutting corners meant death; who hated Jews as much as he admired the false order of the Reich; who volunteered for commando training as a way of getting back home without the slightest idea of what that meant in wartime.

Zdenek spoke to Kral about the problem, but Out-Distance's commander had more important things on his mind. Cyril had managed to survive so far. Personnel matters could be dealt with later, when the mission was done. And that would not begin until they had the signal from the BBC broadcast that said: "Have patience, the day of revenge is coming."

* * *

Ota removed the headphones from his ears and tossed them across the room to Zdenek. "That's it. We've got a go."

"Already?"

"Save your sarcasm for the RAF if they miss. We can do what we came for now."

Kral heard their words as he sat at the table in the half-kitchen. He had established that position as his command post when they arrived: northeast of the sink, his back to the stove, and now he called them to it.

"Final rehearsal," he said, bent over the German military map that had been issued in England. "We'll divide into three teams. Team One is Ota. He'll remain in the city to coordinate sabotage and give a damage assessment of the bombing. Team Two is Zdenek and Ice. They'll proceed to the site chosen yesterday three miles west of the city, set fire to the barn, and afterward board the train for Prague."

Kral tapped the face of the map that was spread over the table where they had taken bad food and good beer for the last three days. "The third team will consist of Cyril and myself. We'll repair to the site two miles east of the city. We'll set fire to the barn to give a back beacon for the bombers, then continue on to the train station." Kral tossed the pencil onto the face of Pilzn, a city that looked much better in contour lines, and glanced around the small circle.

"Questions?"

"A suggestion, sir," said Zdenek as mildly as he could. "I was thinking it might be useful to shift personnel, since we'll all be returning to Prague."

"Your reason?"

"Your team hasn't been in the country long enough to know every danger," said Zdenek. "It would be better if Ice went with you, and I went with Cyril. Especially if the Gestapo's been alerted about the raid."

Ota quickly took up the line. "Good idea. No telling what will go wrong, but something usually does."

Kral looked to Ice as if he had the deciding vote. "They're right," he said. "Keeping our men from the Gestapo is vital."

Kral nodded; the democratic process had been served. "Very well. The composition of the teams will be changed, if Cyril has no objection."

Cyril shrugged without moving much, as if the matter were insignificant. He affected a bored exterior at all times that might not have been his fault. The heavy eyelids made him look as if he were half-asleep; the weak chin and thick lips as if he were always on the verge of a sneer.

"Then it's settled," said Kral. "Zero hour is one-fifteen. We should be in position at twelve-forty-five, and the fires should be going by one."

* * *

As he looked around in the muted darkness of the car, Ice thought: this is a trolley war. Lacking the automobiles and trucks that came from the Skoda Works, their missions moved to the slow glissando of public transportation, wires clicking above their heads, traveling in iron slots as predetermined as death.

Now and then the sparks that trailed from the electrical contacts above the car gusted, illuminating the area. The car was almost empty at this time of night and would not fill until the next shift change at the plant. On the seat beside Ice, his lean face visible in sepulchral glimpses, sat the officer known as Kral.

"What would you say to dying on a trolley?"

Ice could feel Kral shift. "I wouldn't say much."

"That's how Leon did it," said Ice. "Falling off the platform, like a Western movie. The Gestapo squad found him laying in the gutter after he'd blown his brains out. They shot him several times after he was dead, so they could say they'd brought him down."

"Did he mind?"

"I think he was insulted," said Ice. "It's a sin, you know, to desecrate the body of a hero."

Kral shifted again as if growing more uncomfortable with the talk. "Did you know Leon?"

"Yes," said Ice. "The only officer I've met that I liked. It was because he didn't behave like one."

"Are you trying to tell me something?"

"I'm telling you that we're all dead," said Ice. "Some of us will get there faster than others. You'll be one of the first, because you can't rid yourself of the habit of command."

Ice turned in the seat until he was looking into Kral's eyes. "Part of it's not your fault. You seem like a man with a brain. That's the first thing the Germans look for. When they find it, they kill it. Later, they think of a reason."

"I'm surprised they bother," said Kral. "It seems a waste."

"The second thing they notice is tone of voice," said Ice, mimicking Kral's. "They're not very smart, but even a dog heeds that. You talk to one SS or Gestapo as if you're telling him the way to the shithouse by way of Siberia, and you'll be the one to find a fast grave."

"All right," said Kral. "I'm listening to your advice."

"That's all of it," said Ice. "You've spent your life trying to separate yourself from the crowd. Now you have to be one of them down to your shoes. Or you'll die quickly. Like Cyril."

Kral still couldn't rid himself of the instinct that he had honed for years. Ice felt him stiffen in the seat at the mention of the only subordinate that was his freely to command.

"You don't like him either."

"He's a disaster," said Ice. "You must have known it before you took him onto your team."

"I knew about the petition that went up to the minister," he said. "But Cyril went through training well."

"And what do you think now?"

"That he's a very nervous man."

Ice was glad to hear the truth from an officer. He thought it possible, barely, that Kral might survive longer. A week.

"Perhaps we won't have to worry about Cyril much longer."

"What's that mean?"

"Zdenek will make a decision about him tonight," said Ice. "If he decides for the best, the Germans will have another dead body to blame. This time for arson."

Kral put his arm onto the seat forward, twisting his fingers around the metal bar. If that was the way he displayed anger, there was a chance for him. Say, two weeks.

"You should have asked me about this," he said. "Beforehand and very seriously."

"I'm telling you now as a courtesy," said Ice. "And don't think you've gotten off with anything if Cyril comes back in one piece. Do something about him. Immediately. At least get him out of my sight."

"That will make you happy."

"Not at all. That will keep him alive a bit longer."

* * *

Zdenek looked from the watch face to the barn again. Bits of green luminous matter carried over, hemming the outlines of the building. Night vision was a deepening thing. Sight never got better once the pupils dilated, but other senses made up the shortfall. A light wind brushed his cheek and brought the smell of dung from the pens. The sounds that Cyril made as he shifted his weight in the grass arrived like drum rolls. When he spoke, the voice that was hardly above a whisper seemed to shout.

"Shouldn't we go in?"

"Soon."

"Soon is best for coming and going," said Cyril as he moved closer. "That farmer will raise hell when he sees his hay barn go up. He won't ask if it's for the cause."

"I see you know country people," said Zdenek. "Your accent's Bohemian. From the south."

"I was born at Stara Hlina," he said. "Now my family lives in Trebon."

Formerly Wittingau. The town was near the Austrian border. Many of the people there were simply Austrian. The Waldviertel, where Hitler's family came from, lay just across that line.

"What was it like, living with so many of the enemy?"

"I didn't notice," he said. "What does a boy know? Do people carry signs? I'm an Austrian pig. I'm a Czech saint. To tell the truth, I still can't tell the difference. A lot of people can't. One of my relations was drafted into the Protectorate Army. He seems happy enough there."

Zdenek asked himself if he heard those words from another man, wouldn't he think it candor?

"Did you see your relations in Trebon?"

"Yes," he said in a soft mocking voice. "My mother, too."

"A breach of security, Cyril."

"Are you going to shoot me for it?"

"I wouldn't," said Zdenek. "But Ice thinks that no one could be missing as long as you were for anything but a bad reason."

Zdenek moved quickly but carefully toward the barn. The moon was high and quartered, the weather startlingly clear. Ideal for a bombing run. By now the RAF planes had diverted from the raid on the Daimler-Benz Works in Stuttgart and should be heading across southern Germany.

A wooden latch on a rope held the barn door. From their reconnaissance, Zdenek knew that no dogs were in the vicinity. This fellow had a small tractor for the dray work, though where he found the fuel was a mystery. The tractor stood in the barn on the far side of the house, along with the hogs and three cows. This one was more of a big hay shed, and perfect for the work.

Zdenek pulled two bales of hay from the stack and cut the cord with his knife. As he scattered hay across the dirt floor, he saw a dark shadow in the doorway. Cyril. He should have been off to the side, where he was told to stand. A small thing, but damaging to his cause, which was staying alive.

After Zdenek pulled down the rest of the bales and set them in a semi-circle, he checked his watch again. Five till one. He counted the last moments out, and set the fuse on the bomb Ota had rigged. He had guaranteed a five minute fuse, and Zdenek believed in Ota's genius with explosives. The noise would not be heard beyond twenty meters, and the barn would be in flames shortly after the hour.

"Finished?"

"Es wird schon gehen."

Zdenek couldn't see Cyril's face in the dark, but he knew by the sudden rigidity in the man's body that he didn't like being spoken to in German. He understood enough to follow, though.

It was important to put distance between them and the chaos that would ensue, but Zdenek moved faster than necessary. They were across the small pasture near the hill that led up to the road when he heard Cyril's heavy breathing.

"What do you want me to say?" he asked in a voice that was loud and cramped. "I read the advertisement in the paper about buying a dictionary. That was my signal. Until then I knew nothing. I went to the printer's house, and he sent me on to Pardubice. That's the truth."

Zdenek said nothing. He began to walk faster. Behind him, the breathing grew louder, faster.

"I could have gone sooner," said Cyril. "Kral was there ten days before me. That's what you're thinking, isn't it?"

"You don't have to convince me," said Zdenek without turning to face Cyril. "But Ice has taken to notching his gun for kills—and he likes the feeling."

"He scares me," said Cyril. "A lot of things scare me here. We were told so many tales in England. They said the people would help us. They said the war would be over in a year. Then to land

and find a man has nowhere to turn but his family. That's where I was all the time—with my mother in Trebon."

"For almost a month."

"Yes."

"You didn't put your own advertisement in the paper, looking for your team."

"N-n-no," he said, stammering for the first time. "I should have, but didn't."

Zdenek stopped ten meters short of the road. He turned and saw Cyril in shadow, sharpening at the margins. Light? Yes, light at his back. Fire. Distant, just a glow, but steadily stronger. The barn was beginning to burn. The aircraft would be over the target soon, and this mission had a chance to succeed.

"Why didn't you try to contact anyone?"

Cyril bowed his head as if offering it for the kill. "When I was home, I saw my sister, too. She told me the woman that I was in love with before I left the country had a baby. Mine. So I went to see M-M-M-M-Magda. She didn't have the baby any longer. She'd given it up. But she had pictures. It was a boy. That changed everything. And I stayed with her longer than I should have. Much longer. That's the truth. If you don't believe me, there's nothing I can do about it."

Zdenek wanted to know more: was it your baby, fool?

And: how could you tell? How many times did you try to make another? How dare you stop the war at your pleasure?

But could Zdenek really say that? Could he do what prudence dictated and what Ice kept screaming in his ear? Could he do it and live with himself. He had been on the ground for months with no result but survival and the love of a woman. What was the difference between them? Nerves? Wouldn't Cyril be all right in a place where he was welcome and safe?

"You should go home, Cyril."

"Home?" he said, as if he had no idea where that thing was. "Do you m-m-m-mean . . ."

"To Trebon," said Zdenek. "Stay with your family. When you're needed, we'll send for you."

"But the lieutenant . . ."

"I'll clear it with him. Go home. Keep safe and low."

Zdenek turned and began to walk toward the road again and the train station that would take him to Prague. He had not gone many steps when he heard Cyril's steps beside him.

No words in the darkness, no butchered half-words, but Cyril could have spoken and never been heard because at the same time the air-raid sirens began. Zdenek looked back as distant searchlights sprung up in bright alleyways over the city, weaving and colliding, searching out the aircraft overhead.

As they tramped along the side of the road double-time, Zdenek thought he heard the far-off drone of aircraft engines, a deep faint growl; but he saw nothing moving in the bright-dark patchwork of the sky.

Farther on, as they neared the outskirts of the town of Rokycany, the anti-aircraft batteries began to fire. The sound was muted and overlapping, thumping like flesh in a tub. Higher up shells began to burst.

Zdenek looked at his watch. It was one-fifteen.

Where were the Stirlings? Where were the bombs?

Their fire was going good, simmering four hills away, one half of a perfect bracket if the second team had done its job. But it was now one-twenty-two, and still nothing could be heard from the bombers.

At one-thirty, Zdenek began to hear different sounds, loose rumbles that seemed to drift and pop through a labyrinth. But they were far away. Very far and much too friendly.

It was five minutes past the half-hour when they reached the train station. Cyril nodded goodbye, the best thing he'd done, then walked slowly to the other side of the tracks while Zdenek stayed in place on his. Magda's lover still had not spoken, nor had the RAF.

They waited, staring across the vacant rails at each other in darkness, until the anti-aircraft fire began to recede, then like a hand-wound clock, stop. A few minutes later, at approximately one-forty-five, the all-clear sounded.

CHAPTER 15

SUMMARY: ICE TO FRANTA

Follows the damage assessment of RAF bombing in the OUT-DISTANCE operation: there was none. The aircraft did not locate the Skoda Works in spite of our signal beacons, and few bombs were dropped, none finding the target.

We cannot express the depth of our disappointment. Everything from our end was carried out as directed under trying conditions with the best weather. The OUT-DISTANCE and ANTHROPOID teams were exposed to maximum risk. The Skoda workers who cooperated in the mission will be subject to reprisal. Whether they can be counted on again is unknown.

In the event that further missions of this kind are attempted, we strenuously advise that pilots familiar with the area and the position of the works be employed. Anything less is futile.

* * *

"Heydrich left the castle at seven-thirty-two last night," said Libena. "Yesterday, it was six-twenty-five. In all the days you were gone, he never left at a consistent time."

Zdenek looked at the scraps of paper written in Safarik's meticulous hand. Basic white with wood stain, varnish and lacquer. Zdenek moved the scraps around the top of the old mahogany table in the dining room of Libena's home. They were alone, the family was out, but she had not wanted to do anything about it. What she wanted was to talk.

"Heydrich must be busy at his work," said Zdenek. "I wonder what a Protector does besides kill his subjects."

"He entertains women in his apartments," she said. "Mostly Lebensborn bitches."

Lebensborn. The spring of life. The Nazis were good at giving clever names to common vice. Young women brought themselves to strange hotels and barracks to be bedded by Aryan warriors for reasons that only a German needed new words to understand.

"I find it hard to believe that any woman would put herself to the SS like an animal."

"They do," said Libena. "I was on a trolley one day next to a girl who told me she was on her way to the SS school to have herself impregnated. She was excited to be fulfilling her duty to the Germanic race, and being taken care of at the same time. It's not like being a whore to them. They think they're practicing racial selection in a logical way. They go at the proper time of month. When the task is done, they're taken to lying-in places. Their children are given advantages."

"Heydrich must have first choice of the young virgins."

"He has his share," she said.

"Well, he'll not be having many more."

Libena looked at the scraps of paper that bore times like a single train reported for nowhere. She shifted them around until she made two distinct piles: the *withs* and *withouts.*

"You talk like it will happen soon, Zdenek."

"Yes," he said. "This business in Pilzn was the last folly."

"Do you think it's best to go ahead when you're so angry?"

"It's the only thing that will get this job done," he said, speaking the truth that had been plain for weeks. "Ota wants to take the war a day at a time, so he can make love to Anna a day at a time. London thinks we're so hopeless they send us on errands for others. Ice is the only one who really belongs on this team. He doesn't give a damn for any woman—or his own life."

Libena chose one of the scraps of paper from the table. She stared at it as if the numbers meant more than the death of one man. "Time of day," she said. "Time of month. What does it really matter?"

"Are you trying to tell me something, Libena?"

"No," she said after a moment.

She blew on the paper. It lifted from her palm into the air and fluttered toward him. Zdenek had a notion to catch it, say, this one, this is when the monster will die, but he let it collide with his shoulder and tumble down his chest to settle in his lap, knowing that she would find it there, if she wanted.

* * *

Zdenek thought it was suspicious when Emil asked him to meet Jindra, because Ota always handled that tedious job. What help they had gotten in housing, or contacts with people like Safarik, came from quiet competent Uncle.

He had gotten a message that said Ice wanted to see him, but when Zdenek arrived at Auntie's, he found that Ice had left with Auntie's son Atya, Max, and another man, a stranger. Just then Emil came to the door. They didn't say much after Zdenek agreed to accompany him. Most of what filtered through the rain concerned Emil's health, which had deteriorated.

"The doctor says I have rheumatoid arthritis."

"I thought arthritis was a disease of old people."

"Not this kind," said Emil. "The way it was explained is that my immune system has gone amok. It detects the body's own tissue as foreign. And it attacks the invader."

"Can it be treated?"

"Not with the drugs available. I was lucky to get aspirin."

It seemed more than odd—a bad sign—to have a body turn on itself. Radio Libuse was the only link to London. If its commander went down, the link would rely on one radio operator and several couriers working with the Pardubice resistance.

Emil seemed able to walk well enough, though Zdenek noticed that he kept his right hand in the small of his back, clenching and unclenching his fist. Pain would do that. It would make a man do things he normally wouldn't.

That was something to remember as they turned at Kodanska and quickly swung into an apartment building at Number 23. They climbed to the second floor and entered a comfortable flat whose owners were nowhere in sight. In their places sat Jindra, plotting behind that fine mustache, and Kral.

Zdenek shook hands all around but thought: what are you doing here, Out-Distance? Are you still angry because I sent Cyril home where he belongs?

"Sit down," said Jindra. "We're glad you could come."

Zdenek sunk into a horsehair armchair. "It's lucky Emil found me. Or you'd have to play cards with a widow."

"I don't know that any of us are gamblers," said Jindra. "I like to think we're prudent men with reasonable goals."

"In war?"

"In this kind of war," he said. "Nothing is more important than survival in the face of overwhelming power."

Now that he knew the issue, Zdenek looked at Kral, who looked quickly away. He looked at Emil, who rubbed his hands to soothe his pain.

"We've just had a signal from London," said Emil. "They plan to drop five more teams in the next few days."

"Good," said Zdenek. "We have enough officers. We'll have an army soon, if we're lucky."

"There will have to be a great deal of luck," said Jindra. "To date, the parachute teams have had little. The strain they've put on the resistance is enormous."

"We're grateful for the support you've given us, Jindra. But with new teams on the way, it's time to become more active. Hacha gave the Nazis a fully-equipped hospital train for the Russian Front on Hitler's birthday. The next thing we'll see is Czechs fighting beside them. The world will see our shame."

"Is our honor more important than our existence?" he said. "I ask you that question very seriously."

It might have been proper to ask an unanswerable question, but that didn't mean they should have a proper response. "I can't answer that," said Zdenek. "It's not my job, and I don't know that it's yours."

"All right," said Jindra, as if he had reached a point of departure. "That's what we mean to speak about. Your job. We understand that you're close to completion."

"Perhaps."

"You can't give a better answer?" asked Kral.

"No."

Emil stood up from his chair; he seemed to wobble. "We know you plan to kill Heydrich soon. You could at least answer the question with respect."

"I meant no disrespect," said Zdenek. "But since you know the answer, why ask?"

Before Emil could respond, Jindra spoke. "We're not here to fight among ourselves. But let me ask one question."

"Go ahead."

Jindra shook a cigarette from the pack in his pocket. He lit it slowly, coughing twice, tossing the match into the ashtray. "Have you considered what will happen if you succeed?"

"I'm not a fortune teller."

Jindra squinted through the smoke. "If the Protector dies, the whole nation will suffer. The Nazis won't take a hundred lives for one, not when that life is so vital to their cause. Thousands will be arrested, tortured, and killed."

"Possibly."

"Some will be fighters like you," said Jindra. "Others will be innocents. Women. Children. The Nazis do not shrink from atrocity. They'll heap bodies on Heydrich's funeral pyre like the barbarians they are."

Zdenek shook his head quickly, and that seemed to enrage Emil. "You're not listening," he said. "This man is asking you to have a conscience!"

"I have a conscience," said Zdenek. "And a duty."

"No one's asking you to betray it," said Jindra. "Perhaps in the future we'll need to do this thing. But not now. Not when we're weak and scattered."

"I've been here four months," said Zdenek. "Every hour brings us closer to a mischance that can ruin our mission. Every hour the resistance grows weaker. And you ask me to wait."

"Would you like it better if you were told?" asked Kral very quietly. "We can do that, and remove the responsibility."

"You can't," said Zdenek. "My orders come from the president of the republic."

"Damn you!" said Emil. "Everyone's telling you that you're suicidal and stupid. Now I'm telling you that you're murderous. That you have no love for your country!"

Zdenek was in his face so fast that he didn't think the movement. His hand stopped at Emil's throat and the flesh that had turned like a cannibal on itself. Why not do it? Squeeze. Terminate. Zdenek had never felt himself surrounded by so much evil pretending to be good. That pretended to be everything but what it was: crippled.

"It's because I love my country that I carry out my orders!" he shouted. "No one will interfere with that!"

Zdenek took two steps, opened the door and slammed it so hard that the sound blew through the building like explosives.

* * *

He walked through the rain for hours that became miles. The darkened streets passed without the slightest jog of memory, as if the villas and vertical apartment buildings were trapped in a portion of his mind that did not connect with the present. It was as if his senses had been directed to a question that loomed at the head of every block. If Anthropoid succeeded in its mission, the most merciful thing for Prague would be not to exist.

It might be a tomb that Zdenek paced in the blackout night and the lukewarm spring rain. The night before the end of the world for thousands. How would Hitler react when his favorite, the only man with the charisma to succeed him, was killed?

Zdenek walked to the river for his answer, knowing that none could be found. Who could predict the will of a madman? Why had the job been given to him?

He stopped at the embankment, leaning over the railing toward the swift current. Queer feelings here. The sky was so dark and low that it seemed to merge without borders into the land. The land was so dark and crabbed that it seemed unable to slow the water as it churned through the weirs. Everything was in flux.

The whole world was like that. The Nazi Empire was a force that knew no limits. Or failure. The Wehrmacht had begun its spring campaign after being stopped by the Russian winter. Rommel stormed across Africa to the Nile. Behind the army came the SD and the Gestapo, carrying the insignia of the death's head. Their leader was Heydrich.

Would they stop killing when he died?

Zdenek crossed the bridge, listening to the answer that seemed to arise from his footfalls on the cobblestones in the last minutes before dawn. *Hell, no. Hell, no.* When he reached Letenska Street, Zdenek knocked at the door to Anna's flat. Getting no answer, he let himself in with the key.

And found a note. We've gone, Anna and I, to Pruhonice to see the spring flowers. All the best, Ota.

Gone on holiday from the war. What was odd about that?

Zdenek caught a trolley for the ride back to Zizkov. Looking through the thin film of paint on the windows, he felt encapsulated. The sun rose like powder from a jar and the good citizens lofted themselves from the shadows, appearing in ascending files to work for the Nazi war machine.

But there, in front of the train station—the Woodrow Wilson Station—people still secretly placed flowers every night before the monument that commemorated the Republic. Each morning the Germans swept those gay fragments into the trash.

A useless gesture. A symbol.

Zdenek got off three stops after the monument and walked to Auntie's house, where he learned that Max was dead.

* * *

Zdenek looked around Auntie's kitchen at Ice and Auntie's son, Atya, a boy of nineteen, stood by the stove. The third man, Christoph, whose name was Bo Kouba, Staff Sergeant, sat with his head in his hands on Auntie's sofa. He had spoken before he began to weep. Or not quite before.

"How did it happen?"

Zdenek waited for Christoph to gather himself, but he sat hunched into his knees, rocking back and forth, his hands dug into the sides of his head, his fingers hidden in the roots of his dark brown hair.

"They dropped two days ago," said Ice when Zdenek looked to him. "Three teams—Steel A, Bivouac and Bioscope. They all landed near the castle at Krivoklat, then split up. Christoph got here yesterday. He wanted to go back to the sites where they cached their weapons and explosives. So we went—Max, Christoph, Atya and me."

"You didn't tell anyone about it?"

"I left a message with Kral," said Ice, "but we couldn't wait. You know what luck we've had with our supplies. If we hadn't lost the Rebecca beacon in the Out-Distance cache, Pilzn would still be in flames."

"What went wrong?"

"The same," said Ice. "Someone found the cache. Cops were all over the forest. They stopped Atya and me, but let us go after they looked at our papers. Christoph and Max were intercepted, too. Max lost his head and started to fire. He hit two of them before he took a round in the belly."

Christoph looked up without wiping the tears from his brown eyes. "I didn't want to leave him. He made me do it, and when I wouldn't, he just did it. Put that thing in his mouth. I saw the castle in the flash, lit up against the sky. I wish that was all I'd seen."

Zdenek saw the huge black-peaked castle, too, the hunting lodge of the Bohemian kings, as if it were ghosted on a postcard. Without wanting to, he saw the other things as well. No. Better.

"Max did the only thing he could. So did you, Bo."

He shook his head because he had been doing the only thing he could for years, making the journey they all had made—Poland, France, England, and finally falling from the sky back into the homeland. He had lost every time.

"Both the men Max shot were Czech," he said. "I heard one of them scream. He was calling for a woman named Ludmilla."

"The man who stopped us was Czech, too," said Ice. "A cop. I'll never know why he let us go."

"Did he see Atya's real name and address?"

"I'm afraid so."

It was one of the worst things that could have happened—as bad as death but more lingering. If the man remembered where Atya lived, he could damage the network forever. Zdenek believed that Atya was a courageous boy, but he was still a boy, and few men were able to withstand Gestapo torture.

"We'll have to scatter," he said. "I'm sure Uncle can find us new safe-places."

"If that cop wanted to do something, he would have done it there," said Ice. "I don't think we have much of a problem."

"You may be right," said Zdenek. "But we can't be sure that he won't change his mind once he starts thinking about the reward."

"What in the name of hell are we going to do?" asked Christoph in a voice that touched rage for the first time. "We had enough explosives to blow up half the country. Now we've nothing. What do we fight with? Where do we run?"

"We'll find you a place," said Ice. "Don't worry about a thing."

"Don't worry?" said Christoph. "That's what you said all the way on the train to Krivoklat. For Christ's sake, you would have said that to Max when he ate the pistol. Don't worry, old man, we'll see each other in hell!"

"You don't understand," said Ice. "This is hell. We're going to a better place."

"Not me," said Christoph, pushing out of the chair angrily. "I've nothing to accomplish my mission with, so I've no mission. I've no one to give me orders, so I'll cut my own. I'm going to Kutna Hora. I'll send you a postcard when I'm there."

As Christoph walked toward the door, Ice and Zdenek exchanged a panicky look. Could they let this happen? Could he be stopped short of force?

But Christoph stopped himself. He turned with his hand on the door. "Don't worry about a thing," he said, mocking them. "I won't give you up."

CHAPTER 16

The city seemed deserted. Except for the ramparts before the castle decked with German flags, there were no signs of May Day festivities. Before the castle, only an SS honor guard with drawn bayonets stood in the courtyard headed by the Protector.

"Herr Reichsfuhrer, welcome to Prague."

Himmler returned the greeting and the salute, wondering, as he always did, how much mockery lay in Heydrich's tone. It was absolutely forbidden in the SS to use common civilian forms of address, yet Heydrich always used it with him.

"Such a lovely city."

"The most German of all cities, Herr Reichsfuhrer."

There. He'd done it again.

"How ironic," said Himmler. "The Czechs are the most unGerman of people, yet they enjoy the finest of our culture."

"For a time, Herr Reichsfuhrer."

"Indeed."

Himmler passed the front rank and down the line of the honor guard. Heydrich followed two paces back as the cameras whirred for the newsreels. What a fine tableau this would make. The guard was magnificent. All dimensions, shapes and colors determined by rigorous selection.

Himmler saluted the guard—they were his creation—his perfect political warriors—before turning across the monumental stones at the entrance to the castle.

"The Fuhrer is impressed with your work in Prague," said Himmler. "He notices that production has risen while sabotage has fallen."

"Both goals must be pursued at the same time," said Heydrich. "The whip and the sugar."

"A rational approach."

"And one that should be implemented throughout Europe," said Heydrich. "The army is incapable of administering the rest of the occupied lands. They lack the will and the training."

What Heydrich meant was that he should supply both as head of an SS superstate on the continent. Himmler did not disagree with the necessity, and perhaps not on the choice.

"The Fuhrer thinks you should make a tour of the West," he said. "The Judeo-Bolshevik resistance grows stronger every day. We would like your assessment. And your recommendations."

Heydrich's face made a copy of a smile as they crossed the marble hallway and walked up the broad marble stairs. Himmler had learned long ago that if this man gained one upward step each day, he was content. Until the next day.

"The first room on the left, Herr Reichsfuhrer."

No one could have missed the display. Flanking the doorway were two Black Knights of the SS. Within, officials in civilian and military dress stood before long tables.

On the telephone last night, Heydrich had promised an astounding display of ordnance captured at a Czech castle, and he was seldom prone to boasts. The five tables were filled with submachine guns of the ugliest make Himmler had ever seen. Pistols. Radio equipment packed in a large case. Parachutes. And from what he could see, a large amount of explosives.

"Are all these things English?"

"Except for some pistols, which were manufactured here."

"Do we know the aim of the parachutists?"

"No, Herr Reichsfuhrer. The criminal we intercepted last night died before we could question him. But as you can see, the quantity of explosives would allow them to attack significant targets. Power stations, oil tanks, a transportation terminus."

Himmler was sure Heydrich was correct, but among the items with the explosives were curious housings. One looked very much like a telephone stand.

"What's this used for?" he asked. "It seems harmless."

"A sabotage device," said Heydrich. "It's made of black bakelite. Lifting the handset would detonate two hundred grams of plastic explosive."

"Then it's not simply a sabotage device but an assassination device."

"Yes, Herr Reichsfuhrer. An anti-personnel explosive."

"Are there more like it?"

Heydrich indicated the round but somewhat concave object that lay next to the mock-telephone. "This is an explosive designed to adhere magnetically to metal."

"Such as an automobile. Or train."

"Yes, Herr Reichsfuhrer."

"Another assassination device."

"It would seem."

Himmler was impressed with that sort of seeming. The man who climbed in his car unaware, or used an instrument as innocent as a telephone, might find himself in sudden pieces.

"How many parachutes?"

"Seven, Herr Reichsfuhrer."

"And you have caught one man."

"We have the materiel without which they cannot function," said Heydrich. "Soon we will have them, as we have taken every parachutist who landed in this country."

But it took only one, and a half dozen were unaccounted for. Slowly, Himmler walked three steps to the window that overlooked the courtyard, knowing that Heydrich would follow. The day was overcast with a haze obscuring the buildings at the end of Hradcany Square. Very Germanic, indeed.

"I was with the Fuhrer when he took possession of this castle," said Himmler. "He counted it the greatest day of his life. He had finally united Bohemia into the German homeland."

"Yes, Herr Reichsfuhrer."

"He stood at this window accepting the adulation of the crowd. It was a crowning moment, yet the Fuhrer did not tarry. He withdrew himself from public view after a brief time."

"Yes, Herr Reichsfuhrer."

"We know that Adolf Hitler is a man of courage, yet he knew the risk he ran in exposing himself to danger. He understood that Germany could not recoup the loss of his physical being."

"Yes, Herr Reichsfuhrer."

Himmler turned from the window to Heydrich. Impulsively, he did something he never did: touched another man. Lightly. On the arm. "You must fight this thing in your blood," he said to Heydrich quietly. "You must realize that it drives you to flaunt good sense. It is a Jewish thing."

"Herr Reichsfuhrer, please—"

Heydrich always whined when the subject was brought up. He was a man who lived in terror of his origins; who kept all the secrets of the Reich in his hands, including the greatest: that the head of the Jewish Office, the SD, and all departments of Reich Main Security, himself had Jewish blood.

"I know that your car is unarmored," said Himmler. "I know that you ride in the streets in full view of the population. I know that you scorn your escort. All these things will end."

"But Herr Reichsfuhrer, think of the damage to our prestige if the Protector is seen as a prisoner of his own people."

"They are not your people," said Himmler. "The Czechs are historical debris that will soon be collected into the rubbish, like all the others. I will not permit a life as valuable to the Reich as yours to be wasted because of stupid pride."

"Yes, Herr Reichsfuhrer."

"Again."

"You have my promise, Herr Reichsfuhrer."

* * *

They left their bicycles in Libeznice at the church again, but took the food and spare ammunition along. It was an ideal day. The sun had not appeared for seven hours and the clouds were so low and diffuse that they seemed like a stain. Occasional rain slid in as slow and dirty and almost as dense as mud.

Ceiling zero. Zero hour. Zdenek had made up his mind when he saw Christoph pass through the door into a life that threatened them all. The slightest break in his nerves and they were doomed. The recollections of a Czech policeman as he paid his grocery bill would do the same.

He told no one about his plans. Ice was shunted aside when Uncle came with the news that the last two members of the Bioscope team—Vaclav and Eugen—had made their way to Prague. They were to be found safe-places and seasoned to conditions by someone, and Ice was the perfect guide.

So everything was as it was meant to be after four long months—two men walking in the rain along the side of a country road. The cars that might be heading off for the weekend were rare. The peasants who might have been outdoors—the men in fancy vests, the women in tall festival headdresses—kept to their cottages.

"It'll be dark early," said Ota. "If he stays long in the city, we won't be able to see much."

"I'd like to stay over tonight—if it's all right with you."

Ota took the news quietly. "So we camp out."

"We have enough food," said Zdenek. "And it might be safer in the woods than in Prague."

"True."

Zdenek would not have noticed Ota's change of tone unless he had been with this man day by day for months. Like tuning a radio and knowing the frequency was off a bit, Ota's tiny modulation meant: Yes, but—

"What's wrong, Ota?"

"I'm glad you told the officers no," he said. "I don't think I could have done it. Every time I talk to Jindra I end up doing exactly the thing I don't want."

"All we have to do is remember why we're here."

"What if that changes?"

"It can't."

"Anna says they'll go over our heads. They'll radio London to cancel the mission."

"That doesn't mean anything to me," said Zdenek. "Not unless my orders are changed."

"And if they are?"

"It won't matter if the bastard dies today."

Zdenek picked up his pace. They had reached the far side of the village closest to Heydrich's estate. In one of the last cottages—the biggest and best lit—they heard an accordion and a drum. Some whoops and some dancing. Women appeared in groups by the windows. Men stood smoking under the eaves.

Zdenek pulled his cap tighter to his skull. Some of these people had seen him before. They would know everyone in their village and for two villages around and most of the commuters, too. Every day it became more dangerous to be seen in the area doing nothing. It was good that it would be done with.

"Did you say goodbye to Libena before you left?"

"And kissed her, too."

"Zdenek, you know what I'm saying."

"I know what. I don't know why."

"All right. I'm supposed to tell you something. It's from Anna. She wasn't sure if she should tell me, and I'm not sure I should tell you."

"This has got to be horrible."

"Under most circumstances, it would be grand," said Ota.

"I don't want to know."

They walked for a hundred yards. The rain had collected on the road in near puddles. Their shoes squeaked with the suction of the cardboard that was supposed to pass for leather. In time it just left itself behind. Not a footprint. A souvenir.

"All right. Tell me what's wonderful and impossible."

"Libena is with child."

Zdenek walked three more steps with his head held up in an exaggerated manner. Yes, the sky was falling. If it sunk lower it would melt the clothes off their backs. They would be walking naked with scum hanging from their belts.

"This is the twentieth century," he said. "Does that mean she's pregnant?"

"Yes."

What had he expected? They had made love and that was the risk. Life. But she hadn't told him. Others, but not him. Him, she sucked.

"I don't understand this," he said. "If she's pregnant, why doesn't she tell me?"

"She doesn't want you to know," said Ota. "She's afraid it might influence you."

Zdenek saw the woods ahead. He had a fondness for elementary cover and what it lent the soldier. He remembered the sight of the forest in Nehvizdy like a revelation. But Heydrich's woods were as dark and twisted as a spider. It was what men had fled since the beginning of time.

"Positions," he said.

Ota veered to the left side of the road while Zdenek moved to the right. From this point their actions were automatic. Each knew exactly what he would do in every case, and this brought up the foul weather set of options.

Visibility would be marginal. Excellent for cover or escape but not for execution. The top might be buttoned on Heydrich's touring car, which would obscure the view and add a layer of metal struts that could deflect bullets. It would also be hard to toss a grenade where it might do significant damage.

He should tell Ota to go home. The weather made this a one-man job for the one with the Sten.

Zdenek moved three paces off the road into the forest and let his eyes adjust to the deeper gloom. When he could clearly see, he crouched in front of the rocks at the base of the birch tree and dug the cache out carefully.

First, the thorns that he had spent one afternoon layering in with last autumn's leaves—almost all birch, mulched by the hard winter into dense clumps. Then the rock. At sixty pounds, big and awkward enough to discourage browsing.

Zdenek jerked the rock free, rolling it in the small clearing at the base of the tree where it would leave no trace. He took a step to the cache and began to reassemble the Sten. He took the time to do it right because all submachine guns were temperamental weapons with a tendency to jam. The Sten was worse than most because so many of the magazines were bad.

The call was Zdenek's. It was bad to put doubt around the moment of decision, but he did not blame Ota. The fault was Anna's and Jindra's.

Libena had said nothing. At her house, she was herself—the daughter of parents more understanding than God. Her father, Petr, was secretary of the Red Cross and the Masaryk League for Tuberculosis. No one knew more about the bad and only side of the Third Reich and was more willing to do something about it. When Libena told him that they planned to be married, he said good, but in his mind they already were.

People like that kept a soldier in balance. Everyone in the house had guessed the purpose of his mission, and the consequences, but no one said a word. The only thing Petr said was that he knew a man who ran a tubercular sanatorium north of the city. Emphasis on "north." This man might be able to provide a place for them to stay if they needed it suddenly.

Zdenek had already made up his mind to become tubercular when it was over. If nothing else, that would direct pursuit from the people who sheltered them in Prague.

What he regretted was that they could never find a car for their getaway. The best efforts of Jindra had on that issue come to nothing. That, of course, was what made this suicide.

He was sorry that he had not said goodbye to Libena, but he could never do that properly. It was always goodbye between them—every time—and sweet because of it.

Zdenek was wondering what Ota might have told Anna last night when the double whistle came high and shrill from across the road.

The signal. He hadn't seen anything coming but Ota had a better angle southwest. Zdenek could not tell if the shape was the Mercedes touring car, but few others ever passed this way. It was a dark vehicle. The poor light made it seem darker than it was, but it was big. Too big. And growing.

Zdenek stepped onto the rock. Yes, another vehicle trailed behind the first. Christ, there was a third.

The one out front was an Adler 4—armored, full ordnance. Next came a troop carrier—tall but wide, fenders raked. Then more: two motorcycles pulled alongside the third car. Outriders. Zdenek wasn't sure, but he thought the one in the box was the Mercedes. It might have been dark green with a buttoned top, but the vehicles to the front and the flank blocked his view. And it seemed as if more crowded the rear.

More vehicles.

It was a convoy.

Hell, it was a small army.

Part Three:

The Hit

CHAPTER 17

The town of Kutna Hora sat on a steep hill that rose above the surrounding hills like a citadel. It had been a rich place until the silver mines failed. Von Pannwitz, who sometimes collected coins and other artifacts, knew the mark of its mint better than the bleak walls that greeted him.

In a rotting building off the town square, he met four Czech policemen—a lieutenant, two corporals, and a private who looked like the only man of initiative. He was a strapping lout with a back like an ox.

"Superintendent," said the lieutenant, offering his hand in lieu of a proper salute. "Welcome to Kuttenberg. I hope your journey was pleasant."

Von Pannwitz, who was usually good at native liaison, felt tired after the long drive from Brno. The lieutenant spoke bad German obsequiously. No doubt he had heard of the bonuses the Protector had given to the families of the Czech policemen who were killed and wounded at Krivoklat.

"It's my hope we'll all have some reward from this affair," said von Pannwitz. "The Protector takes a personal interest in the capture of saboteurs from England."

A smile. "May we get you something, Superintendent?"

"The prisoner."

"Of course."

Von Pannwitz was anxious because first reports indicated that the man who had been taken was a parachutist. Armed with a service pistol, he resisted a check of his papers at the railway station. Once subdued—and this was the telling point—he refused to divulge information.

The three parachutists found yesterday in Brno were mute in the beginning. One shot a Czech policeman and escaped, but the other two were taken. With proper encouragement, they cooperated.

The group, called Bivouac, had landed at Krivoklat with four other men. The massive amount of explosives belonged to them and a second team—Bioscope. While Bivouac went into hiding, Bioscope stayed behind to retrieve the supplies.

Yet Miks, the parachutist who killed himself in the ambush, did not belong to either team. Gerik identified him as the man who dropped with him in Slovakia. Even with his head blown apart, he looked like a heavyweight boxer.

Conclusion: the parachute resistance still functioned. They maintained contact with each other and the new teams that had dropped. Which meant that they had reliable radio contact with London. A transmitter. A courier system. Secure safe-places. An organization.

It was most likely centered in Prague. The Bivouac team knew nothing of the cell, but they had given good descriptions of the parachutists who jumped with them. Von Pannwitz was sure that the man held here was one of the Bioscopes. If he was also the man who escaped from Krivoklat, he could lead them to the heart of the organization.

Momentarily, von Pannwitz lost his optimism when the door opened and the Czechs led their prisoner into the room. Though handcuffed, he was clear-eyed and hostile. Good procedure dictated that he should have been stripped naked, shunted from cell to cell, deprived of rest—psychologically altered.

"Leave him here. Everyone will go from the room except that man." Von Pannwitz pointed to the enormous private.

"At once, Superintendent."

That was always an exaggeration with Czechs, but von Pannwitz had found the police were efficient when it was in their interest, and they left in an orderly fashion.

"Sit down."

The prisoner waited until the door closed before he sat in the straight chair in front of the desk. He did not fail to note that the largest of his jailers had positioned himself before the door. Or that he was as big as the door.

Not exactly fear in his surly face, but at the threshold. It was amazing how brave a man could be until his balls were liquefied in a steel press made for that purpose. One size fit all.

"Your name is Christoph Barouch."

The prisoner did not answer. He moved his brown eyes from the desk to the window that let in weak spring light.

"Perhaps you don't remember, having used the name so little. It's the one you were assigned in England." Von Pannwitz paused. "Or would you rather I call you Sergeant Kouba?"

He turned his head lazily back toward his interrogator. "I don't give a fuck what you call me, Gestapo man."

Insolence was the thing that preparation always removed. Had it been done, von Pannwitz would not have to now.

He sat on the edge of the desk and picked up the telephone receiver. "We found explosives in your cache that look much like this. That's cowardly. What if an innocent person picked up that telephone? A woman? A child?"

"What if it was your mother?"

Von Pannwitz brought the receiver across the prisoner's head obliquely. With his hands cuffed, he could not deflect the blow, which was hard but not at full strength. Nonetheless, he blew off the chair, landing on his shoulder without a sound.

When von Pannwitz pointed, the private moved from the door, picked up the fallen man as if he were weightless, and righted him into the chair.

Von Pannwitz waited a second, then hit the prisoner again with the receiver, this time full face. And harder. He went down again. The cuffed hands that he held to his face made it seem as if he wept blood. He looked deeply into his hands as if he could not believe the quantity.

"Yes, it's yours, asshole."

One of his teeth fell onto the floor. Finally, he spit a gob of dark blood and looked up.

Von Pannwitz lit a cigarette. "We can continue this. And more persuasively. Or you can tell me who gave you shelter in Prague. Where are the parachutists?"

No answer. Instead, the prisoner tipped his little finger toward the cigarette. Not much of a movement, but the first.

Von Pannwitz took another cigarette from the pack, lit it and passed it. The prisoner accepted it in one hand, but with handcuffs it seemed as if he used both. His hands moved to his face as he inhaled, peering between his fingers as if at another world. Exhaling deeply, he pushed thick smoke into the room.

"Good," said von Pannwitz. "You could have many more. You might be free in time."

As the prisoner exhaled the last, his eyes lost focus. The whites flashed like blinds, his head fell to the side, and his body followed, sliding from the chair and sliding the chair back. He struck the floor without breaking his fall with his arms.

A faint? A delayed reaction to the blow on the head? Von Pannwitz finally understood when the body rose and began to convulse, spine arching, heels knocking on the floor.

"Poison!" he screamed. "Poison!"

Von Pannwitz went to his knees, sliding on blood. With the body lurching under him, he put his hands into the open mouth, forcing it wider as he inserted his fingers deep into the esophagus. He felt the normal sensation of violating smooth flesh, but nothing foreign. No capsule. And now no movement.

"Respiration!" he said to the private who stood over them. "Give him artificial respiration."

The private bent, shifted the prisoner's body, and crouched with his knees wide apart. Slowly, he began to apply pressure with his hands on the prisoner's back, leaning forward with his tremendous weight.

"Get a doctor!" said von Pannwitz to the men rushing through the door from the anteroom. "Immediately!"

One corporal ran off hurriedly, but von Pannwitz saw that it was already too late. The labors of the behemoth produced no independent movement of the body. The poisons issued by the British were usually fast and fatal.

"Why was this man not searched?"

"He was, Superintendent," said the lieutenant. "I swear."

Perhaps it was true. Provincial police were not equipped to deal with these matters. The poison might have been hidden in a body cavity, or even a false tooth.

Von Pannwitz watched as the huge private continued his labors on the dead. Astride another man's hips, sweating, groaning, his muscles bulging. Inward. Outward.

Yes, von Pannwitz allowed himself to be excited by it. The nothingness of it.

The waste.

* * *

"Look, here's Captain Midnight."

Zdenek didn't want to look and see Kral, who Ice called Captain Midnight. Mounted on the seat of a bicycle, he seemed ungainly, his body rising far above the handlebars, his knees spread wide so his long legs wouldn't knock about.

"You don't suppose he's lost?"

"Oh, he is," said Ice. "An officer without a command is like a fly in a shitstorm."

Kral put his bicycle up against the tree that shaded the café table where they sat. It was a gorgeous spring day, the sun low and cooling, all the trees shedding pod and gaining leaf.

"May I join you?"

Zdenek said nothing.

Ice should have said nothing, but as usual couldn't control his mouth. "You know, I gave up my dog when I moved from Zizkov. He always followed me around, and it got to be inconvenient. I mean, there you'd be, fucking on a feather duvet, and you'd hear panting. Oh, she's finally getting into the spirit of the thing, you'd think. But, no. It was that damned Moula standing in the doorway, drooling, waiting his turn."

Kral looked at Ice as he always did—as if he was seeing a para who had jumped but never landed. And that wasn't a bad way to think of Ice.

"I understand you boys don't like me," he said, as he took a seat. "I suppose that can't be helped."

"It could be helped with a nine millimeter," said Ice. "But we dislike killing Czechs."

"The Gestapo don't mind," said Kral. "We've just gotten word that the entire Bivouac team was taken in Brno. Two of them were tortured until they gave names."

Three more men down. Zdenek didn't know what to say. Being practical seemed callous, but since Ice was good at that, he left it to him.

"Can they hurt us?"

"Indirectly," said Kral. "We've also had word of Christoph. He was taken in Kutna Hora. He's dead. A suicide. We're sure that he gave no information."

So Christoph was as good as his word: he had gone silently. But that meant four men of the seven who dropped at Krivoklat were lost. Two of the Bioscope team were living at safe-places in Prague. And one man unaccounted for.

"What about Steel A?"

"He reached Pardubice safely," said Kral. "What he might do there no one can say."

"I think you should join him," said Ice. "You'd have someone who would listen to you then."

Kral, a very serious man who liked to think he did serious work, refused to look at Ice. "There's one more thing you should know. Jindra sent a message through Radio Libuse to London requesting them to cancel your mission."

Zdenek said nothing. He had known something like this was coming since Ota said that Jindra planned to go over their heads. Kral was Jindra's chief accomplice now.

"I agreed with the request," said Kral when he was sure he would have no response. "Emil also."

"Emil's a sick man," said Ice. "What's your excuse?"

Kral still did not look at Ice. "I came here to talk to you, Zdenek. Do I have to listen to this idiot?"

"We agree on everything," said Zdenek. "I don't know what that makes me."

Kral brought his chair closer to the table. A tall man, he seemed to lengthen. His arms spanned the table and his shoulders nearly reached the lower branches of the tree on the walk.

"I like to think that if I had your orders, I'd act as you have," he said. "You've been correct. What I'm asking of you now is what I would ask of myself."

"I'll listen, Kral."

"We'd like you to delay your mission. At least until we have word from London."

"And you think they'll cancel."

"Yes."

"What if they don't?"

"Then we'll do everything we can to help you carry it out."

Zdenek had learned to play poker in England, but he had never seen a better hand. Since May Day the security around Heydrich's estate had been impenetrable. Just going out toward Panenske-Brezany was foolhardy. And today they received word that Anthropoid had left the country bound for France. That was the reason Ota had not shared this interview. He was off to discover if anyone knew when Heydrich would return.

"All right," said Zdenek, thinking it could not take long for London to decide what they had already decided, and certainly no longer than it would take Heydrich to exhaust the delights of Paris. "We'll wait."

For a moment, Kral did not react. He might have sensed a trap; he might have been genuinely astonished. "You will?"

"But I want to know the minute that you have word from London."

"I promise you that."

Kral stood up as if he were still unsure of his good luck, or his persuasiveness. He put his hand out. Zdenek took it without feeling too bad.

"Thank you very much."

"Goodbye, Kral."

They watched him get back on his bicycle like a kite being assembled. Almost before he was out of hearing, Ice began to laugh.

"That was excellent, Zdenek. You gave him nothing and got his promise of support."

"Which may be nothing."

"True," said Ice. "But it was worth being here to see."

"I don't want you getting used to the place. I've got a job that needs immediate attention."

"At your command."

"We can't count on security letting up at the estate," said Zdenek. "Find me a place where we can hit the target in Prague. Do it before Anthropoid returns from France."

"You don't have to worry about a thing, Zdenek. I'll get just what you need."

"I know that."

CHAPTER 18

When Zdenek saw the place Ice had chosen, he thought: this is where it will happen.

The street was quietly suburban, laying on the border of the Kobylisy and Liben districts in northern Prague. The houses were separated by trees and gardens. Just up the road a field opened where the top of the hill began to level. It was the last place where anyone would imagine sudden death.

The way from Panenske-Brezany led through here. It was the Prague-Dresden road, centuries old. Nothing had changed but the surface—from dirt to cobblestones that might have been quarried in the pit at Nehvizdy.

The most important thing was the grade of the hill and the sharp bend. It was a steep incline slightly above thirty percent coming into a near U-turn that led down to the Troya Bridge a mile away.

Zdenek remembered the tests they had made last October in England. An old Austin rolled down a ramp and around a corner into an ambush set by the team. The hit was usually judged successful at twenty miles per hour or less. Beyond that, results were questionable, especially with grenades.

"How fast can he go through the turn?"

"Twenty. Twenty-five," said Ice. "More than that and we won't have to waste bullets."

Zdenek crossed the street, which was wide in the turning. A bit narrower would have been better, but few things were perfect when improvised.

Oberscharfuhrer Klein, a good driver, would downshift into the turn and probably brake, too. The car would decelerate rapidly until the middle of the turn, when Klein began to accelerate out of it. There.

Zdenek stepped onto the curb of what he already thought of as the site. Here. Near the lamppost in front of a wrought iron fence. At intervals of fifteen feet along the fence, stone pillars obscured the road as it turned up the hill. The trees behind the fence made it impossible to see what was coming and the foliage would thicken with every spring day.

"We'll need a lookout," said Zdenek. "A man to stand at the head of the bend and give the signal."

"Ota should be good at that."

"Ota's good with explosives. We're a team trained to act as one. If you want to join us, you'll man the post up there."

"That's not quite what I had in mind."

"There's no discussion on this. None. If you want conversation, talk to Kral."

To Zdenek's surprise, Ice did not continue the argument. He believed in his destiny as if it was his heart. Allowed to follow it, he did the work better than anyone else could have.

"We'll have to look around the area carefully. We need to know if there's a police post nearby."

"There isn't," said Ice. "I checked."

"SS barracks?"

"Negative."

It seemed too much to hope that they could get away easily, but they might be able to vanish into the surrounding streets and get clear of the area. A lot would depend on traffic and the time of day. Not many cars, it seemed, but trolley tracks ran down the center of the street, two sets side by side that almost joined near the middle of the bend.

"How often do the trolleys run?"

"I don't have a schedule," said Ice. "But I'll get one."

"They could give us a diversion," said Zdenek. "A lot of confusion. Milling around. But it will be a mess if the target and the commuters arrive at the same time."

"There's a hospital down the road to Liben—the Bulovka."

Zdenek did not know if that made him feel better, but he felt no worse. Ice seemed to have calculated everything.

"Would you hold back?" asked Ice. "Knowing that innocent people might be killed?"

"If I had a choice, yes."

"And if not?"

"I'll let you know when the time comes."

"Are you sure it will?"

"I've never been more sure of anything," said Zdenek. "We're meant to do this thing. And we're meant to do it here."

* * *

They went to ground when they found the place where it would be done. Zdenek and Ota stayed with Professor Ogoun in Dejvice near Prague Castle, while Ice lived in Hanspaulka with a communist family. They kept in touch with each other and no one else but Anna. Only Uncle knew their locations.

A ferocious conspirator, he seemed never to run out of places to warehouse paras, or to run out of paras. When he came to the house one afternoon in mid May, it was with word of the latest arrivals.

"Two teams dropped in the south at the end of last month," he said. "We've had no word of any of them until today, when a man showed at Auntie's. He contacted Pardubice through the newspaper code. Emil sent him to us."

"Then he's legitimate," said Zdenek. "Not a plant."

"Yes."

Zdenek nodded as they sat in the two chairs in Ogoun's study. The professor taught at the Modern School for Girls, but the bookshelves in his study were lined with histories of civilizations whose chief value was their antiquity. He often said that a man could find out all he wanted to know of Germans by reading Julius Caesar. Nothing ever changed. Character was character.

"His name is Blackie," said Uncle. "No last."

"Bags under his eyes," said Zdenek, remembering the face from training. "Very serious."

"Yes," said Uncle. "He comes alone. He said that his mission was Tin. A two-man team."

Uncle looked as if he expected a reply. The thin man was smart enough to understand the numbers by now. Three-man teams were sabotage, one-man teams resupply. Only Anthropoid and Tin so far were two.

"Blackie lost his partner in the drop and hasn't been able to contact him," said Uncle. "His mobility is limited. A bad leg and possible internal injuries. The doctor's looking at him."

"Have you found him a place?"

Uncle nodded. "I'll tell you if you think that's wise."

Zdenek shook his head. "Tell him to get well soon."

"Perhaps he should take his time recovering. We wouldn't want him to interfere with your mission."

"That's his business," said Zdenek. "Tin has its orders."

"And you?" asked Uncle. "Do you still have yours?"

"We've no word from London," said Zdenek. "Anyone who expects our mission to be cancelled will be disappointed. You should tell Jindra that."

"I have," he said. "But everyone worries when they consider the consequences. We're not all paras."

"I worry, too," said Zdenek. "But this decision was made a long time ago. It might have been carried out long ago—if we hadn't been so concerned with ourselves."

"Then we'd be having this conversation in hell."

"I think we are, Uncle. Indecision is hell, and I've had enough of it."

He smiled. It was as if nothing changed in his face but the thought in his mind. "Should I ask about your escape plan?"

"There is no escape plan, Uncle. There never was."

* * *

They took turns making the rounds in the morning so they might know of Heydrich's return. Zdenek usually boarded the trolley in Dejvice for the trip to Mala Strana where he enquired of Anna for news that might have come from Novotny on those scraps of paper that had ceased to exist for almost two weeks.

But this morning, Zdenek walked. The sky seemed limitless, blue not like a mood but with the brightness of clear water. The lawn of the Royal Gardens, in which no blade of grass rose above another, alternated with tulips, azaleas, and almond trees. These gave way to Chotkovy Park, which gave way to Ledeburska Gardens, which gave way to Waldstein Gardens, which led after common pavement into Letenska Street.

They were going to have to do something about that after the war, he thought, as he knocked on Anna's door. It should be possible to walk through all of Mala Strana feeling grass underfoot, trampling the buds off the trees, never confronting reality.

"Come in, Josef."

Libena held the door like a barrier that could be removed easily—or never. She had spoken in exactly the tone that should be used between lovers who had not seen each other alone for a short but incredible length of time.

"I thought—"

"Anna's with her mother," she said. "I could tell you the good woman is sick. Would you like that?"

He shook his head. He could have done something else, he supposed.

"Josef, I exist."

No doubt of that. Her skin was so white that it glowed like ice. One faint blue vein on her temple that he had seen before but never quite thought of as beautiful.

"Come in," she said. "You don't look right out there."

Zdenek moved into the small room by large sections of his mind. Did he expect to see Anna emerge from the even smaller kitchen?

"Would you like something to eat?" she asked, following the direction of his eyes. "Have you had anything today?"

"Yes, I did. The professor's wife makes a fine breakfast, and we have two extra rations cards from Uncle."

"Then there's no reason why your mind should wander."

"Yes, there is."

She sat down on the straight chair by the window. Too hard, he thought. She should be more careful.

"Are you angry?"

"No," he said.

"What are you?"

"Confused," he said. "I find it hard to understand why you couldn't tell me about this . . . problem."

She crossed her hands in her lap and made a fist with the one that was barely visible. "You're angry. I knew you would be. I thought it best not to worry you."

"You decided," he said. "I had to find it out from Ota, who had it from Anna, who might have heard it in the street."

"He exaggerates when he's angry," she said as if talking to herself. "That's all right. We understand."

He took a step to stand before her in the chair. "Libena, there's just two of us here. We exist, and so far that's all."

She smiled as if she were her age. "It doesn't mean we can't do anything, you know. It certainly doesn't mean that you have to stay away."

"Yes, it does," he said. "I can't think of anything else. When my mind should be on other things, all I see is you. Now, I see you and a shadow."

"I can put your mind at rest," she said, holding both hands to her belly. "I'll destroy the . . . shadow."

She meant it. He could tell by the way her voice quelled her emotions, holding them back like her hands held her belly. And he knew that if he became angry she would lose control.

"That won't help. It would make me feel worse."

"Then I'll bring forth the shadow," she said cheerfully. "There's nothing to worry about. My father knows. He's willing to assist my decision. Our decision. Whatever way we choose."

"You told your father, too."

"Yes. He doesn't like the idea of a Czech Lebensborn, but he likes you. And he likes what you're doing."

Zdenek would not have believed that of any other man, but he could imagine her father saying it. "You should have the baby, Libena."

"That is your wish?" she said in a voice that wavered. "That would make it possible for you to do your job?"

"Yes."

She leaped from the chair, throwing herself forward with no mind for herself or new life. Her shoulder struck his chest so hard that he thought he would be knocked to the floor. Her arms went round his neck, suspending all her weight.

"I love you!" she said, almost shouting. "And it doesn't matter about us. Not really. I don't want you to think about it. I want you to kill that bastard. Kill him, Josef! Do it for our child. For all the children."

"When the time comes."

She slackened in his arms and tipped back, mischievous again, beginning a smile. "Did I forget to tell you?"

Libena's hand moved inside her blouse, tweezing aside her breasts. Zdenek was mesmerized by the globe-like flash of white flesh, he was as hard as iron, when she handed him the slip of paper. It was the ragged kind that a carpenter carried with him in his work.

The handwriting, artificially small and precise, said: "Six-forty-seven. With."

CHAPTER 19

Canaris, being a German naval officer, did not swim, but he enjoyed watching the Heydrich children splash about in the pool. He remembered when he had first seen Heider in his carriage being pushed by his parents along Dollenstrasse. His father clicked his heels and asked what Herr Kapitan (Canaris) was doing in the neighborhood.

Living, of course. It was an accident that the two families found themselves within yards of each other, but none that they got along. The men had known each other since 1923, when a young naval cadet reported on board the cruiser Berlin to work for Wilhelm Canaris, the naval intelligence officer.

They renewed their friendship in Berlin. Admiral Canaris, now chief of Military Intelligence, went to Heydrich's house for musical evenings, where his wife Erika played second violin to Reinhard's first. General Heydrich, the head of the SD, came to their home for Canaris' cooking. His favorite dish: a saddle of boar in a croute of crumbled black bread and wine.

"How was the food in Paris?"

"Excellent," said Heydrich. "The French do some things well."

"You stayed at the Palace?"

"No," said Heydrich with the smile that always seemed wrong. "The Ritz."

Canaris knew where Heydrich had stayed. He knew how many times his former pupil, who was a satyr, had visited the brothel reserved for the general staff.

"Do you plan to return to France soon?"

"We have our hopes," said Heydrich. "I'll see the Fuhrer on the twenty-eighth. He will decide whether Europe is to be run by the military or the police."

"The army or the SS."

Heydrich smiled again like a fissure in ice. "Who else but the SS can deal with the Judeo-Bolshevik enemy?"

"Is that what you call the French resistance?"

"That's what the wise man calls it. The Reichsfuhrer will have it no other way."

"There must be something in Germany that does not arise from Himmler's ass, which is to say his mouth. I've never understood how you deal with the man."

"That's easy," said Heydrich. "I imagine him in his underpants."

That would work, thought Canaris.

"Is Himmler still obsessed with shipping all the Jews to the east?"

"Yes," said Heydrich blandly. "There's no higher priority in the Fuhrer's mind."

The strange thing was that Canaris had come to believe that. He knew about the conference where a Final Solution was set out, but he thought that Heydrich, intoxicated with the scope of his new assignment, spoke rashly at Wansee.

Yet had he ever done that? When the first reports came from Russia saying that SS Task Forces had murdered thousands of Jews, Canaris doubted his own intelligence. When the thousands became hundreds of thousands, he knew that a war of extinction had been opened. That it would carry over to the rest of Europe seemed plausible. Knowing Heydrich, it seemed a fact.

"Will all the Jews be . . . deported?"

"As quickly as we can."

"Pending a new railway system."

"We'll make do with the one we have. You shouldn't worry, Wilhelm. I promise your people will be involved as little as possible."

"That's good," said Canaris, feeling his temper rise like the waves of distortion off the pool. "The army dislikes the mass murder of unarmed civilians."

"Which is why we've taken over the work," said Heydrich in a tone that was almost playful. "We know how hard-pressed you are."

Canaris did not return the jibe—the first reference to why he was in Prague. In the guise of an intelligence conference, he had been required to cede control of foreign intelligence to Heydrich.

It all had to do with the Fuhrer's will, which was inscrutable, and a rogue V-man named Major Thummel, or Rene.

"It's Germany that will be hard-pressed," he said. "Every human being in Russia is our enemy. When we first entered the Ukraine, the people welcomed us. Until the Task Forces began to kill everyone. Women. Children. Enemies. Friends, if they found themselves in the wrong place."

"Those units may have been overzealous, but they were under my orders."

"To slaughter?"

"The Fuhrer decreed racial war. That is what we have."

"And if we lose?" asked Canaris. "Will we be exterminated as a race? Have we asked our people if they mind?"

"The Fuhrer does not ask the people," said Heydrich lazily. "He *is* the people."

"Adolf the Unanswerable."

"Don't be a defeatist, Wilhelm." Heydrich gestured toward the plate of hors d'oeuvres. "Tell me how you like the cheese. I brought it from France—a goat Brie."

Canaris obliged. He took a bite of the cheese. It was very strong. Only a coarse man could enjoy it.

"Wonderful," he said. "Who thought of putting the cucumber with it?"

"My chef. I want you to give me instructions on how to make that brandied herring dish of yours. I'll relay them."

"Allow me," said Canaris. "I'd like to see your kitchen."

Canaris was glad to leave Heydrich lounging by the pool. He would have been happier to leave Prague, and happiest if he no longer considered Heydrich a friend. It was clear that nothing could stop the SS from doing what they wanted with the people of Europe.

Which meant: nothing could stop Heydrich. Reichscommissar was the term being bandied about. Overlord of all the Occupied Countries. A Protectorate for the continent. Canaris could think of nothing worse for himself or Germany. Not many men were capable of systematizing insanity, but Heydrich had done it. He had incarnated it. Power was his cult—the only thing he worshipped.

"Georg?"

The chef looked up from the cutting table as if he did not recognize his name. "Sir?"

Canaris halted before the web-faced man with the knife in his hand and diced carrots under it. He seemed nervous at losing the anonymity that was easy to cultivate in a kitchen.

"Are you familiar with Herring Alexander?"

The chef nodded. "Beluga caviar?"

"Then you know," said Canaris. "And there's no need to go into it."

He tipped his head swathed in a tall white cap. "I'd gladly listen, sir."

"My wish is that all gifted chefs prosper," said Canaris. "I hope that you find worthy employment in the future."

"The future, sir?"

"When your master leaves for France."

Georg absorbed the information without speaking, but did not miss the import. His stroke upon the carrots ceased to be fluid or automatic.

"Tell me, is your brother well?"

Georg, whose Czech name was Jiri, reacted like a man who had been unmasked. "Yes, sir."

"He's being held at Terezin Concentration Camp, I understand."

Georg nodded. Plainly, he did not trust himself for more.

"I have a friend at Terezin," said Canaris. "They call him a traitor to the Reich. But they've kept him alive, and I hope some day to intervene in his behalf."

For the first time, Georg left off the carrots. He rested the knife by its tip on the table and looked around the kitchen. "It's not a good place, sir. The small fortress."

"But survivable."

Georg nodded.

Canaris drew closer. He took a handful of carrots from the butcher block. "You should know that when your master leaves on his trip, he might not return. It's possible that you will never see him again here. Your opportunity will . . . pass."

"Sir?"

"Look around, Georg. There must be someone in Prague who can make use of your talent. Your knowledge."

* * *

Ota knew who had knocked at the door before Mrs. Ogoun opened it. It was not so much that the proper sequence had been given, but the rhythm it was given in. All radio operators had a distinctive signature when they ran code—a fist—but Ice's signature was more like the random sounds in a dream.

Ota heard Ice chatting with the lady of the house in his lunatic way, which meant that she wanted to take off her drawers by now. Why did women fall for that line? *All* of them.

"Wonderful landlady you have," said Ice, as he closed the bedroom door behind him. "You should see the one I'm staying with. Dishpan eyes and a mustache."

"You're not supposed to be here, Ice. Never in daylight."

"Don't I know that?"

"All right," said Ota. "What is it?"

"Two things," said Ice. "Number One is that Uncle has word from Georg. He wants a meeting tonight at ten."

Ota didn't ask why. If Georg felt that he had to leave the estate, bypassing the charwoman who lived in Klicany—the matter would be of primary importance.

"What else?"

"Not much."

Ice put his foot up on Mrs. Ogoun's best bedspread—the lady wouldn't mind if she knew who had done it—and rolled up his left pant leg. Releasing the thread that tacked his cuff, Ice accepted the small cylinder of paper that fell into his hand.

"This is by way of Radio Libuse. They were upset at receiving it. It's addressed to you in a code they can't break."

Ota took the cylinder from Ice's hand, which lingered at its task. "Thank you."

"That's all?"

"Yes. You can go now."

"But you'll need help decoding the message. I'm an expert, if you remember."

"I'll manage."

Ice was as angry as Ota had ever seen him. The long jaw and broad forehead articulated the deep structure of his bones until they seemed frozen.

"I think you're carrying security too far, Ota."

"That's impossible," he said. "But don't worry, Ice. I'll let you know which way it goes."

He did not slam the door as he left. No conversation took place in the hall with Mrs. Ogoun. Ota saw a shadow pass along the wall, stretched by the skylight. He heard the outer door click shut. Locked.

From his pack Ota took the one-time pad that had been issued in England. It was a simple code in transposition that anyone could decipher if they had the key. He spent less than three minutes at the work, because the message was brief.

VERBATIM: FRANTA TO ANTHROPOID
May 20, 1942

This is to reconfirm your mission and target. The timing and execution are as always in your hands. We wish you luck and Godspeed.

CHAPTER 20

"Who was this man?"

Georg still seemed spooked by the experience that had caused him to risk his life coming to the cottage in Klicany. He looked around the room lit by candles and hung with Jesus renderings. He shook his head as if it were part of the pious glow.

"His name is Canaris. He wore a naval uniform."

Zdenek looked at Uncle, who would know the name if anyone did. "Admiral Canaris is the head of foreign intelligence for the German Armed Forces," he said. "It's not surprising that he could read Heydrich's future in carrots."

"But how does he know about us?"

"It's clear that he knows something of us," said Uncle. "But perhaps we shouldn't grant Canaris too much foresight. He understands that there's a resistance. He knows Heydrich can be careless about security."

"He didn't say much," said Georg, lighting a cigarette off the candle. "No names. But he gave the impression that he knew every secret. All about my brother anyway."

"That he was at Terezin."

"Yes."

"Did Canaris say that he'd visited the camp?"

"No."

"Suppose he did," said Zdenek. "He could have talked to Rene, who might have had word from Leon. He knew our target."

"I don't think Leon would have broken security on this matter," said Uncle. "It's more reasonable to assume that Canaris received word through his spies. I'm sure the admiral has his sources in England."

That caused Zdenek to revisit all his worst nightmares. A traitor in England was beyond their ability to correct. He had been having ugly feelings since they sent over a traitor in Gerik and a weakling named Cyril.

"There's a lot I don't understand," he said. "Why does the head of Military Intelligence want Heydrich out of the way?"

"Rivalry," said Uncle. "Heydrich's taken over all the Reich intelligence offices except for Canaris' department. That's why the admiral was here. To agree to his own dismemberment."

"Did he lose his ass?"

Uncle shrugged. "I'd guess that Heydrich beat him to death with Rene. I don't see any way Canaris could win this war. Any way but one, that is."

"Our way," said Zdenek.

"Yes."

Georg stubbed out his cigarette and accepted a fresh one from Uncle. "I suppose I shouldn't have been so nervous about meeting you. I could have come yesterday, but I wanted to be safe. Heydrich has a nose for conspiracy. He lives it."

"Are you certain no one followed you from the estate?"

"Yes," said Georg. "I would have been careful even if the admiral hadn't left for Berlin this morning."

"Are you sure he's gone?"

"He went to the airport," said Georg, who held his cigarette up like a signal. "Now, wait. There's something you can work with. When Heydrich leaves for his plane, he goes alone. He and Klein only. The escort car stays behind. Always."

That was the best news Zdenek had heard in months. Now all they needed was to know when Heydrich would leave for France again. If the trip were as important as Canaris seemed to think—if it was a one-way ticket—someone at the castle would know.

* * *

When Novotny entered the anteroom that preceded Heydrich's office, he saw at once that the red bulb above the door was lit. That meant the Protector was engaged. The watchmaker had no reason to stop before the hauptsturmfuhrer's desk except to plead ignorance. Always best.

"I have to go inside," he said to the man with the SD patch on his sleeve. "The mantel clock."

"It's broken again?"

"It hasn't been broken since the last emperor died," said Novotny with a smile. "But it will stop tomorrow morning unless I service the springs."

"All right," he said. "But you'll have to wait."

Novotny did that. Putting his toolbox aside, he sat in the chair nearest the hauptsturmfuhrer's desk. It was not as pompous as the one that Heydrich used to sign his death lists, but more functional.

"I've been meaning to ask, what's the best thing to give a Czech girl?"

Novotny shrugged. "With rationing so tight, what about food? Say, a goose."

The hauptsturmfuhrer laughed. It was not the grossest sound that Novotny had ever heard. The murderers of the SD were among the best educated Nazis. They were intelligence men, after all.

"I had in mind something more lasting," the hauptsturmfuhrer said. "She has access to what's perishable."

"Thinking of a watch?" asked Novotny. "I have a fine selection in my shop. Come any time. I'll give you a good price."

"Perhaps I'll do that."

Novotny was sure he would, racial selection being what it was. His best business was not cuckoo clocks but the women's watches that he called, privately, the Mounds of Venus. They could have settled on a price, which was standard, if the box on the desk had not squawked, well, like a goose.

"Yes, sir," said the hauptsturmfuhrer to the machine. "At once, sir."

The murderer rose from his desk, ticking his finger at Novotny to tell him to stay in place. "Decide what you want for the best you have," he said. "I'll be right back."

Novotny rose, too, as if out of respect for the offer. He watched the black uniform with a broad white belt disappear into the doorway across the hall before he moved to the desk with a heart that could not beat.

Novotny knew what he wanted and where it was kept. Top side left. A bound leather folder held the papers that tracked the Protector's appointments for the coming days.

The top sheet in lined segments listed the schedule for Tuesday. It seemed harmless. Meaningless. Turning the sheet, Novotny scanned the next page, which was Wednesday.

The twenty-seventh.

There it was, circled in red ink. The Protector's departure.

The end.

CHAPTER 21

Heydrich awoke with music in his mind on what would be the most satisfying day of his life. He felt that.

Last night in the Banqueting Hall of the Waldstein Palace his father's piano quintet had been performed by musicians from Halle—his birthplace. Heydrich had written the program notes. He chose the musicians. Better ones could have been gotten in Prague, but the symbolism would have been lost.

The meaning was this: for years his father had been dogged in the streets of Halle by boys calling him a Jew. He suffered in every way from the accusations. Good citizens did not receive the Heydrichs. Money was always slow coming in. The brilliant music that should have been known throughout Germany—and the world—fell into utter obscurity.

So the past had been rectified. His father vindicated. It was the best of several good things that had come to Heydrich in the last week.

"Do you think they really liked father's music?"

"Of course."

Heydrich turned from the mirror to his wife. She looked like a pumpkin, all swollen again. His fault.

"I meant—the Czechs."

"Why worry about them? You'd do as well to ask the cook."

"But they have taste in music," he said. "When Mozart went to a pauper's grave in Vienna, the people of Prague turned out by the thousands for a memorial service in his honor."

"They'd do the same for you, I imagine."

"Perhaps," he said. "If I die in the next few hours."

"Don't joke about that," she said. "Just be sure you spend some time with the children before you go. They've seen you for a week in the last three. They won't see you again until—"

"I'm not quite sure."

"Until then."

Heydrich offered Lina his arm, which she took as they left the room. God, even her limbs were weighty. Why did he think of her as slim and athletic? She'd not been that for years.

But had he the right to criticize? His belt was tight at his waist and his tunic bunched at his hips. He had put on weight in Paris. A little more in the wrong places and they would be calling him by Himmler's secret name: *Reichsheini.*

"I promise that I'll dandle Silke on my knee."

"The boys," she said. "You must talk to the boys. They're growing wild out here in the country."

"Klaus and Heider will have time to become sophisticated in Paris," he said. "Their mother, too."

"Are you certain of the appointment to France?"

"I've shown here that an SS state is efficient when properly handled," he said. "The Fuhrer is more impressed than Himmler is worried."

"I don't like that man when he's worried," she said as they reached the staircase. "He's dangerous."

"Lina," he said. "So am I."

* * *

As they churned up the long hill that led to Liben, Zdenek could think of nothing but his motorcycle. At Trenchin before the war he had owned a Jawa 175 with a saddle fit for a king's nuts and a top speed that he never discovered. For two years he ran races in Slovakia and Moravia. His best finish had been a second in '37 at the free-for-all from Brno to Ruzomberok.

250 CCs, anytime. Not like this. The morning was clear and bright. It had seemed friendly when they started out on the trolley, business-like and cool, but after picking up the bicycles in Zizkov, and stopping at the Khodl's, sweat began to drip into the waistband of his suit. The raincoat, the pistols, and the Sten in the briefcase on the handlebars added weight. The higher the sun rose in the sky, the heavier Zdenek peddled.

His watch said eight-ten. Heydrich usually left his chateau at nine and never before eight forty-five. There should be plenty of time.

"I'm going to walk it up."

Ota nodded, drifted a bit on the pedal, then got off his bike. "This is damned primitive. I'd say it's embarrassing, but we've had so much of that lately I've gotten used to it."

"Feeling more yourself this morning?"

"Better," he said. "I'm always better when the sweat breaks. It's the waiting that's hard."

"Did you say goodbye to Anna last night?"

Ota shook his head. "Bad security. Bad luck, too."

Luck was the thing. When Zdenek thought of all the men who had parachuted into the country—when he thought of how many of them had gone down—luck seemed the greatest part of it. None had carried out a successful mission. Most had not had the chance to fail before they were taken, tortured and murdered by Heydrich's Gestapo.

"We've been lucky from the first," he said. "We found the quarry and the right people found us. If I hadn't been hurt, we would have marched into Prague and the Gestapo's hands."

"Be careful," said Ota. "When a man starts talking about fate, he's halfway in the ground."

We're more than halfway, thought Zdenek. Every step brings us closer to the end. Let it be a good one.

* * *

Ice saw them coming up the hill, pushing their bicycles until they reached flatter ground, where they remounted and wheeled toward the streetcar stop. Assassination on schedule.

A Number Three trolley passed, and momentarily the two men vanished. They reappeared suddenly as if they had moved backwards—Ota in a black suit with a black hat, Zdenek with a light green raincoat and a suit. Commuters. They were headed the wrong way for a trip into the city, but no one would notice.

The bicycles veered across the street toward Ice just as the trolley stopped and left off its passengers—a flock of nurses who began to walk toward the Bulovka Clinic.

The two commuters parked their bicycles separately, one against the fence railing and the other against the first lamppost down the hill. They undid the crocodile-skin briefcases from their handlebars and moved toward Ice.

"Report."

"Nothing," said Ice. "No police. No one that looks like a Gestapo. A man's sitting in the tobacconist's kiosk just up the hill, but he's not doing much business, or much watching."

"Stand a little to the left," said Zdenek. "Ota to the right."

When they shifted to block the view from the pavement, Zdenek took up his briefcase. Using their bodies and his raincoat as a shield, he opened the case to reveal the Sten gun that had been broken down in three pieces.

Ice watched as Zdenek reassembled the submachine gun. He inserted the breach-block into the receiver, then put the butt with the recoil spring behind it. That step made the Sten an ornery weapon. The spring had to be compressed and slid upward along the groove until the stock locked in place.

Click-snap. Sixty-five seconds for a job that would have taken Ice long minutes.

"All right," said Zdenek. "Let's find our marks."

Ota moved to a lamppost several yards from the corner, where there was shade from the trees but no good view to the top of the hill. He was the reserve—the man not to be seen.

Zdenek and Ice crossed the street together, staying close to obscure the bulge under the raincoat. When they reached the other side near the trolley stop, Zdenek took a position at the edge of the knoll below overhanging brush. From there, he had a clear view up the hill.

"I'll look for your signal."

"Good luck, Zdenek."

He smiled. "No excursions, Iceman. If you have to piss, I want two wet shoes."

"I wouldn't piss to put out Germans who were on fire."

Ice turned and began walking up the hill, which grew steep immediately after the big curve. The sun rose higher and hotter. It was a beautiful day, perhaps the best of the year.

* * *

"I wish you'd drive the other car. Not the coupe."

"It's not as fast," said Heydrich. "And not as much fun."

"Fun," said Lina. "Is that what you're after? You drive around the countryside with the top down like a movie star. You expose yourself and dare them to attack you."

"My Czechs won't harm me," he said. "Besides, they know what would happen to them if they tried."

"You've consulted the lunatics among them, have you?"

"There are no more lunatics, Lina. They've all been deported."

He kissed her before she could reprise, then turned quickly down the line. Heider. Klaus. And last, Silke.

He kissed her better than he had her mother, because she was his fascination. A Nordic beauty with Nordic wiles. He did not tire of her as he did the boys. They were living machines. She was a machine for living.

"A surprise when I return," he said into her ear.

"A pony," Silke whispered. "Better than Klaus'."

"We'll see."

Heydrich turned toward the touring car as the bell above the balustrade sounded—ten o'clock. While Klein moved to the front of the car, Heydrich laid his jacket across the front seat.

"You may do the same, Klein. It will be a hot day."

"Yes, Obergruppenfuhrer."

As Klein removed his jacket and placed it beside his master's, Heydrich turned and waved.

"I'll call when I reach Berlin."

"Safe journey," said Lina.

* * *

When the clock on the Liben Reformatory struck ten, Ota looked at his watch, which was correctly set. Already three minutes after the hour. Heydrich had never been this late according to the times that Georg and Safarik had logged.

Ota looked toward Zdenek, who stood across the street by the brush to receive the signal from Ice up the hill. He put his left hand palm down to the ground. Nothing. No signal.

The team had been conspicuous for the last hour, occupying the same ground, letting five trolleys go by, but luckily no police patrols had passed them afoot or by car. Ota had been thinking for the last twenty minutes that Heydrich might cross them at the last moment. On a whim, he could go directly to the airport, ignoring his appointments at the castle, leaving them hanging one last time.

Ota checked his briefcase one last time. He carried two grenades with fuses he had shortened last night to explode on impact. That was dangerous, of course. Under normal conditions he would not have done it because the grenade was rather heavy, and at forty centimeters, rather awkward, packed with enough explosive to pierce armor. He had to be sure, however

What you didn't want to do was drop them. You didn't even want to bump against something, or you might find yourself blown through the iron fence like cheese through a grater.

That was why Ota kept the bombs in the briefcase. There was no sense exposing them until they were needed. The hit was Zdenek's with the Sten. Only if something went wrong would Ota throw the bombs. Otherwise, he was to clean up the car. Heydrich, on his way to Berlin, would be carrying papers with him that were of too much potential value to leave behind.

Was every garbage man this nervous? Did the sweat run down his pants-legs into his socks until he felt like he was standing in water?

* * *

The touring car ran at good speed from Libeznice, entering a lane of chestnut trees that loomed on both sides of the road, completely blocking the sun. It was straight road, light entering sideways from the fields or not at all. The feeling of piercing the space was intense, as if they hurtled into nothingness.

"Faster, Klein."

"But Obergruppenfuhrer, it's not safe."

"Did I ask you that?"

"No, Obergruppenfuhrer."

Klein depressed the accelerator and the Mercedes responded nicely. A distinct forward pulse at one hundred and ten KPH. He had not armored it, as Himmler insisted, for that would have robbed the car of everything that was good about it.

Too many things had the life taken from them by excess caution. That was not the same as losing life, but for Heydrich it was similar. He always felt much closer to God in an airplane or a speeding car than in church.

He felt the rush of blood at the end of the trees. The sun began as a coin of light until it became a door, a bright passage. Suddenly, they blew into the open countryside of Bohemia. The heart-land. Peasants haying. Giant ricks flung across the plain like fortresses. Straw fortresses. That, Heydrich decided, was a metaphor to the people who lived in this land at the sufferance of the Reich. These stolid Czechs would trade freedom for subsistence forever.

No doubt the French would be different. No doubt they would be the same. The delights of Paris put the thrill of a fast car on an open road in perspective.

"At your own pace, Klein."

"Yes, Obergruppenfuhrer."

He backed off the accelerator slowly, as if a too-quick descent might mean a loss of face and more. He knew that his predecessor—a too-cautious man—had gone on to gassing Jews and commissars with the Task Forces in Russia.

They passed through the village of Whatever on their way to Whereupon. Soon the houses began to thicken at the side of the road. Some became villas. All acquired flowers. In the distance, Heydrich saw the suburbs of Prague announced by a light shroud of haze.

* * *

Ice felt exposed as he stood alone on the pavement at the steepest part of the hill. There were no trolley stops this far up and only one street leading off Kirchmayer Boulevard. So many trolleys had come and gone that by the fourth pass he memorized the faces of the conductors. They had seen him, too.

That could make it bad for getting away and staying away from the Gestapo. If their leader went down, they would begin a manhunt that would turn into nonsense every previous definition of the word. Zdenek and Ota would have a fair chance of getting clear on their bicycles; but Ice had no machine. He had made up his mind to stay until the monster went down. The minute that he gave the signal, he would head toward the turning. He would get off afterward, if he could, on foot into the city.

The thing that he couldn't do was move more than two paces in any direction. Line-of-sight between his position and Zdenek's was tight because of the curve in the road. He stood with his hand in his pocket clutching the lighter. It was huge—as big as a cigarette pack.

During practice runs, he had almost blinded Zdenek with the reflection. An overcast day, or rain, would have made it a bit strange, but on this perfect spring day the sun's rays would carry.

They flashed off the windows of the trolley that came down from the top of the hill—sheets of light that shimmered like water. For a moment, Ice saw nothing else, but he sensed another vehicle coming behind the trolley, drafting it, then swinging out wide to pass.

A dark green touring car with flags on the fenders and the top down and two tall figures sitting in the seats like adults on ponies. And no escort car at the rear.

It was 10:32.

* * *

When Zdenek saw the signal—three quick bursts of light—he crossed the street fast, walking but almost at a run. He still had the raincoat folded over the Sten gun, but as he moved toward the opposite curb, he withdrew the magazine from the side pocket of his coat.

He could have loaded the weapon two hours ago, but he did not want the extra weight when he had little idea of when the target would appear. Nor did he want a bad profile. Unlike most submachine guns, the Sten loaded from the side and stuck out at an angle that made it almost impossible to conceal. He would have been walking around with thirty-two rounds in a clip that hung out the left side like an oar.

But quick. Zdenek jumped onto the curb and pushed the clip into the receiver, where it slotted automatically.

Two more simple movements. Zdenek pulled the lug back into the cocked position. Last, squeeze the trigger.

* * *

Klein had let his mind wander on a route that he knew well. This was the neighborhood where his wife lived and where he joined her for his days off, but he chided himself for his inattention because his first and only rule was to protect the Obergruppenfuhrer's life, if necessary with his own.

And suddenly there were choices. A woman moved from behind a streetcar and began to cross the street in front of the Mercedes, stopping only when she saw she had no choice. Then a man, the stupidest man in a country full of ignorant people, set off from the curb as if he were bent on suicide.

Klein braked hard as the man jumped into the street and put himself before the hood. Instantly, Klein realized that this one knew nothing about suicide. In his hand he held a weapon. A submachine gun.

Shit, they were dead.

* * *

Zdenek threw the raincoat aside as he moved from the pavement, jumped into the street, and brought the Sten up to his shoulder. There, right there, was Heydrich. Zdenek had seen him perched in the frame of the Barleycorn sight so many times that the image seemed to freeze. Time did not stop. It entered a place where it revolved forever, like a record riding the same warped groove.

Just bump it out of the track. Firmly squeeze the trigger and blow it all away.

Instead, Zdenek heard the click of the trigger, then the bolt slamming home into the closed position—metal to metal into the back of the gun barrel.

Dead metal to dead metal. No cartridge.

No fire.

The dark green Mercedes drifted past him as if caught in the same slow dream. He saw both men looking at him like fish from a tank, the enormous driver in the front seat and Heydrich in the back.

Zdenek did not think he had time to reload, so he ripped the lug back to recock. He pulled the trigger again.

The trigger clicked again. The bolt slammed. Nothing.

Zdenek felt panic rise in him like steam. Mindlessly, like a recruit, his finger pulled tighter at the trigger, deep, so deep that metal met bone. Where was Ota?

From the car that was so open and close it had almost brushed him going by, he heard Heydrich's shrill high-pitched voice: "Stop!" he said. "Stop the car!"

* * *

Ice couldn't understand what happened. He was running down the hill, and Zdenek was standing to the left of Heydrich's car in a classic small-arms pose, and nothing, absolutely nothing was happening.

The car drifted on for a moment until it stopped moving with a jerk of brakes. Heydrich stood up, along with the driver. He reached for the pistol at his belt.

Ice took his pistol from his belt as he ran faster, lunging down the hill with strides so big they were slinging him forward head first. He could no longer see Zdenek, but beyond the curb, emerging from the shadows of the trees, he saw a figure moving fast.

Ota.

Ice was within thirty meters of the car when Ota's forward momentum stopped and his arm carried on in a half-arc. Ice was within fifteen meters and closing when the bomb detonated in a shriek of white light, taking his legs from under him, throwing him down.

CHAPTER 22

Heydrich had always been amazed by explosives. As a boy, he had broken down cartridges and set the powder off in the garden of his parents' house. Before entering the Freikorps or the Navy, he knew all the explosive charges used in every shell, bomb and torpedo in the German Armed Forces.

Therefore, Heydrich knew that he had been wounded by a powerful blast of explosive, although he had not seen the bomb or the man who threw it. He had been blown from his seat, the door had been blown off, the entire rear of the car gutted. The air was filled with debris—pieces of leather, metal, paper—his papers—and white puffs of stuffing from the upholstery.

"Obergruppenfuhrer!" called Klein. "Are you hurt?"

Heydrich had screamed when he was hit, as any man would have but in exactly the way that the Protector of Bohemia and Moravia never should have. The pain was extraordinary, intense in sharp bursts in his back, more generalized and steady in the rib cage. Heydrich spoke without parting his teeth.

"Get after those men, Klein! Get them, do you hear?"

* * *

This is it, thought Ota. Blind in a whirlwind.

In the blowback of the explosion he had been hit so hard that he fell against the iron fence railing. He knew the instant the grenade left his hand that his throw was not good enough—online but short. He knew that if it landed outside the car the chance of success was poor and the chance of being blown up himself very good.

And the worst happened. The grenade hit just in front of the rear fender, blowing a hole in the side of the car and throwing fragments back at him.

He had been hit in the chest and face. Ota did not want to touch his face because he did not want to know how bad it was, but he forced his hand up to the slippery blood and cleared his vision.

Dense smoke poured from the touring car. The air teemed with strange white debris, floating lighter than air and settling on everything like feathers. Was he really seeing that? How badly had his sight been damaged?

Not enough to mistake the huge figure looming from the smoke. A giant. Yes, it was Sergeant Small. Ota lurched for the bicycle. His third step told him that he was able to move well enough in his limbs and the fourth put him over the seat with his revolver in his hand.

He heard the first round from Klein's pistol crash and strip leaves through the trees. When Ota turned the bicycle awkwardly into the street, he saw with blurred vision Klein point-shooting again.

Ota snapped off a shot across his left arm, nearly throwing himself off the seat with the recoil. When he recovered his balance, he leaned into the pedals hard and jumped the high curb into the street.

He heard the noise of Klein's pistol but felt nothing except the rolling bounce as he hit the cobblestones in the street. The crossroads were directly ahead, jammed with milling commuters who had fled the trolley in confusion. Surprised to find the pistol still in his hand, Ota raised it into the air and fired twice.

The crowd scattered, parting miraculously. Ota saw a clear lane across Kirchmayer to the street that led down into Liben.

Jamming the revolver in his coat pocket, he put his head down and began to pedal. The sweeping downhill gave him tremendous strength, fantastic speed, wings. He felt wind blowing strong in his face, like a cold hand on his hot wet hair.

Christ, the explosion must have blown the hat off his head. He hated leaving anything behind. The homburg. The briefcase with the second bomb. Ice. And Zdenek.

* * *

The smoke ballooning from the back of the car carried up the hill to Zdenek, vanishing as it reached him. When it began to thin back to the source, what he saw completed his nightmare. A jammed gun. A badly thrown bomb. And now the huge figure of the driver leaping from the car, firing his pistol at Ota, followed by another who arose like a pale wraith from the smoke, staggering, his pistol like a dark wand in his hand.

Heydrich. He was alive.

Zdenek threw down the Sten. He reached into his pocket for the Colt and brought it up for a good look when he heard a shot and felt something sizzle off the pavement at his feet. It might have hit his shoe or just thrown chips of cement, but it seemed to come from nowhere.

Zdenek lunged to his right for the cover of a lamp-standard, trying to keep Heydrich in view through the smoke, and instead seeing Klein coming up the hill in a crouch that made him the size of a normal man. The driver fired again. Again the round struck the pavement just to the left.

Zdenek brought his gun-sight back to the figure weaving at the side of the car, but Heydrich was no longer there. He had moved to the front of the car—away from the fuel tank. Zdenek saw a flash of blond hair as it appeared above the hood, then only a hand as Heydrich slid down over the radiator, clutching the bright ornament on the hood.

It was over. If the wretched bastard wasn't hit hard enough to take him out, he would never be. If Zdenek could not get out of this place immediately, he never would.

No going across the street, where he could use the crowd at the trolley stop to confuse his trail. Nor downhill past the driver and Heydrich, directly into the face of the pursuit that was sure to come.

Zdenek made his decision. He stepped from behind the pole and fired twice at Klein, bad shots, hurried. The driver ducked behind the door of the car, returning fire.

The next few feet up the hill were critical, because Zdenek would be exposed until the road curved sharply. He put two more rounds into the car door, thinking that .38 caliber was enough to pierce metal but not have much left.

He sprinted, wanting all the power left in his legs and getting less than he could believe. It was as if he was running uphill against a grade that grew steeper with every step.

One loud discharge at his back but with no effect. Another that sang off the prongs of the iron fence. Zdenek turned in behind it, hoping that Klein was not marksman enough to put two rounds in the same place, knowing that if he cleared the bend he would be headed for some chance at safety.

He hit the head of Na Kolinske with nothing at his back and little breath in his lungs. He did not understand why he was exhausted, but the tension of the last three hours, the waiting of the last two, and the frustration of the kill were like a barrier in his mind that seemed to suck the strength from his body.

He needed something. He passed a man in the street loading wood into the back of his horse-drawn cart, but saw only fear in his eyes. The man dropped the wood in his arms and raised his hands into the air.

Zdenek kept running in mud, jamming the pistol back into his pocket. He thought that he might have a fifteen second lead, depending on how fast that great ape could climb a hill. A turn brought him into Na Zapalci, which was filled with small houses, almost every one fronted by even smaller gardens, with shops here and there. The thing to do was get off the street, into one of the shops with the door open, escape by the rear, and double back to the trolley line.

All the shops looked the same except one where concrete had been poured in the garden space. More modern? More likely to have a rear exit?

Zdenek turned into the shop on the run, bounding down the flight of steps through the door. A butcher shop. Dead meat for sale. He had found the right place.

"Morning," said Zdenek to the broad man in the bloody apron. "Do you have a back door?"

"What's it to you?"

"I need it," said Zdenek. "Please show me the way."

The man shook his head. "There is none. The only door to Brauner's Butcher Shop is the one you came in."

Brauner. A German. So Zdenek had done it: dead-ended himself in a chase. Ignoring the butcher, he drew his Colt from his pocket and quickly went back through the only door in the shop. He stopped one step onto the concrete and looked up to street level along Na Zapalci.

He saw Klein because the SS man was the biggest thing in the neighborhood. Seven feet tall, maybe more. He held a pistol in one hand and in the other he held the carter that Zdenek had passed at the head of the street. That man pointed toward the front of the shop. There. That's where the assassin fled.

Zdenek ducked back into the doorway, flattening against the wall. He was looking into the street with concentration when the butcher suddenly passed by, blocking his view for an instant, then crossing the concrete and taking the steps in one bound. He screamed: "This way! Here! Murderer!"

As Klein came running up the street, Zdenek checked his load. He fed two fresh cartridges from his pocket into the chamber of the revolver. All right. No automatics, this time. Nothing to jam. You want to trade fire with me, you bastard, let's do it.

Zdenek could have dropped Klein as he came up to the gate in front of the steps, but the Oberscharfuhrer wasn't stupid. He still held the carter in his hands like a trophy, and he kept the man between himself and the door to the shop. When he was within three feet of the gate, he lunged toward it, fitting most of his bulk behind it.

Zdenek gave a two count, then showed himself for an instant in the doorway. He knew he would draw fire—three quick rounds. The first smashed into the counter behind him, the second went high into the front of the house, and the third dug a splinter of wood from the doorjamb.

He shifted the revolver to his left hand—a bit weaker but usually accurate at short range. He jumped across the doorway to the far side, firing twice, hitting the post both times, keeping Klein's head down. Now Zdenek had the angle.

He knew that Klein would return fire, and he waited as two more rounds crashed into the shop through the plate glass window. Then Zdenek flashed and fired.

The first round should have killed the overgrown son-of-a-bitch, but it caught him high on the thigh at a height where a normal man kept his heart. The second round went wide into the hedge, but by that time Zdenek stopped counting. When Klein yelped, he pushed hard out the door, took the steps in one long stride, and fired again as he passed the gigantic body that was sprawled behind the gatepost.

Another hit. Too low again for a kill but enough to take the monster down hard. Klein was so busy calling on his maker for the first time in his life that he didn't notice his target had bolted into the street.

Now Zdenek moved free and clear. He felt good legs under him and good wind in his lungs. No one was going to catch him this time.

* * *

When Ice awoke, he found himself a block from Kirchmayer. Strange, but he was walking.

He remembered two flashes. The first from the mirror in his hand. The second.

Was it a bomb?

His trousers were ripped. Good trousers.

A bomb. Nothing else flashed like that. Nothing sounded like that. He had hit the ground within the flash. Fallen. There was blood on his trousers, too.

Ice stopped by the wall that rimmed the side of the inn. He rolled up the trousers of his left leg to the knee. Something had sliced him above the calf. Not a large wound, but deep and ugly and fresh. Very fresh.

The bomb. A fragment chewed him up. And if it did that to him, what had it done to the target? Yes, the target.

Ice rolled down his pants and moved toward the boulevard and the rolling sounds that lapped along the hill. Twenty yards away—at the hairpin turn—a string of trolley cars sat idle. A lot of people stood around as if they were breaking away. A lot of confusion for a sunny day.

Ice began to climb the hill, moving toward the trolleys and the open car that sat at the opposite side of the road with a tire flattened and a door hanging at an angle. A small van passed, belching smoke from a two-cylinder engine. It swung to a slow stop as it neared the touring car.

A blonde-haired woman ran from the car to the van. Ice was reminded of Tatana.

It was coming back to him like a message in coded groups. The windows of the three trolley cars had been smashed. And high in the trolley wires were two SS jackets, hanging as if they dropped from the sky.

Hadn't he seen the jackets before? Folded neatly over the seat of the touring car. Ice remembered flashing the signal and seeing two men in the car. One had looked back at him, turning as they passed.

He was the man who was walking toward the Tatra van. A policeman helped him walk, because he was hurt. Everyone had been hurt.

This one was badly hurt. He seemed unable to walk upright, like a man. Holding his back, he shuffled in a laborious crouch, as if he clutched each cobblestone with prehensile toes. Like an ape. A blond ape.

Anthropoid.

The name flashed in his mind. It was a code. Instantly, reflexively, his hand went into the side pocket of his jacket, wanting the pistol.

Nothing. Lint. He had been running down the hill, yes, and Ota threw the bomb, and something struck his leg and knocked him hard to the ground and his pistol skittered off.

Just then Heydrich stopped by the door of the van. He looked toward Ice as if he recognized some part of him, but his eyes moved quickly away. He crouched lower into the front seat of the van, bending his narrow horsy head, still holding his back.

It was bloody. Anthropoid was very badly hit.

Die, thought Ice. Die, he prayed, as blue smoke kicked from the back of the van.

CHAPTER 23

Ota watched the front of the building through the window. On the first floor was a bar, and when he saw the men coming up the walk with empty jugs to be filled with beer for lunch, he knew the crowds on the streets would be at their height. It was time to disappear among them.

"How do I look? Tell the truth now."

Mrs. Novak, who had been married for two decades, probably was incapable of giving that to a man. She peered at him as if he were across the darkened room instead of sitting at his side with the bottle of iodine in her hands.

"Your forehead has stopped bleeding," she said. "What I mean is—stopped running freely."

Ota took the hand-mirror and looked at his face. The wonder was that he had not been hit in the eyes. Had he closed them at the moment of impact, knowing when that would be?

"It looks fine," he said, taking the cloth cap from the back of the chair. "If it doesn't bleed again, I'll be all right."

"For what? You look like the Gestapo had you already."

Ota pulled the cap down low over his brow, covering the worst of the damage. With the blue jacket that came from Mrs. Novak's closet, and the raked cap, he could pass for a railway man with a grudge against the rest of the world.

"Thanks for everything. And if I could ask one more favor."

She nodded without hesitation.

"I left my bicycle outside Bata's store. Perhaps you could have someone pick it up."

"I'll send one of my girls when they get home."

Now would have been better, but Ota was in no position to be anything but grateful for what he had already gotten. A place to hide while he recovered his breath and mind. Attention to his wounds, and clothes that did not drip blood.

He had arranged this safe-place through Auntie's husband, but when plans became a reality that none could imagine, it was hard to guess how a woman with three daughters—a woman so poor that she had to borrow the iodine and a hand-mirror from the next-door neighbor—would react.

"If I tell you how brave you are, you won't think badly of me when I'm gone."

"I'll never think badly of you," she said. "Just be sure to have someone look at those wounds before they infect."

"Goodbye, Madame Novakova."

Ota left the cheerfully dingy room, passed into the darkened hallway and down the long dark staircase. He could tell what everyone would have for lunch by the smells that snuck under the doors and how many children by the cries that pierced the papery walls.

He would have to find someone to look after his wounds in a professional manner. Fragments of the bomb were still embedded in his face and chest. What they were composed of was unknown, but they were likely to infect, because they were meant to kill. No one but Zdenek and Ota knew that last night he had taken care to lace his bombs with poison.

* * *

Zdenek bought a bunch of violets at the florist's shop on the corner that led to Vitkov Park. He hated buying anything at a place with an "Aryan Shop" sign in the window, but the flowers were not so much for celebration as an offer to trade. He badly needed a raincoat to replace the one he had left on the street in Liben.

As he walked the familiar streets of Zizkov, Zdenek turned over in his mind the sequence that led to the moment when he aimed the Sten at Heydrich and pulled the trigger into nothing. He remembered the sound—the click-thud.

The trigger had pulled easily, releasing the spring load. That was the click. In the Sten's peculiar sequence, the trigger did not directly activate the firing pin, but freed the breach-block, which moved forward and stripped a round from the clip. The firing pin struck the cartridge, exploding the round.

Nothing like that had happened this morning. The bolt slammed into the back of the gun barrel. Metal to metal, yes.

A bad magazine. The answer was to jack another clip in and fire again. Zdenek had not done that because he didn't think he had the time.

Because he didn't believe it had happened to him.

Because, for a moment, he stopped thinking.

Nothing else in the city had stopped. Nothing in the streets said that Prague had changed. All the way to Zizkov people rode the trolleys and walked to lunch without showing the awe that would have told Zdenek that his mission had been a success.

But he knew that Prague would soon become a death trap. Only one man in the city—in the country—was capable of finding safe-places.

Uncle's flat lay on the first floor of the building, which was good for a man who followed in the rhythms of the resistance. He lived with his wife and son, who went to school in Liben. As Zdenek knocked quietly—giving the signal—he asked himself for the last time what everyday life had to do with this? What right did he have to involve women and children? And what choice?

"Zdenek."

"Uncle, I wasn't sure you'd be home. I brought some flowers for your wife."

He took the violets like a gun, inhaled the fragrance, and stepped back. "Well," he said, "shall I light a candle for the dead?"

Zdenek moved to the chair by the window and sat down heavily. No doubt he would be sitting by windows for the rest of his life.

"We hit him, Uncle. But it was messy. My Sten didn't fire. Ota's grenade fell short."

Uncle lowered himself into the matching chair that also gave a view onto the street. He still held the violets in his hand as if they were dangerous.

"I heard nothing on the radio," he said, as if that tightly controlled medium mattered. "That could be good or bad. If the Germans think the attack is beneath notice, they won't want to draw attention to it."

"They noticed," said Zdenek. "Heydrich was wounded by Ota's bomb, which means he's a lot worse off than they think. And I shot the driver twice."

"I see." Uncle placed the flowers in a porcelain vase on the tea table, taking his time with the arrangement. "We'll have to assume they'll respond quickly. Were you seen?"

"By any number of people," said Zdenek. "Heydrich was more than an hour late, and we stood on the street for almost three hours. It's just a question of whether anyone will volunteer information."

"You should do everything possible to change your appearance. Clothing, hair color, perhaps glasses. Start a mustache."

Zdenek nodded. "I came for a new coat, if you have one."

"No problem," said Uncle. "What we must worry about is the place where you'll hide."

"I'll stay with Libena tonight. We'd planned on it."

"For now that's good," he said. "But I'm thinking of later. The Germans will search all of Prague. Every room. Every coal bin. And I've seven paras on my hands."

"You've done enough for us already, Uncle."

"I know that," he said, smiling. "And I've been thinking about this for some time. You could be scattered throughout the city, which would make it more difficult for the Germans to find you. But then I'd worry about morale. One man who cracked under the strain could bring the whole network down."

"So you think we should be together."

"That would be best."

"Do you know a place?"

"Yes," said Uncle. "I'll need time, though. You'll have to make it through the next day or so on your own—before all the arrangements can be made."

"How do I thank you, Uncle?"

"You've already done that," he said. "You've made a monster mortal. Now all the others know it, too."

* * *

Rastenburg, East Prussia 12:15 PM

"An urgent call from Prague," said Bormann. "Deputy Protector Frank."

Hitler took the receiver from his secretary's hand. He disliked the phone because it was the opposite of a loudspeaker. That wonderful piece of technology had brought him to power.

"Yes, Frank. What news from Bohemia?"

"Fuhrer, I beg your indulgence to deliver a terrible report. This morning as Obergruppenfuhrer Heydrich motored into the city, he was attacked by assassins and badly wounded."

Hitler felt the words like a thickening of his blood. That was a strong premonition of death. "What is his condition?"

"He is being operated on as we speak," said Frank. "We will know more when the doctors have done what they can. The Protector has numerous internal injuries, including a badly damaged spleen."

"But he will recover."

Frank's answer was not quick. "If all the bomb fragments are successfully removed, his chances will be better."

A bomb. Hitler heard the word fall from the others like a tree in deep snow. Bomb. The most pernicious, the deadliest weapon. Silent until it was the last thing heard in this world.

"You will keep me informed of the Protector's progress," he said. "Any change."

"Yes, Fuhrer."

"I also expect to hear what is being done to respond to the outrage. Who are the criminals who perpetrated this act?"

"We have no present idea, Fuhrer. The assassins fled the area immediately."

"And Heydrich's escort? What did they do while their chief was being attacked?"

"The escort was not present, Fuhrer. The Obergruppenfuhrer often did not travel with one. It was his way to show disdain for the Czechs."

"Was the car properly armored?"

"No, Fuhrer. That, too, the Obergruppenfuhrer refused."

"The *fool*! The damned arrogant *fool*!"

Hitler did not hear Frank's response. He toppled the phone onto the desk and turned to the situation map of Russia. The map. Pins and topography. Proof of his second-hand existence. Hitler hated this place in the woods of East Prussia—the deadness of the surface in daylight and the endless nights underground. Now he realized this was all he would know for the rest of his life. He would never be able to leave Wolfschantze—or any of the other Wolf lairs—in safety again.

"Frank," he said, taking up the phone. "You will, as Acting Protector, arrest twenty thousand Czechs immediately. All political prisoners in our custody will be shot immediately."

"Yes, Fuhrer. And the sugar?"

"A reward of one million marks for the assassins," he said, coming immediately upon a number that fit. "You will find the perpetrators of this outrage, Frank. You will ransack the entire country until you have them. Turn the SS loose. The Gestapo. The SD. At last—at the very bottom of the sewer—you will find a Jew. Find him. Find him! Find HIM!"

Part Four:

The Catacombs

CHAPTER 24

Zdenek took a trolley to Charles Square, where he entered an antique store toward the river. The shop was open because the Germans had decided to let people go about their business in daylight. No one challenged him from the time he left Auntie's, although the Hacha government had that morning matched Hitler's offer of a reward for information about Heydrich's attackers. Now it was two million marks.

The newspapers and radio had circulated fairly accurate descriptions of Zdenek and Ota, and a photograph of Ice had been posted all over town again. They had even gotten half his name right this time. Zdenek knew that many people in their acquaintance or anyone who passed them on the street could have betrayed them, but in spite of the colossal reward, no one spoke out.

The first night the Germans tried to search the whole city. After shutting down all public transportation, all places of public meeting, and leveling a nine o'clock curfew punishable by death, the Gestapo and SS terror squads attacked defenseless families who waited quietly in their homes. Many people were beaten, more imprisoned, and some murdered, but none were paras. Fresh German troops poured across the borders by the thousands, bent on searching every house in the country, but so far the seven remained hidden with Uncle's people.

Zdenek did not know where the thin man found them, but they were unbreakable. Example: the man who came into the antique shop to look at the selection of crystal. He was dressed and in fact well dressed in a dark suit and gray homburg hat. A black goatee sharpened the somewhat puffy lines of his face. When Zdenek placed a crystal decanter on the shelf next to the counter, the man turned and left the shop.

Zdenek followed at twenty paces. They moved roundabout for several blocks, down to the river and back up again, Zdenek on one side of the street, his contact on the other, until they reached a church on Resslova Street that was hardly more than one long block from their starting point.

It was an elegant building almost as tall as it was wide, standing on a broad busy corner in the New Town. Its windows rose a full story above the sidewalk and its bell tower looked toward the bridge that crossed the Vltava River two blocks away.

After entering the church by the side door, the man in the goatee seemed to disappear. When Zdenek crossed the street, he reappeared, flashed the door open, and admitted Zdenek to a small office that could have belonged to anyone except for the small statue of the Virgin that sat on a ledge behind the desk.

"My name's Vladimir Petrek," he said. "I'm chaplain here."

"Zdenek Vyskocil."

Petrek heard the name as if he would try to forget it. He was a darkly handsome man with thick hair parted in the middle and bright eyes that expanded in the dimmer light indoors. His intense gaze seemed to lend him a touch of mysticism that the Eastern Church cultivated so well.

"Welcome to St. Cyril and Methodius, Zdenek. We take our name from the saints who brought Christianity to the Slavs. I mention this because what they brought is the only thing that distinguishes us from the Germans."

"They think it's race."

"They're wrong," he said. "Czechs and Germans are identical except for their psychology."

"Speaking of that, Father. I hope Uncle made it clear what will happen if the Nazis find us here."

"We're aware of the chance to be martyred," he said. "All our people from the bishop to the sacristan swore an oath that you were not to be given up. We'll honor your sanctuary to the end."

"Let's hope it's not for long."

Petrek smiled with teeth nested in his beard like piping. "History hasn't made it easy for the invader," he said. "Come into the church and you'll see."

Zdenek followed Petrek down a narrow hall that led from the rectory to the church. He had no feelings about any place of worship except for the memories of his childhood at the chapel in Rajeske Teplice. The sermons were always of bleeding Jesus and his victory in defeat. The churches were always filled with old Slovak women, who made the best Catholics, because they craved doom.

His feelings did not change when they entered the chancel. The altar rose in a thronging of purple and gold that might have been beautiful to believers. The arched ceiling that rose above the nave shimmered like a sky, cloud-white with cherubim floating in the mist. The feeling that arose was of suspension—of a half-world set in the middle of the city like a jeweled egg. Very still, very cool.

They passed from the altar down the aisle between the pews silently, shoes whispering on wide strips of coconut mat. Ahead were the wide nail-studded doors where the congregation entered and above it the gallery for the choir.

"This church was built in the early eighteenth century," said Petrek. "But like most things in Prague, it was erected on the site of an earlier structure. A monastery. The foundations were left intact."

He stopped before a narrower strip of matting that had been laid from the front doors toward the side of the building leading to the church quarters. Reaching down, Petrek moved the matting aside to expose a large flagstone with an iron rung.

"This is the only way into the crypt that isn't shut up."

They reached together for the ring, each taking half, and heaved in unison. The flagstone came up as if it had a will to stay, heavy and bulky. Zdenek saw nothing but darkness gathered in the hole and felt nothing but a still cold that rose from it. That's not right, he thought. Heat rises. Cold sinks and stays.

Something like fear touched him. It was the same feeling that he had as he stood before the frigid hole in the fuselage of the Halifax, counting out the seconds to his fall.

"It's quite a way down," said Petrek, pointing his flashlight in the hole. "Seventeen feet. There, you can see the ladder."

Zdenek saw the top rung hanging in the light. You wouldn't want to miss the thing at almost twenty feet, he thought, as he squirmed into the hole.

It wasn't wide—a bit broader than Zdenek's shoulders—but his foot found the rung. And the second. It became a bit colder with every downward step, then his hands found the sides of the ladder as cold and slippery as icicles as he hurried down the last rungs to the floor.

Zdenek had strange sensations as he watched Petrek descend the ladder, the flashlight wavering in his hand. On the right, in front of the ladder, was a kind of hive made of stone. The wall was honeycombed with many small compartments that were about the size of a man laid out on his back. Graves. A graveyard again.

"I can see you've met the monks," said Petrek, putting his light onto the stone compartments. "The Old Ones."

Zdenek saw that three of the compartments, which must have been burial places, were mortared shut. That left many still awaiting customers.

"Are they all saints?"

"We like to think so," he said. "No one knows their names or how long they've been here. They might be Peter and Paul."

Zdenek gestured toward the whitewashed wall on the left side of the ladder, which was illuminated. Hung on a steel hook was a crown of thorns large enough for the heads of three men. Or Jesus Christ.

Petrek shone his light there. "Our Easter pageant."

Zdenek followed again as Petrek began to walk along the crypt as it tended toward Resslova Street beyond the wall. On the wall high up near the ceiling was an oblong patch of light that could only come from outside.

"That's a window?"

Petrek put his light toward the ceiling. "It's more of a ventilation slot," he said. "It gives a little fresh air and a little light."

"Where does it vent?"

"To the street," he said. "It's set about ten feet above the pavement, so no one can look in."

That was good. A stove out that slot would keep off the cold, which was amazing for the last week in May. Penetrating and layered. Zdenek felt as if he were turning brittle.

They moved back along the length of the crypt. If he had not lost his sense of direction, too, they were mirroring the way they had entered the church, moving away from the gallery and the entrance doors toward the altar. Four huge pillars flanked either side. Between the second and third were more tombs set in the walls, some enclosed. At the end of the crypt, following the beam of light, lay a staircase. It was narrow and steep and led up in twelve steps exactly to the level of the floor.

"Where do the steps go?"

"Into the church before the altar," said Petrek. "But the staircase hasn't been used for years. There's a heavy stone slab mortared in place."

Borrowing Petrek's flashlight, Zdenek made his way to the top of the stairs. The mortar was tight around a large stone slab that would take explosives to dislodge. No one could enter the crypt by the stairs unless they announced their presence with a bang.

So. Two entrances. One stanched by a half ton of rock, the other so small that no one could enter it quickly or silently.

"This should do very well," said Zdenek. "When can we start to move the men in?"

"Any time."

"What about later today? I've got wounded."

"We should take them first," said Petrek. "The Germans can sense blood, you know. They were like animals when they came through this district last night. Howling. Actually howling. And if the Protector should die—"

Yes.

* * *

Heydrich awakened from a dream in which white things were missing from their places. Strange, but his first conscious thought was of "Amen," his father's fourth opera.

He had been named after the main character—the superior man Reinhard, who falls in love with the maiden Dora. Through many trials, they remained true to each other, though their marriage was thwarted by an evil peasant. In the finale, Reinhard was slain by the peasant, and Dora ended by poison the life that she could not continue without him.

Heydrich opened his eyes. He saw two people, both looking at him. An SS gruppenfuhrer. And Lina.

She was fat.

He was Gebhardt. Himmler had him performing experiments on Jews at KZs. The idea was to save German lives by the knowledge gained, but the Jews almost always contrived to die in his hands. Therefore: Reinhard was in danger. Imminent danger.

Heydrich didn't feel that he was. His mind was utterly calm, and his body seemed to exist on a plane that was identical but somewhat removed. Sideways.

Morphine. Yes, it was morphine.

"How do you feel, darling?"

"I feel nothing," he said. "The pain is elsewhere."

"That's good," she said, running her hand over his brow.

Heydrich was disconcerted. She had been sitting quietly, obesely in a chair, but suddenly she was at his side. This was operatic, unreal. Yes, something was missing.

"What is my condition?"

Gebhardt, the false doctor, appeared. His face ballooned toward Heydrich. "Obergruppenfuhrer, you have developed an infection. We think it originated with pieces of the car's upholstery that entered your spleen from the force of the blast."

"Tell me what that means."

"I have recommended against removing your spleen under the circumstances," said Gebhardt. "It means that we will control the infection through drugs."

"It means you will try."

"Yes, Obergruppenfuhrer."

The British had developed a new drug—a wonder drug—called penicillin, but none was available in Germany. Thus, Reinhard must die.

"A peasant," he said.

"Obergruppenfuhrer?"

Heydrich closed his eyes. "A peasant slew him."

* * *

Ota was first into the crypt because of his wounds. Although the swelling on his face had diminished, a dark crease at the corner of his left eye was readily visible to anyone who cared to look, and there were bound to be more interested observers as word of the gigantic reward passed to every soul in what was now a very poor country.

Ice was next with a leg that was infected and beginning to fester. He thought he had taken care of the wound well enough, but it refused to heal. When Ota told him the bomb had been poisoned, Ice was furious until he realized that Heydrich would be having the same problem in a much warmer place.

Eugen and Vaclav—two-thirds of the Bioscope team—were happy to enter any secure area. On the first night of the terror, they had nearly been caught when the Gestapo raided their flat. They escaped by climbing into the airshaft and dangling three stories high by their fingertips until the search ended.

Likewise, Kral narrowly escaped capture. The woman he was staying with in Dejvice put him in a cubbyhole behind her sofa when the SS came calling. Although she and her young daughter had been closely questioned, they kept their mouths and emotions so well controlled that the Germans left without the thorough search that would have gained their prize.

Blackie, whose mission was Tin, had no problems during the frenzy. Every night, he went to the basement of the apartment building in which he was staying and climbed into the furnace. Blackie put down his little stool, hung his pistols from the flue, and waited for the business that never came. He was, he said, disappointed in the enemy.

That would have been talk coming from anyone else, but Blackie, of all the paras, was the only one who looked as he was ordered to be—an assassin. It was the square-ended nose that did it, but the lead-weight eyes helped. The way he handled a pistol sealed the impression.

All the men had reached the sanctuary of the church by Sunday, yet no word came from the Bulovka Clinic. Although the Nazis had sealed the hospital, allowing no Czechs within a floor of Heydrich, Uncle had managed to insert a spy there. This nurse said that huge quantities of morphine were missing, but whether it was being fed to Heydrich, or an addict on the general staff, remained unknown.

Zdenek cursed himself and his Sten gun so often that the phrases became an incantation. Each day that passed seemed to increase the chance that Heydrich might survive. By mid-week, Zdenek found that he could not sleep in the crypt. It was the preternatural cold, yes, but it was also a criminal sense of failure.

On Thursday afternoon, which was June 4, 1942, one day more than a week after the hit, the signal for a friend tapped the rock above the tombs of Peter and Paul.

Everyone jumped. It was not the time of day for a supply run. The main doors were still open for parishioners.

Kral, lying on a mattress in one of the unoccupied tombs, hoisted himself out and doused the candles. Vaclav and Eugen, along with Blackie, went to cover the steps. Zdenek climbed the ladder with Ota and Ice covering his back. He tapped the return signal. Two slow. Two quick. The rock began to move, grinding like gears, until it suddenly freed itself in a swarm of light above. Petrek's face appeared, peering down from a dim halo.

"It's all right," he said. "I have news."

Zdenek yearned for it to be the word they had awaited so long, so eagerly, and with an untold portion of dread.

"Is it Heydrich?"

"Yes," said Petrek. "He died early this morning."

CHAPTER 25

June 9, 1942

About three o'clock, Libena came with food and warm clothing. Zdenek thought she looked far too big everywhere until she stripped off the extra coat and two sweaters and the scarves that she had brought for the seven men in the crypt.

She looked herself then, carrying spring into the church, her hair shining like an afterglow of the scarcest thing in his life—the sun.

"Let's go upstairs," he said. "We can be alone."

They climbed the steep winding staircase that led to the choir loft overhanging the interior of the church. The wall that faced the street was all windows, but it was easy to stay out of sight in the niches. They spent time finding one, and more time touching. Zdenek felt giddy with a woman's body against him. Her warmth was astonishing. It was like the day she had come to transport him from the ice of Nehvizdy. Nothing had changed in the meantime but the world.

"Here we are among the angels," she said. "What a lovely place to hide."

The cherubim flitted about heaven in the vaults like heedless pagans. The smell of old incense seemed to rise from the altar like an aphrodisiac.

"It's a hideous place," he said. "You shouldn't have come."

"You're not happy to see me."

"No."

She laughed and moved his hand to her belly. "Tell that to the intruder."

Zdenek felt nothing beneath his hand but a more generous warmth. She could be lying about this, he thought. That was a wonderful idea. It could happen here among the choir books.

"Is it a boy or a girl?"

"It's still deciding," she said. "When this is over and you're safe, I'll know."

"How?"

"I'll go to the woman that Mrs. Sramkova knows," she said. "The medium."

"Keep your hand on your purse."

"I knew you'd say that, Josef. You're too rational for a Slovak. The first time I saw this woman was at a Red Cross meeting. Auntie was there, and she asked a question about her oldest son—Atya's brother, Mirek—who disappeared without a trace when the Germans came. This woman closed her eyes and said: "He's by the sea. In dirty overalls. A mechanic in the Air Force."

"Of course," said Zdenek. "He's in England with the RAF."

"We didn't know that until you came to tell us. No one knew except this old woman when she closed her eyes." Libena smiled as if she could still be wistful. "Do you know what else she said?"

"We have until dark, Libena."

"That there would be a great outrage." Libena looked up as if her pause had fallen from the rafters. "A killing. Many people would lose their lives."

Do I need this, Zdenek asked himself? She's lost her mind with worry. The father of her child has a foot in the grave up to his balls. She came all the way across town carrying enough clothing and food to guarantee she would be torn into pieces smaller than the child in her womb if a cop had a whim to search a lovely young girl.

"It seems this woman has a gift," he said. "Many people have lost their lives already."

"I suppose a vision is easy to have in wartime," she said. "It's true that many have died, but the country has never been as united as it is now."

"I'm glad to hear that. It will mean a lot to the others."

"Tell them they're the greatest heroes this nation has ever known," she said fiercely. "The Nazis are cowering. They took

Heydrich's body from the clinic in the middle of the night because they were afraid of an uprising."

"What did they do with it?"

"They put it at Prague castle for a while," she said. "They made people come from all over the city—all of us from the Red Cross—to parade before the catafalque. They hung a huge SS flag above the coffin. Pine trees all around. Flaming urns. It's what they're good at. Celebrating death. And they're still at it. They sent the remains to Berlin for more pomp."

"When did that happen?"

"Two days ago," she said. "They'll bury him today."

Zdenek heard that as if the bell aloft had begun to toll. He had been waiting for a reprisal—the one that would make all the others look small. He had no idea what form it would take, only that it would happen after Heydrich was in the ground.

"You should leave the city. Leave the country, if possible. Your father may be able to get you out through the Red Cross."

"Just like that."

"We all dropped with plenty of money," he said. "Uncle has some of it. He'll get you papers to Portugal. You can find passage to America. No one can harm you there."

"But where would I go?" she asked. "I don't speak English."

"That doesn't matter. You'd be safe there."

"And you?"

"I'll join you as soon as I can."

"When the war is over."

"Yes."

She turned her eyes again to the cherubim hovering in the ceiling, as if they were more real to her. Angels and mediums might be the natural companions of her condition. Zdenek knew before she turned and put her head on his chest that she would never agree to go anywhere.

"It's going to be all right," she said. "We'll take care of you, and God will take care of us."

* * *

Reich Chancellery, Berlin.

His double preceded him into the city, arriving by the front gates in an open car while Hitler entered from the rear in an armored van. He had been told that the new plating would deflect any bomb except the sort that had killed Heydrich. That one, it seemed, was too powerful, developed by the British for use against German tanks in Africa.

At the funeral, Hitler pinned the medal of the German Order on Heydrich's corpse. Overcome with an anger that passed for grief, he spoke very few words, but he listened patiently while Himmler babbled. When it was all done and the body loaded onto a gun carriage and the funeral march from Eroica began to play, Hitler withdrew.

After the Czech delegation returned from the cemetery, he had them brought to his office in a group. Daleuge and Frank, the new Protector and his Deputy. The ambassador with the garish name that he could never recall. And President Hacha, looking like a boar without tusks, living proof of a degenerate nation.

The best thing Hacha did was bend his back. He bowed to Himmler and Bormann, then nearly fell upon the enormous desk that Hitler often thought of as his altar.

"Fuhrer, I offer my sympathy," he said. "I condemn from the depths of my heart the assassins who performed this cowardly deed. I would never have expected the British of stooping to such methods."

Frank put himself forward, as he had from the first moment of the crisis. "President Hacha means that the weapons found at the site of the assassination were English. The submachine gun. The bomb, detonators, and fuses. If the Fuhrer recalls, that is the reason we decided against massive retaliation."

Hitler spoke quietly. "True. In the beginning, we felt it best to give the Czechs the benefit of a doubt."

Hacha's mouth opened as if he would say something, but he did not. Himmler smiled—an unconscious gesture, always.

"In the beginning," said Hitler, "we wished to believe that the people of the Protectorate had no part in this outrage. But now—almost two weeks later—we find that the Czechs have lent no hand in bringing the assassins to justice." Hitler rose and slapped the papers on his desk. "Reports say the common citizen approves this outrage! That he laughs!"

"Fuhrer, I assure you—"

"No one mocks German power!" he shouted. "I refuse to accept any further damage to the interests of the Reich in the Protectorate!"

He stared at Hacha. "Perhaps you don't know that we have already resettled millions of people. From all over Europe, Germans have come home to take their place in a Jew-free Reich. From the Tyrol out of Italy, from the Baltic Lands and Russia. What is to stop us from repopulating the Protectorate? If the Czechs will not hand over the killers, we must assume that they do not wish to live in peace! That they are hostile to the Reich concept!"

Hitler sat back at his desk and folded his hands. "If that is the case, I will be forced to use extreme measures. Every compromise solution will be ruled out."

"Fuhrer," said Hacha, his voice, like his back, bent with pleading. "Do not act in haste! Please, allow us to take this message to the Czech people. They will see the danger!"

Hitler was sure that Hacha would launch an immediate program of public education. "I will agree to your suggestion, Mister President. Czechs are intelligent workers. Practical. They will be more so when they have an example of German resolve." Hitler snapped his fingers and pointed at Frank. "A name. Give me a place-name."

* * *

The village of Lidice sat on the rolling plain northwest of Prague. One Baroque church, a school, a gymnasium that had been the home of the subversive Falcon organization, and approximately five hundred inhabitants.

Von Pannwitz arrived near dawn with the propaganda team from Berlin, who were terrified of driving at night in enemy territory. Goebbels' warriors. All they wanted to know was where they should set up for business—so von Pannwitz went looking for the officer in charge.

He found Hauptsturmfuhrer Rostock having coffee with Bohme, the head of the SD and a truly great thug. Bohme was gracious enough to offer more coffee, and von Pannwitz foolish enough to accept. It tasted like the tin cup—and nothing else.

"The propaganda team wants to know where to put their gear."

"Behind the barn," said Bohme. "In the field."

"What sort of propaganda will they make out of this?" asked Rostock, who was young—too young to have eyes like that. "It's a police action."

"Remember that nothing is more important to the Reich than a stable home front," said Bohme. "Germany cannot be defeated in battle. It must be done by stealth."

"But to publicize it," said Rostock. "These things happen in Russia all the time. No one shouts it out."

"The decision has been made," said von Pannwitz. "These men came in by special aircraft. They'll leave in the same way once they've got their pictures."

"Pictures," said Rostock. "You mean they'll make a *record*? What the hell are they thinking of? It can't be my men. It's bad enough, what they'll be doing, but to have it recorded!"

"This is a Fuhrer Order," said Bohme. "Do you understand what that means?"

Rostock did.

* * *

Zdenek must have dozed off, for he was awakened by a flash of light and a crash of gunfire. He rolled across the wooden planks, the Colt in his hand, coming up under one of the choir benches, awaiting the next volley. Where had it come from?

The darkness in the gallery was incomplete. From the top of the high school across Resslova Street a thin spill of new light ran down the building's gray stone front. In the niches, Zdenek could see the figures of Vaclav and Ice under their blankets. They had not moved. Inconceivably, they had not seen the brilliant flash of light; had not heard the sudden din of firing.

Crawling along the wooden barrier that separated the gallery from the church, Zdenek looked out into the street. He saw nothing. Not a soul. Not a light in a window.

Carefully, he rose and looked out over the barrier toward the altar. A very Christian quiet prevailed. Jesus hung in blood from his cross. All the doors were closed, or so it seemed. No early priests were making sunrise rounds.

Nothing was out of place but the noise that had exploded in his mind. Where had the flash and the gunfire come from?

What had he dreamed?

* * *

This fucker was twitching in the legs like a bad relay. He had both hands held out in front of his chest, and a damned nice set of boots.

Rottenfuhrer Steinhaus had a weakness for good boots, no matter what kind of rank flesh they covered. He had been a poacher before the war, making a living in the Teutonburg Forest until the SS decided that a man who was a good shot and even better at breaking the law made the best kind of recruit. Until this morning, Steinhaus would have agreed.

What made him change his mind? A set of fine calfskin boots on poor legs?

No. What made it bad was this: Steinhaus had a long-barreled Luger with a thirty-two round magazine that he thought would do for the housekeeping. He hadn't expected much of that, but it was such nasty shit, this business. You'd think that SS line troops would be crack shots—you'd think that Steinhaus' squad would be the best in the SS—but killing a man was harder than it seemed. Killing Czech peasants was damned near impossible.

They were feeding them in by groups of ten from the barn and at least three from each group didn't go down well in the volley. That meant Steinhaus had to move along the line giving the coup de grace. Manually. They all lay on their backs, which meant he had to put the Luger right in their hairy fucking ears.

His right arm was covered with blood and bits of bone. His pants did not bear looking at. He would have to feed in another clip soon.

"Get on with it, Steinhaus. We have more coming through."

"Yes, hauptsturmfuhrer."

Steinhaus finished this one, the spastic, with a round that ended his twitch, but strangely, did not force his hands apart. He still lay there with fists clenched as if holding invisible reins.

Ride on, fucker. Send me a postcard when you reach the other side.

CHAPTER 26

NOTICE OF THE CRIMINAL COURT IN BOHEMIA

In the course of the search for the murderers of SS Obergruppenfuhrer Heydrich, unshakable proof was found that the inhabitants of Lidice near Kladno had helped a number of possible offenders. The proofs were found through investigation without the help of the local population. Their positive attitude toward the assassination is emphasized by further deeds hostile to the Reich: the circulation of anti-state leaflets, the hiding of arms and ammunition, the possession of an illegal transmitter and rationed goods, and the fact that some inhabitants of Lidice are abroad in the service of the enemy. Because the inhabitants violated the law in the worst possible manner, all adult men were shot, the women sent to a concentration camp, and the children taken away to receive a suitable education. The buildings were razed to the ground and the name of the village has been erased.

* * *

Zdenek held the blood-red edict in his hand for much longer than it took to read it. He had seen these things in public places all over Prague. Usually they announced the death of one man or woman. This *bekanntmachung* told the end of an entire village. A world.

"What does that mean—the children will receive a suitable education?"

"If they have fair hair, they'll be put into the Lebensborn program." Uncle clasped his hands as if suddenly conscious that they knelt in a pew. "Germanized. If not, they'll be sent to concentration camps, too."

"Children," said Zdenek. "I've never heard of that village before. None of us have ever been there."

"They know that," said Uncle. "No transmitter was found, or any serious weapons. The purpose of this atrocity is to show us Nazi power. They're making a hecatomb for Heydrich. A demon sacrifice to terrorize the people."

"Yes, Uncle. But they want us."

He smiled patiently. "Well, they can't have you. Very few people know where you are, and those who do are the finest. Mass murder will only make them more determined. In time, we'll find a place out of the city for all of you."

"A little village in Bohemia?"

"Stop that," he said in a schoolmaster's voice. "It's the Nazis who are terrified. If they don't have our factories, the Russian Front will collapse. So they play the game of gradual response. Our choice is to lay down and do nothing—or resist." Uncle covered Zdenek's hand with his. "Perhaps it will help you to know we learned from the castle that if Heydrich had lived, he planned a new round of terror. Mass arrests. Executions. Perhaps even a village or two."

It didn't help, but Zdenek wanted some good word to carry back to the crypt. The longer the men stayed underground in the cold the more erratic they became. He had no idea how they would react to the news that a village had been wiped from the earth as the price of their freedom, but the mood would certainly worsen.

"Tell me, Uncle, when were the men shot?"

"In the morning. Yesterday. Early."

"At dawn?"

"I believe so. They wanted all the men, so they waited until the night shift changed at the steel mill in Kladno. And daylight was better for pictures of course."

"Pictures?"

"They want to see their work," said Uncle. "The proof of their inhumanity."

* * *

No one slept much that night. Kral said nothing for a long time, while Vaclav and Eugen, who were quiet men, wept quietly. Blackie cursed so hard in the same phrases that it seemed like a kind of prayer. Even Ice was quiet as he sat on a straight chair and cleaned his weapons. He had fieldstripped his pistols a hundred times in the last two weeks, but he took them apart again, one by one. When he finished oiling the slide on the last, he spoke.

"We've got to do something."

"Ideas," said Zdenek.

"Blackie had a mission when they threw him out of the plane," said Ice. "A target. I say we hit it."

"Let's go," said Blackie.

"You can't act like that," said Kral. "Unthinkingly. If we kill another man, they'll destroy another village."

"It's not unthinking," said Ice. "It's his orders."

"But not yours."

"He lost his partner," said Ice. "It seems like he should have a replacement out of the stock on hand. God knows we've plenty of that."

"You're as barbaric as the Germans," said Kral. "How can you spend the lives of innocent people without a thought?"

"I have plenty of thoughts for them," said Ice. "More than for you, asshole."

"Stop it!" said Ota. "Stop wrangling!"

Because Ota never said anything harshly, they stopped. It seemed like he meant to say more as he began to pace between the vent that was blacked-out every night, and the ladder to the trapdoor that was always closed. "I've been thinking about this a while," he said. "From the moment we did it. The first night, when the Germans were searching the city for us, I wandered the suburbs alone. Twice, I stopped at the houses of people I knew. Both families asked me to stay. They knew by my face how dangerous that was for them. So I told them I had to go."

Ota continued to pace as if retracing his movements. "It was safer for everyone. Trapped inside a house with the SS surrounding the block was something I didn't want to think about. Put the baby up, Mrs. Laches, and pass the ammunition. She probably would have, too.

"I figured out after a while that the Germans were posting a sentry on every block they meant to search. It wasn't hard to skirt them. I kept to the sides of the roads—and the ditches. All I had to worry about were the dogs, because they were spooked. Dogs give back the moods of their masters. What they picked up that night was fear—the kind that puts you down deeper in the darkness. Where there's nothing.

"That was when I realized what we'd done. I'd been walking the streets of Prague for weeks—I'd worn out three pairs of shoes—but I never felt like I was walking in my sleep. It wasn't just that I could hear my own footsteps and nothing else. I felt like I'd been cut loose from everything, wandering in the night with a brand on my face.

"When I heard the singing, it was like that. I was in the Kobylisy district, and I began to hear voices like one voice—far off—mixed with the sounds of trucks. With no traffic, I knew the trucks had to be German. I was off the street, but I climbed up the hill to some trees because the trucks had their lights on—the blackouts and tripods, too. They put a strange blue cast on the road. Not quite light. Something in between.

"The strange thing was, I knew where they were going. When we first got to Prague, we stayed in Kobylisy for a week or so. Do you remember, Zdenek?"

He nodded. He could see the houses and weed lots now, better perhaps than he had then.

"The trees were on the hill right near the firing range," said Ota. "That's where the trucks were going—down the road to the range. And there were people inside the trucks, singing.

"I moved to the bottom of the hill, so I could cross over and get out of there. I didn't put it together—the people in the trucks, the firing-range—until I found a culvert running under the road. When I came out the other side into an ashpit, I heard the first volley. It was like the sound of my footsteps jammed through a loudspeaker. Like *I* was causing it.

"That's when I knew they were shooting those people—the ones who'd been singing in the trucks. They sang on the way to their executions." Ota stopped pacing. "That's when I knew those people were braver than I was. And I knew I could never let them down."

CHAPTER 27

Auntie weighed as much as most men, and perhaps more than some of the paras in the catacombs who had little solid food for more than two weeks. The ladder groaned as she descended into the crypt preceded by the smell of sausages from the bag on her arm. Ota and Blackie helped her off the last long step onto cold ground.

"Anna's coming," she said. "Mrs. Krupka from Pardubice, and Atya, too. We've brought you good things to eat, and a bottle of wine."

"The last supper," said Ice. "Who'd believe it?"

"We should have a place setting for Peter and Paul," said Ota.

"I don't want to hear that kind of talk," she said, as she began to dole food onto the rack of planks they used for a table. "You've got to live up to the name you made. All over the world, people are talking about the heroic Czech paras, and you've nothing to answer with but a smart mouth."

"All over the world?"

"The one where things happen, yes. Hitler's armies have taken the Crimea and are running toward the Caucasus. Rommel has defeated the British across all North Africa. Heydrich's death is the good news for the Allies—all of it."

"What do they say about Lidice?"

Blackie had spoken in the way he had—as if nothing but death could please him. But he was not prepared for the way that Auntie had.

"What they say is that Hitler made the biggest mistake of his wretched life." Auntie looked around the crypt at each man as if in accusation. "He meant to destroy a village in Bohemia. To erase its name and its people from the earth. Instead, he made it immortal. Lidice is on the lips of every decent human being everywhere. In the newspapers, the radio, the newsreels. In America, they changed the name of one of their villages to Lidice. In Mexico, too. There will be villages called Lidice everywhere that people value freedom."

Auntie took up the sheath knife that Blackie had left on the table. She began to carve up a piece of sausage as if she were doing much more.

"They're calling it the turning point of the war," she said to the sausage. "Sure, it's propaganda. The death of one bloody Nazi isn't going to make the German Army run and hide. But ask yourself how things really turn. With a dramatic event. It can be as big or as small as you like. Show people what they're fighting, which is what Hitler did when he butchered Lidice, and they'll fight until that thing dies."

She dumped the sausage into the mess tin in front of her, which happened to be Ice's. "Jews are dying in great numbers in the camps. The same night that the Nazis destroyed Lidice, Hitler sent a thousand Czech Jews off in a train marked The Assassination of Heydrich. These monsters can do anything they want—except find the men who killed their apostle of violence. Every day you remain free—even though you don't think you are—Hitler loses the power over men's minds."

Auntie took up the mess tin filled with food, offering it to anyone at all. "And you want to ruin it now. You want to kill a nobody and then kill yourselves."

* * *

That had been the plan, and it did sound wrong when Auntie mocked it. In fact she had come close to killing it with a few words. They usually didn't fire up the kerosene stove except in the mornings for coffee, but they made an exception when Mrs. Krupka, Atya and Anna came with more food and all the good news they could bear. They made coffee, using Ota's vest as a strainer.

The word that came via Radio Libuse was good. The President had sent them a personal message of thanks. It had arrived some time ago, before the destruction of Lidice, but the words still meant something, especially to Zdenek and Ota.

Ota tried to explain that to Anna when they went up to Petrek's office to heat water to bathe the wound on his face. Twice, a doctor had been in to treat the infection, which had to be cleaned twice a day and usually was done once in tepid water with strange things floating in it. Finally, as the water began to steam, Anna let out her secret.

"Jindra's working on a plan to get you out of here," she said, applying the warm compress to the left side of his face. "He'll be by soon with the details."

"Soon?"

"The German amnesty for information about you expires on the eighteenth," she said. "He wants to move before then."

Ota looked at her through one eye. She seemed dimensional even so. "I don't know if we'll last another five days in this tomb," he said. "Everyone's jumpy and depressed."

"Are you in such a hurry to die?"

"What if the Nazis destroy another village?" he asked. "My own, perhaps. Or yours."

"And create more martyrs?" she said. "Don't be absurd. The Nazis like to lose propaganda battles less than they like to lose them in the field."

"Absurd. Is that what I am to you?"

"Yes. I remember a man who made love to me like three men. If anyone had told me he was a coward, I would have killed them."

"A coward?"

"A suicide."

"Three?"

She shrugged. "Two and a half."

"This coward hasn't had a proper bath in weeks."

"I noticed," she said, removing the compress and putting it back in the steaming water. "Take off your shoes and trousers. Put them over the chair."

"Anna."

"Do as I say."

She picked up the pot of water that had simmered on the hot plate and moved it to the floor by his chair. Because he had not moved, she unlaced his shoes and stripped off his socks and undid his trousers. With less efficiency, but more intent, she pulled them down.

Beginning at his feet, she began to wash him slowly, after letting the cloth cool a little. It took Ota some moments to realize that what she was doing had a purpose that he could imagine but not believe. The long days in the catacombs began to melt away, the cold drawn out in rhythmic waves as the compress had drawn the poison from his face.

She moved up his legs, accelerating, but not once looking at him. She was at his knees, then she was between his thighs.

"Hello," she said to the thing that had sprung long and hard like a hose suddenly put to a hydrant.

"Anna—"

"Relax," she said. "Feel the warmth."

Ota closed his eyes because he was afraid it would go away to be replaced by pain. He felt the warmth, felt the gentle circular movements, felt clean, felt the clammy cold of the catacombs shed like skin, felt a surge in his body that he could not hold back. He opened his eyes again late, very late, and felt her rise between his legs as he was coming, chasing the pale filament as it flew.

* * *

Mrs. Krupka was the most beautiful woman in Pardubice. Make that Czechoslovakia. Ice had been stunned by her beauty from the first, and in the depths of the catacombs, he was overcome. Delicate bones, golden hair, and green eyes tilted in the way that ignorance described Slavic beauty.

"How is your husband?"

"Well," she said. "He worries about me, of course."

"I would, too."

"Why?" she asked. "The Germans have never stopped me for any reason. I've only had my papers checked twice, even during this round of terror."

"They're too busy staring."

"At what?"

"Perfection."

She laughed and shook her head. "Do the things you say ever bring results?"

"What do you mean by results?"

"What every man means."

"If I was every man, I wouldn't be here now. I wouldn't be frozen half to death, wounded—"

"Wounded?"

"The leg."

She looked at him as if she were peeking round the corner. "Which one? I didn't notice."

Ice touched his left thigh lightly.

"You do that look very well. I'm hurt much worse than you can imagine, it says. And there's only one way to assuage the pain."

"Assuage," he said. "That sounds good. How is it done?"

"Slowly," she said.

"I would have guessed that."

"What else do you guess?"

"That we'll never see each other again."

"I believe you said that the last time I was in Prague."

"I can't be wrong forever. Give me a chance."

She turned her head away. Even her profile was soft and understated. Seraphic. How would it translate, he wondered?

"Give up this stupid plan you have of killing the Minister," she said.

"Is that a proposition?"

"Yes."

* * *

"Libena will be here tomorrow," said Auntie. "She said to tell you that she's feeling fine. She could have come with us, but decided to go with her father. He's searching for a place where you can stay after you leave here."

Zdenek was glad to hear that the plan to move them from the crypt was not being mounted by Jindra alone. "I'm sure the others will agree to wait," he said. "Having a deadline will make a difference."

"How do you feel about it, Zdenek?"

"I'll look forward to living. This is a poor substitute."

"Then you won't mind leaving here feet first."

"What does that mean?"

"Jindra told me that he has a friend who may be willing to lend his hearse for the plan," she said, smiling. "It would mean loading all of you into coffins and transporting you outside the city in them."

Zdenek's first thought was that the plan seemed ingenious. Arrive at the church for the funeral, load the coffins, and head for the cemetery in Switzerland. Doubts began to appear when he thought of laying in a sealed box at the mercy of the SS at every checkpoint on the way out of the city.

"I wish Jindra had been able to find four wheels when we went after Heydrich. It would have made this unnecessary."

"He's not one for suicide. For surviving, yes."

"You say that like a para, Auntie. Like a man. What do you have up your sleeve?"

She tapped the brown cameo pinned to her breast. "I saw Emil when I was in Pardubice. He gave me his cyanide capsule."

* * *

"Your mother looks drawn," said Kral to Atya. "She might be losing weight."

Atya looked across the crypt to the table where his mother sat with Blackie, Eugen and Vaclav. He had always known her as an enormous being long after he had grown tall.

"She's exhausting herself cooking for seven," he said. "And two more at home. When she doesn't come to the church with supplies, she makes drops for the others. And she works at the Red Cross and—"

"I'm surprised she came back," said Kral. "The Gestapo must know it's her bicycle they found at the site."

Atya shook his head. "I'm sure they don't. We were out of the city for almost a week—mother and I—and no one came to investigate. Maybe they can't trace the manufacturer's number. They have to rely on betrayal. That poor old bike's been in the big window at Bata's downtown, but no one's identified it. Two million marks. That's a million marks a wheel."

"It's unbelievable, the support we've gotten from the people," said Kral. "It seems impossible the Gestapo haven't penetrated our networks."

"There's been nothing," said Atya. "They picked up a leader of the communist resistance, but he had no connection to us."

"And Jindra's network?"

"New members every day," said Atya. "They have problems vetting so many, that's all."

"You've seen nothing suspicious?"

"No," said Atya slowly. "Except for the man from Kolin."

"What man?" said Zdenek.

"I didn't see him myself," said Atya. "But you know Mister Spinka, the caretaker in our building. He said a stranger came to the flat looking for us. Wanting to pick up a briefcase."

"He was from Kolin?"

"Yes," said Atya. "But we don't know anyone there. The only person who mentioned it to me recently was Cyril."

Kral heard that name with pain. No doubt he had done his best to forget Cyril, and Out-Distance, though it was his mission.

"What did Cyril tell you about Kolin?"

"It was after I'd picked him up in Pardubice and we were on the way to Pilzn to meet you," said Atya. "Cyril told me that he had a relative there who hid him for a time. He seemed to think it was someone he could count on."

"Is that all he said?" asked Zdenek.

"Yes."

"Do you think this man came from Cyril to contact us?"

Atya shook his head. "I don't know. We've heard nothing from Cyril. Absolutely nothing."

CHAPTER 28

June 16, 1942

"Commissioner."

"Yes, Horst."

"We've got one off the street. He claims to know everything about the assassination."

Von Pannwitz was on his feet instantly but not without reluctance. Since the amnesty had been declared, the intake of anonymous letters had grown from zero to several hundred, but the product stayed the same—non-existent. This might be the first dividend, or another zero.

"Where is this man?"

"With Superintendent Jantur."

They walked quickly down the hall, turning at the stairs that led to the interrogation rooms below. These basement places were where so much of the real work—the productive work—of the Third Reich was done.

"What did he say when he appeared?"

"He wished to speak with someone in authority. He said that he recognized the briefcase in the window at Bata's store—the one left at the scene. And he identified it when it was put with twenty others."

"That's encouraging."

"Yes, sir, very encouraging. But he stutters. Superintendent Jantur couldn't understand a word of his German, and the Czech interpreters are having problems, too."

"You mean he can't speak his own language plainly?"

"Apparently not, sir."

The thing that was usually done with a man who had trouble talking was beat him. As von Pannwitz entered Interrogation Room Four, he saw that had already been done. The man was being put back on the chair now. A little blood. His lips looked bad but not swollen; they were simply big. The black mustache made him look like a thousand other men but unlike himself.

Nodding at von Pannwitz, Jantur continued the interrogation. "Tell us where you saw the briefcase."

"At the house of the Svatos family in Prague."

"On what street do they live?"

"M-M-M-M-Michalska."

"What number?"

"I don't remember."

Jantur said nothing. But he began to turn his eyes to the Assistant on his right.

"Please, sir. I don't remember. I saw the sub-m-m-m-machine gun at the Svatos house. In that briefcase."

"What kind of submachine gun?"

"A Sten."

Jantur looked at von Pannwitz. The make of the submachine gun had never been made public.

"Whose briefcase was it?"

"It belonged to the assassin of Heydrich."

"What is his name?"

"He called himself Zdenek."

"That was his cover name?"

"Yes, sir."

"And your cover name?" asked von Pannwitz. "What is it?"

The stutterer turned and looked at von Pannwitz as if surprised. Jantur turned at the same time, disconcerted. This was his interrogation, but von Pannwitz was head of the investigating commission.

Jantur bowed.

"Your cover name," said von Pannwitz.

"Sir?"

"You're a parachutist, too," said von Pannwitz. "All the agents use cover names. We know because we have them in our custody. Or in our morgue."

Only a fool would enter Gestapo headquarters without knowing he would be forced to tell everything. This one was at least that. And weak.

"Cyril," he said. "I was called Cyril."

* * *

When Kral returned to the crypt after meeting Jindra in Petrek's office, he seemed subdued but vindicated. He put his sweater and gloves back on and sat on the cot.

"The transfer will take place on the eighteenth," he said. "In the late morning. There'll be a mass for the dead, after which coffins will be loaded into a hearse. The hearse will take us to Kladno. From there, Vaclav, Eugen, Blackie and Ice will make their way to the Moravian hills to join with partisans."

"And us?" asked Ota. "Where will we go?"

"I'll remain here to direct the resistance," said Kral. "You and Zdenek will go to Oubenice, where a small plane from London will land and retrieve you."

Ota and Zdenek glanced at each other with a look that said: England? They had not anticipated that: a return in triumph. Medals. Promotions. Would they be sent on speaking tours?

"Why's everyone in a hurry to see us off?" asked Ice, who never seemed to mind the cold as much as others. "Once we leave here, we'll be at risk."

Kral winced. The contours that always seemed to fret his wide brow sunk skull-deep. "Petrek informed me that he's had orders from his bishop about us. It seems the good man fears his church will become extinct if the Nazis discover we've been hiding here."

"You mean he wants us out?"

"As soon as possible."

* * *

Because of the deep cold, Zdenek often slept in one of the open tombs, two slots down from the disciples. It was lined with papers and a mattress, padded with several blankets, but even so he usually awoke shivering. And remembering.

That night—after Kral had come with the word of their salvation—Zdenek had an insistent dream. He understood that he lay in a coffin, which moved around the streets. Presently, he saw The Man from Kolin following him. He was dressed darkly, like a Gestapo.

Zdenek wanted to get away. Gestapo were coming and the water was rising all around, but his strange conveyance stopped as they came to The Border. From behind a counter, a man in an official cap looked down into his face. It was not a police cap but something like the ones that Czech border guards had worn in the days of the republic.

Zdenek strained to see the man's face but could not. The cap was too low on his forehead. It seemed as if he must know this bizarre official.

"You can't pass," said the man. "Not without a life."

* * *

Marie Moravcova awoke dreaming or thinking of someone talking about elevators, or heaven. She saw light seeping at the edge of the window as it always did, no matter how many times she refitted the blackout curtains.

It was dawn. The clock with hands that glowed in the dark said five twenty-one. Marie luxuriated in the feeling of having survived another night. The Gestapo always came at four in the morning, after you had waited for hours for the sound of the car door slamming in the street and the boots on the stairs and the rifle butts on the door and had just gone to bed knowing you were safe when in the very dead of night the doorbell rang.

The doorbell rang.

The doorbell rang, just once, and then impatiently, again.

"Marie?"

"I'll get it, Alois."

She was on her feet pretending to be calm. That was vital no matter what was wrong. It would be something. It would be about the boys.

She put on her robe, thinking what a burden it was to be a superwoman. She encouraged it, but that was to give the others hope. They liked thinking that someone else was larger than their lives. Without fear. Without needs.

The doorbell rang again. Marie stopped halfway into the room and listened. No sound from the hall. No feeling from beyond in the hall. She took two steps, undid the lock, and pulled the door open.

They knocked her flat on her back. Someone stepped on her hand and three or four of them were trampling alongside her head, yelling at the same time: "Where are the parachutists?"

All the men in black had pistols. One of them pointed in her face and the others were turned toward the door of their bedroom and Atya's room. Boots had gone in both directions.

Marie looked one way: her husband was doomed.

She looked the other: her son, wearing the new pajamas that Ota had bought him, was doomed.

The Gestapo still screamed for the paras. They hauled in Alois and Atya and slammed them hard against the wall. They pulled Auntie to her feet and pushed her face against the wall.

At least six of them were in the flat now and three more coming and four putting their heads into the two bedrooms and waving their pistols at the linen.

Marie looked at her husband from the corner of her eye. He looked back. It shouldn't be necessary after all these years to say anything, certainly not a thing that they talked about and agreed upon and wanted to share, but she spoke anyway.

"I'm sorry, Alois."

"No talking!"

She felt the pistol at the back of her head and she almost began to sing the first lines of "My Country." Go ahead, you son-of-a-bitch, shoot. Do it for me.

"Where are the parachutists?"

Another voice said that. He was short and fat and as ugly as a man with enormous eyes could make himself. Gestapo technique. Screaming, snorting, playing the animal until it was not an act.

"Turn and face me," he said, spinning her around by her arm. "Do you know who I am?"

Shc shook her head.

He smiled with a wet widening mouth—a maw. "Superintendent Oscar Fleischer."

His name meant butcher in German, and he had spent his timc in the world justifying it. Everyone in Prague knew of him.

"Where are the parachutists?"

"I don't speak German."

He put his face next to hers. "I think you understand every word I'm saying. But we'll have a translator for you."

Marie was surprised that with her face turned back to the wall she knew so much of what they were doing to her home. She heard drawers in the bedroom chest roll out. The kitchen cabinet slammed shut, some glass breaking. The closets. The windows thrown up. It made her angry, and tearful, to hear her things being treated as if they were nothing, which they were.

"Where are the paras?" said a voice behind her in Czech.

"Tell them to be sure and check the sugar bowl," said Alois. "You never know until you look."

Marie held her breath for the pause as the voice translated Alois' words into German. "He says that he doesn't know of any parachutists, sir."

Fleischer accepted the words as they were relayed. "I'd think it would be easy to remember the men who were fucking your wife. That's what parachutists do. Tell him he'll remember that—and everything else—when we get him in the basement."

Marie waited for the translation, but it did not follow. Instead, she heard a man call from Atya's bedroom for Fleischer. When she was sure he had left the room, she whispered in German.

"May I go to the bathroom?

The big Gestapo man by the door said, "Piss in your drawers, bitch."

"Please, sir, I must."

"Shut your mouth!" he said, and taking half a step, swung his open hand against her face.

She hit the wall. Her nose smashed the edge of the portrait of the train that Alois rode all over the country in his work. The frame shifted and hit her again. She held onto the wall by the molding.

But the big man was gone. He moved off to follow Fleischer into Atya's room.

Slowly, Marie turned her face toward the interpreter. He was Czech, surely, and a human being, perhaps.

"Please, sir," she said plaintively.

"Go ahead, Madame," he said. "Hurry."

She moved immediately toward the bathroom, passing Alois and Atya. She tried to hold the eyes of her son but hardly had the chance because she could not afford the brief moment that might keep her from reaching that door.

These will be the worst hours of your life, my son. Is there anything I could have done to prepare you for them?

Marie closed the door behind her. She opened the catch on the cameo and took out the brown capsule. What was so difficult about this?

It will be worse, so much worse, for the ones I love.

CHAPTER 29

When they returned with the woman's body in one of her ragtag carpets, von Pannwitz knew that he would have to act at once. While the old man and boy were being processed, he rerouted the attack squad back to Zizkov.

This was the most important phase of the operation. One of the key figures of the resistance cell had to be taken alive before the assassins were alerted.

This would have been necessary if Cyril had known their location, but he swore endlessly that he did not. All he could give were the names of the people who had helped them. Moravcova (Auntie). Zelenka (Uncle). Von Pannwitz had waited until dawn to raid Moravcova's in case the parachutists were hiding at one of the Zizkov houses, but they had not been in the woman's flat, and reports from the surveillance teams watching both locations were negative.

Zizkov was not one of the smart sections of the city. Known as a breeding ground for subversives, mostly reds, it would have been a sealed ghetto like Lodz if von Pannwitz had his way. The man code-named Riha lived on the first floor of a building across the street from Moravcova's. Von Pannwitz would have preferred to wait until Riha showed himself, but the neighborhood was already tense. After parking the cars out of sight, the flying squad mounted the stairs, stopping at a door with a plaque that said: Jan Zelenka, Schoolmaster.

Von Pannwitz rang the doorbell.

No response.

He rang the bell again and heard footsteps, tentative steps, then saw a blink of light appear in the door at eye-level. A peephole.

"Smash the door!"

The man with the sledge brought it down on the knob, sending pieces of metal splattering down the hall. The next two threw themselves at the door, splintering wood and throwing off one hinge. As they were about to hit the door again, it suddenly swung open and a woman stood, alone, with a detached brass knob in her hand.

Von Pannwitz pushed her aside in time to catch sight of a man running one last step into the bathroom. "There he is!"

Herschelmann and Kahlo fired their pistols, nearly taking off the woman's ear. Three, four, five shots splashed like paint against the bathroom door as it slammed shut.

Von Pannwitz followed his men into the room while they flanked the entrance to the bathroom. He held up his hand, certain that he had heard a voice from within.

"Don't shoot!" said a man in German. "I'm coming out!"

So easy. Then why had he run to the bathroom?

Von Pannwitz had a bad feeling as the door opened and the schoolmaster stepped into the hall. He was a thin man with a starved but comical face that seemed poised on a smile.

Then Zelenka did smile. He threw open his arms, not in surrender, but as if welcoming them. When von Pannwitz moved toward him, the thin man suddenly stiffened, his body twisting, his shoulders strangely lofted. He seemed to move upward, willing himself to a higher place, climbing in the air. And then the convulsions began.

He fell into von Pannwitz's arms with the smell of bitter almonds pulsing from him.

* * *

Night arrived in the crypt as it always did, with subtle distinctions among the rubble. They blacked out the ventilator slit and lit more candles. The pinochle game broke up. The last of the food was parceled out until morning coffee.

The rapidly dwindling supplies were a source of concern to Zdenek. They had gorged themselves, so to speak, when Auntie brought the sausage and soup with liver balls and fresh bread and cake. But the next supply run had been three days later, which was two days ago.

The last they had seen anyone outside was yesterday at noon when Uncle came to say hello without any perishables. He promised to return today with some clips of nine-millimeter ammunition that he had gotten from a policeman in Kladno, but for some reason he had not met his promise.

Zdenek tried to see all this as a consequence of relying on Jindra. He had premonitions of trouble from the time he heard of the plan to evacuate the church, but had not anticipated that the problems would extend to every part of their subterranean life. They could certainly use the ammunition if serious fighting broke out. Food could be done without for days, if their bodies did not have to cope with the stupefying cold.

"You can have my sweater," said Ota. "It'll be warm in the choir loft tonight."

Zdenek nodded his thanks. Tonight Ota, Kral and Eugen had a turn at real sleep in the gallery, and the chance to thaw.

"Be sure to set a guard," he said to the three. "At least one man until dawn."

"You're worried because no one came by today."

"Yes," said Zdenek.

"That's happened before."

"Twice," said Zdenek. "But not since Auntie returned from Pardubice."

"I think she simply gave out," said Kral. "She's carried this entire operation on her back."

"Auntie doesn't give out. If she had trouble, she'd wait for it to pass."

"So you think she's come under pressure?"

"I don't know," said Zdenek. "But we can't take chances. There might be twenty people who know where we are. That's far too many. Anyone can be broken if the Gestapo takes them. And that could happen with just a bit of bad luck."

No argument there. Zdenek felt better when the three passed up the ladder to the church a few minutes later. At least they would be cautious and alert.

Having Ota there with the grenades was a plus.

* * *

Von Pannwitz found Superintendent Jantur as he left the interrogation room where the questioning of Moravcova's son had been conducted. Contrary to regulations that mandated a distinct separation between interlocutor and his subject, Jantur had small specks of blood over the front of his shirt.

"What success, Superintendent?"

"None," he said. "The boy won't talk."

"And the father?"

"Worse," said Jantur. "We broke his balls, but he just sat there and moaned. It happens sometimes when they see their family go down before their eyes. All they want is death. The pain makes them feel they're closer to it. We should leave him alone for a day or two—no sleep or food—then hit him hard."

"We can't afford delay," said von Pannwitz. "There must be a breakthrough soon."

"Not with that old man," said Jantur. "Never."

"Then keep on with the boy."

Jantur flashed his competitive eyes at the man who had been chosen over him as commissioner. "What in hell do you think I've been doing? We've had him underwater so much, if he has more, he'll grow gills. There's no skin left on his back or teeth in his mouth. Now tell me, Herr Commissioner, what do we do next?"

Von Pannwitz felt his vast anger move behind his eyes as coils. Like the movements of Schoolmaster Zelenka in his last moments. He knew it was exhaustion—almost three days without sleep—but it bred from the last reach of necessity, an idea. Von Pannwitz knew at once that it was psychologically sound.

"Where's the woman's body?"

"The woman?"

"His mother," said von Pannwitz. "The body was brought here this morning."

"I don't know," said Jantur. "I'm sure it was logged in."

"Have it brought to me in Interrogation Room One. First, be sure that the boy has been stupefied with alcohol."

"Then he won't feel a damned thing."

"He'll feel what I want him to," said von Pannwitz. "In the way I want him to."

* * *

Zdenek accepted the last bad cup of coffee from Ice. He sipped it, pulled his sweater higher, stamped his feet and chafed his fingers in the double gloves. He had never been this cold—not even in Nehvizdy. He sometimes thought he felt the river through the walls—a hoary pulsing current—though he knew the Vltava was too far away to be felt as a force.

It was his imagination and his dreams. Both were overwrought and strangely heightened by the confinement. At times they seemed to be the same. Waking, sleeping. Past, present, future.

It was as if a clock were running backwards, but from what point? Where did tomorrow start?

Was everything he had been told in his life—and knew to be true—wrong? Or simply prelude.

To what? When it was over, they put you in a box like the Disciples. You and your legend. Here rests the man whose gun jammed when he had the greatest killer since Genghis Khan in his sights. This is the man who by his stubbornness became responsible for the deaths of more of his countrymen than Attila the Hun.

Zdenek had seen the killing at Lidice without being there. He had actually felt the force of the volley as it ripped through the air toward the targets. How?

Sleeping in a coffin, he had traveled in a dream-coffin to the borderlands, where he encountered a misplaced official who turned him back. What did that mean?

"I've been thinking," said Ice. "What kind of plane do the British have that can fly from England, land in a grass field, and take off again with enough fuel for the return flight?"

"They don't have anything like that," said Zdenek. "Not as far as I know."

"So you're counting on a surprise to get you away," he said. "A secret weapon."

"We'll be out of here soon," he said. "We've got plenty of money, firepower, and help along the way. That's more than we had when we landed."

Ice smiled. "It's a life."

* * *

Atya awoke with everything going sideways. On a reel. The drift was continual, sickening, could not be stopped. He tried to focus on the bare lightbulb in the ceiling, holding onto the bright globe until his eyes throbbed, but the harsh light seemed to glide away, streaming in a smeared phosphorescent band.

Everything slid. The bright globe repeated itself endlessly, superimposed on the ceiling, the walls. As if he were drunk.

And in his pajamas. Atya looked at the pattern of light blue stripes. It was familiar but smeared and jittery. Where had he gotten the pajamas? They were much too fine to have come from the house money, of which there was constantly none. Someone must have made him a present.

Atya moved from the place on the floor where he lay and felt the crust all over his back. The smooth material pulled and returned pain like stitches. He had stitches when he got in that beer hall fight and pulled the Hitler Youth's thumb off his hand and got hit from behind with the glass that shattered and took a piece of his skull with it.

His back felt like that now, all the way to his shoulders, but it didn't really hurt because he was drunk. No doubt of it. He should go to the water-tank and dunk his head. It was more like a fish tank that seemed to brim with fluid and echo the wavering movements of his mind. Sickening.

Something floated in the water. Atya pulled himself to his knees, feeling the stitches spring like brittle cuts along his back.

His balls ached, too, distantly, as if the flesh and pain belonged to someone else. All this must belong to someone else.

He wobbled to his feet. Taking one step, or two, he reached for the edge of the tank. He saw a face. Long dark hair floated over the eyes, the brow, tangled around the chin.

It was his mother's face.

Atya blinked away the image, closing his eyes tight. When he opened them again, the image returned.

Once, twice, and the third time it held.

His mother's face floated in the water.

His mother's head. He looked up, feeling panic rise like a wave from the ocean that he had seen only in films. In the corner of the room was a chair in which his mother sat.

She was sitting as she had always sat on the chair in the kitchen, but she was naked, with no head.

Her head was in the fish tank, floating.

"Unless you want to see your father like that," said an unfamiliar voice, "you'll tell us what we want to know."

CHAPTER 30

Ota heard more activity than usual in the streets around the church at four in the morning. Some vehicles seemed to run down from the direction of Charles Square and stop out of sight of the window that overlooked the street. The sound of the engines died and the gears did not continue to change and whine. They might have been idling.

That was uncommon, but no reason to panic. This was Gestapo Hour, the time when they came through the door and took whatever was on the other side for torture. Several raids had taken place in the area since they arrived, but the Nazis had never invaded the sanctuary of the church.

Ota tried to filter out the irrelevant sounds. Standing by the window but behind the inner wall, he put the stethoscope on the glass and listened out.

More traffic. More dense. Like trucks.

Ota waited, listening intently, though the sounds began to diminish. He was still unsure whether the vehicles had passed on or stopped.

He moved the stethoscope lower on the windowpanes. Because they were blind in the crypt, they had been using the instrument since the doctor came to look at Ota and Ice and was persuaded to part with his equipment. The stethoscope provided relief from the monotony of seven men living in a closed space. On Sundays, it brought in the choir loud and clear.

Then Ota heard steps. Steady thumps. Not shoes. Boots? He looked carefully out the window and saw the shapes of four men in civilian clothes turn the corner of Resslova and Vaclavska and pass out of sight.

That was unusual. The men wore street clothes with boots. Not Gestapo. Possibly SS or SD, though there was no way to be sure.

But something about the way they moved seemed wrong. Like a unit. Like one with a purpose.

Suddenly, the footsteps stopped. They did not slowly echo away, but halted as a group. Ota thought he heard a distant sound—a doorbell, probably. And if it was, the door lay close by.

He scurried low across the planks to Eugen and Kral, taking them by the shoulder and shaking them from sleep. "We've got company."

Kral, who operated by wire and gears, sprung instantly to his haunches. "In the church?"

"In the street."

"We should warn the others," said Kral. "They won't know a thing down there."

Kral never seemed to accept things as they were, so Ota tried to be patient. "They'll know something's wrong when they hear it. We can't chance opening the trap door. That could tell the Germans exactly where everyone is."

"How many are out there?"

"I heard vehicles. Quite a few. I saw four men."

"You're sure?"

"I'm sure we have strange men on the streets. If they're a recon team, that means forty behind them. Or four hundred."

Kral looked out of the darkness of the choir loft with his bright eyes in shock. "If the Germans are here in force, they know something specific."

"That seems obvious."

"We'll defend this position," said Kral, ignoring sarcasm, as he always did. "Myself on the stairs. One of you on each side of the loft."

A good plan because it was the only one. From his pack, Ota took one of the two grenades—a bomb was called a grenade when it could be thrown—and handed it to Kral.

"There's just one way they can reach us," he said, nodding toward the stone staircase. "If they come up the stairs, blow it. This explosive is powerful enough to seal off the bottom of the stairway."

"And seal ourselves in," said Kral.

"It's a three-second fuse," said Ota. "Remember."

* * *

Although he had more than seven hundred Waffen-SS at his disposal, von Pannwitz chose to lead a picked group of SD and Gestapo men into the church. This moment belonged to Reich Security and the memory of the man who had exalted it.

The sacristan, who had been awakened and handcuffed, led the way down the hall until he stopped at a closed door. He was a taciturn man with a squirrel's frightened but defiant face who probably should not have been knocked about quite so hard.

"Where does this door lead?"

"Into the church."

"Where's the key?"

The sacristan jerked his head toward his pants pocket. "I can get it for you if I could move freely."

Von Pannwitz nodded to Kahlo, who put the sacristan against the wall and looted his pockets until he had the keys.

"Here, Superintendent."

"And the lights?" asked von Pannwitz.

"Just inside the door," said the sacristan. "You'll be able to see everything well enough."

Von Pannwitz switched on the lights and entered the church—the first time he had done so voluntarily since leaving theological school. He beheld Christ's irrelevant temple. This version was peculiarly ornate in the way of Eastern churches—a great many wall hangings and icons, banks of unlit candles, an immense altar, and a screen that separated the nave from the chancel.

"Begin at the altar and work back to the choir loft," he said to his augmented attack squad. "You can be sure they're here somewhere."

Von Pannwitz assumed that the assassins would be armed, but he was not worried about escape. The SS and police reserves had cordoned the surrounding blocks all the way down to the river, guarding the side streets, building exits and sewers. It was possible that an old building like this might have many passages running from it.

Now to close, and with the element of surprise theirs, capture. Von Pannwitz was thinking of how it would happen as his men fanned out to the altar and Kahlo jumped as if he had been shocked. At the same time the gunshot cracked and Kahlo's arm swung back wildly, throwing flesh and blood for three meters.

Suddenly, the church filled with noise. A gunshot, two gunshots, three, then many more quickly beyond counting. The attack squad was milling about in confusion, firing their weapons at everything. A second man was hit, clutching his leg, going down as he screamed.

"Pull back!" shouted von Pannwitz. "Quickly! Pull back!"

* * *

"Do you need me?" cried Kral from the stair.

"Negative, sir."

"What happened?"

"They retreated into the corridor. About twenty in all. We hit one or two fairly well."

"You're keeping score?"

"Of course," said Ota. "There's no point otherwise."

Eugen laughed quietly but like a lunatic. He was scared out of his mind, like Ota, but taken by the beauty of it. Those fuckers had run. They had been hit. They were not going to take this position without a direct assault by troops who knew what they were doing.

And Ota still had his grenade.

* * *

Von Pannwitz held his pistol to the sacristan's head. "You lied to me."

"No, sir. I never did."

"You knew the parachutists were up there."

"I knew they were there occasionally, sir. I didn't know if they came tonight."

"Came?" Von Pannwitz looked at the translator, who nodded. That seemed to mean they had arrived at the church from elsewhere.

"Where do they come from?"

"I don't know, sir. They don't confide in this poor fellow. They show up at night to sleep sometimes."

"How many tonight?"

"Three." He hesitated. "Three, sir."

Although von Pannwitz had no idea how many shots had been fired, or from what positions, the number agreed with his private count. The two assassins. And the lookout.

"How do they get up to the choir loft?"

"By the staircase," said the sacristan. "It's in the back."

"Show me."

* * *

"How many shots?" said Blackie, as he listened to the new silence above his head.

"Fifty," said Zdenek. "Seventy-five. It could have been more. Most of them came from around the altar, but it was hard to tell."

"There were hits," said Blackie. "I heard screaming. Two men at least."

Ice fastened on the last of Blackie's words as he returned from the stairs. "It's serious. They're outnumbered badly. We should be up there."

"No."

"They need help."

"We can't help them," said Zdenek. "All we can do is go out that hole and be picked off one by one."

"We die up there or down here," said Ice. "I don't see the difference."

"Chances are they don't know we're here," said Zdenek. "They might not for quite a while."

"What does time mean to us?"

"That we should start digging."

* * *

Von Pannwitz's men did not approach the winding stone staircase through the nave, but went by a door that opened from the rooms at the back of the church. They could not be seen, and barely heard, as they reached the bottom of the stairs. But there they found a metal grille blocking the entrance.

It was padlocked, and the sacristan did not have the key. He claimed that it was given to the parachutists each night, who locked themselves in until morning.

Von Pannwitz did not have time to ream the truth from that filthy bastard. He gave orders to force the grille with rifle butts. He knew enough about assault tactics to regret forfeiting the element of surprise. A few seconds later, as the grille swung open, creaking, clanging lightly on the stone like the gate to the underworld, von Pannwitz knew more.

As the first man climbed the stairs, he heard a queer rattling sound, then a bump and a bump. His men were already moving away fast when the canister hit the last step.

* * *

Ota had been hoping that Kral would hold the grenade a count before dropping it down the staircase, or that he would toss from the top, but the lieutenant had to show his nerve. He took two steps down the staircase to get a better angle on the stairs as they curved the ninety degrees toward the bottom, then he let it go.

The grenade blew the same instant as Kral dove back up onto the gallery floor and rolled. The noise that came with it up the staircase was tremendous, booming once, booming again, but the explosion threw little debris.

Not good enough. The blast had certainly caused some damage to the men who were trying to force their way up the stairs, but the grenade must have reached the last stone step before it blew. That meant the staircase was probably still free if not clear.

The Germans still had access to the choir loft, but that was not all the bad news. Seconds after the blast detonated, the high wall of windows that overlooked the street shattered and blew into the gallery like chunks of ice. Hundreds, thousands of rounds of machine-gun fire poured through the windows and ricochets angled everywhere, chopping, chopping. The air that had just begun to turn light filled with screaming fragments of stone, plaster and metal, forcing Kral behind the pillar near the top of the stairs.

After the first long fusillade, and a pause for control, Ota ducked a quick look out the window. He didn't see much and ducked out again. The machine gun opened up again, rattling from the first floor window of the high school across the street. He was not sure, but he thought he saw some men on the roof, too.

It wouldn't have done much good to return fire with his pistol, so Ota slid back into position behind the front of the gallery. Just as he reached cover, a heavy burst of large caliber fire hit the windows and exploded, throwing one of the big chairs halfway across the loft.

The men on the roof. They had light cannon.

"They own the middle," shouted Kral. "As long as we keep to the pillars, we'll be all right."

All right? Compared to what? A funeral? Ota would have given both his nuts and a willing partner for the Sten gun that Zdenek dropped at the turning.

He looked over the loft into the church. A dozen men were coming, moving like crabs from cover to cover. They were all in civilian clothes but heavily armed.

Decision. Ota thought he recognized the man in charge by the descriptions of the Gestapo chief that Ice had given. He had fired at him when they first entered the church, but hit the man in front of him.

The bastard didn't show himself the second time. When did you realize that a man could be killed if he went against other men who were armed and meant to take as many of you as possible before he died? What does this do to your strategy?

Ota waited until most of the Germans cleared the screen in front of the altar before he lobbed the last grenade. It was a good toss, better than the one that took Heydrich to his grave. The blast lit the church like an oven, bleaching the angels in the ceiling to ghosts, throwing pews like paper, blowing out the windows, the doors, everything, including the lights.

* * *

SS Gruppenfuhrer von Treuenfeld responded quickly to von Pannwitz's call. He left his command post at the high school and made his way to the church. Heavy fire still came through the two rear windows. Thick smoke from the smoldering wall hangings obscured the interior. The altar was overturned, the relics and statues and candelabra scattered and burning. Plaster dust hung in the air like thick fog, vaporizing in puffs of green smoke and flame.

"Have the heavy weapons cease fire," said von Pannwitz in a voice higher than he liked. "It's chaos in here. Your men are firing at everything. I can't even get the wounded out."

"How many are you fighting?"

"At least three."

"Not an army then."

Von Pannwitz did not appreciate the sarcasm. His squad was nearly half of what it had been. Four wounded, one dead, and the rest so shocked by the force of the explosions that they would not answer for hours.

"We need troops with combat experience," he said. "These men are parachutists trained in England."

Von Treuenfeld nodded. "So you think they're the ones who assassinated the Protector?"

"Yes. They must be taken alive."

"We'll do our best."

* * *

The first SS squad moved low and quick into the area of dense smoke behind the altar, where they began to put out rifle and submachine-gun fire. Then they started to move men out into the open.

Ota hit the first one out, a lucky shot, and it seemed to surprise them. For a moment the heavy fire slackened. These were soldiers. They wanted to know exactly what was out there and they didn't want to know late.

Ota moved behind the wall toward Eugen three paces, fired, moved another pace, and fired.

No hits and a lot of return, most of it high. The SS were keeping their heads down, using the cover of the altar and the doors from the hall, because the high ground in the gallery gave the angle. But they were counting.

"They'll rush the stairs now."

Kral nodded. He had a pistol in each hand and several clips for each. They all had plenty of ammunition.

Ota reared and fired at the altar, emptying his pistol before he hit the floor and rolled back along the gallery toward the windows. No machine-gun fire had come from across the street since the SS moved into the church. Taking a chance that they were under orders not to fire, Ota turned his back to them and worked his way into the niche that looked out onto the rear of the church.

Reloaded but did not fire. Waited.

There were two doors from the corridor into the church—one that came in behind the altar and a second well back in the nave. They would use the second one for their assault because it was closer.

As he was thinking that, four men ran from the corridor toward the staircase to the loft. Ota fired from twenty yards with a bench-rest. Eugen fired from fifteen yards with a slightly worse angle but with almost as good effect. Two down and four more coming. One of those down and five more coming when finally Kral began to answer.

Good. Good. Firing down that winding staircase was like firing into a funnel. The screams that followed sounded up the stone staircase at ten times the volume. Within seconds, the SS men came blowing back out the bottom.

Ota was firing and Eugen was firing and Kral was firing and the SS were in retreat, hobbling and wounded, not bothering to return the fire that they couldn't see, wanting just one thing—to get out of the death trap that was their way to the top.

The only way.

The men behind the altar retreated into the corridor, too, and for the next ten minutes the silence in the church was broken only by the hiss and pop of things burning.

Ota had been worried that the fire would spread everywhere, but the thick stone walls did not take the flames. The smoke thinned, clearing the nave, and morning light began to drift down through the highest windows. None of these things worked for the enemy.

They came again at full light, charging from the corridor carrying armor plate from one of the personnel carriers in the street. Ota stayed tight in his niche, firing at the ones who followed, while Eugen went to join Kral at the steps. With two men firing into the staircase, the narrow winding space filled with so many ricochets that it didn't matter if the SS were armored from head to foot. They retreated again, using the plate as a shield as they crossed back to the corridor.

"Report!"

"All clear," said Ota to Kral. "They're back in their hole."

"One wounded here," said Kral, holding up his arm. "But I'll manage."

Ota looked at the blackening stain that had begun to foul the sweater along Kral's lower arm. At the distance, the wound did not seem serious unless they were still in this loft tomorrow. Ota would have gone across to the staircase to help, but Eugen had already begun to tie off Kral's arm with a piece of his shirt.

"Why don't they come with everything they have?" said Eugen. "All they're showing us is their balls."

"That's what the SS does," said Kral, who seemed elated to be losing blood. "It's what they use for brains."

"That's what the SS does when they've orders to take men alive," said Ota. "We'll be able to hold them off until their orders change."

And that will be all, Anna.

* * *

She carried the tin with the leek soup and the package of salve from the doctor that she would be leaving with Father Petrek. Anna smiled every time that she thought of his office. Such a nice man to have such uproarious things happening in his best chair.

She noticed that the motor traffic was thicker than usual in the area, a little crazier, but thought nothing of it as she rounded the corner to Resslova. Just as she did, Anna saw the barricade in the street a block away.

She slowed, wanting to stop, but kept walking. Before she had taken many steps, Anna heard the first loud noise. An explosion. A bomb? It traveled some distance, coming twice down the street, like an echo but closer.

As she approached to within twenty feet of the barricade, Anna thought she heard small sounds, too. Rapid. Like stitches of sound. Many. So many.

Anna stopped. Another loud noise, direct and without its ghost, boom-popped. The stitches of sound, which she now recognized as gunfire, began again.

The church? She moved to the side of the street, to the curb, to look between the armored cars that blocked the way.

It was the church. She could see down Resslova Street for two blocks to the scattered cars and trucks that surrounded the building.

"Move on," said the SS man who came toward her with a black machine pistol. "It's none of your business. Move your pretty ass along."

* * *

Eugen was dead. He had been hit by a grenade that shattered the lower half of his body, but he kept firing until the SS reached the top of the stairs. Silently, staring at the men who were moving toward him, he put a bullet through his head.

Ota and Kral fought from the niches behind the columns as long as they could, but when two bodies piled up at the top of the stairs, the SS used them as cover to heave grenades down the length of the loft. Poor tosses, but bothersome, noisy, putting smoke and the stench of it everywhere.

The niches were deep, carrying from the crypt below up to the rafters, but if one grenade found the angle, it would be over for them. Over and maybe not dead. Trophies.

The only fallback was the rafters above. The church was tallest toward the bell tower at the rear, and the rafters ran off it with headroom. If they could gain some time and space, they could make the jump from the ladder-back of one of the chairs.

Ota had one option left. The Molotov cocktail that he rigged yesterday. He wasn't sure how the blast would go with two parts gasoline to one paraffin, but he knew it would blow and put out cover. Giving Kral the signal, he leaned out from behind the niche and let the beer bottle fly.

The explosion was muffled and unseen but for the heat, which came on like Nazi hell. The walls all along the gallery took the taint of fire and behind it smoke gorged out thick and blue-black, penetrating their space and choking through the rags they had wound around their faces.

Now there were screams. Violent screams.

What was wrong with the smell of burning flesh when it was your enemy's? And why was it not even better?

* * *

Because it was his turn with the iron bar, Zdenek tried to keep working through the din that rumbled above their heads like rolling thunder. One explosion. Automatic weapons fire in volume. Handguns at an increasingly faint distance but still making the count.

Zdenek jammed the bar into the wall and felt it pop all the way through. He levered the bar and dumped three stones from the wall at once, jumping back so they wouldn't break his feet.

He knelt at the foot of the pile and lit a kitchen match. Yes, this was bad. The worst. Clay.

Zdenek took some in his hand and squeezed it. Dry, but still spongy. A city could be built with this shit, but lacking something as simple as a shovel, they would never dig through it. Using the iron bar was like punching sand.

And he had hoped for a secret passage. Or a sewer.

Suddenly, the noise from above changed character. It came from the gallery, and higher up, more distant, and the automatic fire ratcheted a notch.

Ota. They had been together so much for three years—for the last six months inseparable, living like twins in the womb of war—that Zdenek thought he would know from the pain in his heart when his friend died.

He was still alive, yes.

For how long?

* * *

Kral was still active, hit twice but doing good work as he moved with Ota's help into the rafters. They spidered over the ceiling joists toward the buttresses, where a small platform of planks sat on top the crossbeams. Saddling the crossbeams, they covered their asses with mere wood.

The SS had been stunned by the slow blast as it blew across the loft, but when the smoke cleared, they came out again, one man posting and a second forward, using the overturned benches for cover, expecting another petrol bomb.

Ota waited until they were big enough in his sights that it didn't blot them. They jumped into the gap easily, but correcting for altitude was difficult. Lower. Always lower, and watch the recoil.

He and Kral fired almost at once. Ota saw the helmet of his mark blow like a nutshell, but the man didn't go down quick. He heaved backward, his weapon followed under him, his body covered it, he spun, pointed, and began to fire as Ota returned two more rounds and pinned him to the floor.

He screamed: "FUCK! FUCK THIS PLACE!"

Didn't they always say: I'm hit? Help me, I'm hit. For God's sake.

No God in the SS. No help. The others kept to the niches and still didn't seem to know how many guns faced them. It was like that when fire came from above. Too tall, too sudden.

Ota heard shouts. Orders. He couldn't understand the words but results came fast as the SS began to direct concerted fire at the rafters, chopping out strips of wood and stone like shale.

Ota and Kral began firing, keeping up a return as well as they could, but the SS did not back off. The discharges were constant, rising, rising. Most of the ricochets carried through the buttresses and ran higher. The rest battered around the crossbeams or off them, hitting Ota once, twice, in the legs.

It was surprisingly easy to ignore the pain. Why? Because it was just a step in the process? He wasn't going to be able to stand again soon, but where was the need for it? What law of the church said that a man had to have a left calf or a right ankle when he left this world? If you don't like it, send me back for them.

Now the SS were posting forward again, slower, more carefully. Constant bursts of fire. Impossible to draw down. Impossible to keep them off.

The end would come when they got into place well enough to lift a grenade into the rafters. The opening was narrow, less than four feet, but stick grenades with handles gave leverage to an average arm and made it better than it should have been.

There were a lot of average arms down there. At least a dozen men had forced the stairs. They had to be careful that the grenades didn't fall back onto them and they had to let fly quick unless they liked holding them live behind their ears.

Ota saw a man with blond hair who looked like Heydrich flash into the open, his helmet thrown back to allow him a free swing, his arm careening back and then swishing forth.

The toss fell short, the grenade hit the beam and sent gray uniforms clattering back along the planks behind the pillars. It blew late, falling all the way to the floor, hesitating, one, one-and-a-half, then blowing, lifting Ota three inches off the beam, taking out a row of benches and pulling down plaster like shrapnel. Thick white dust blew past them into the recesses of the roof and beyond.

The beams were white.

Kral was white.

Ota knew the SS would come up again, following chaos like its dogs, but they would find it hard to regain the angle. He and Kral fired and fired again, bracketing that six-by-twelve space. Hits? Who could tell?

The Germans stayed head-down, weapons high and firing blind, walking their submachine guns across the ceiling by feet and then by inches until the planks began to shred like cork and the debris climbed so thick and fast in the air that it became hard to breathe and even harder to see.

"When they stop!"

Kral nodded. He seemed to nod.

They held tight to the beams, making themselves as small as they could, waiting, feeling the plaster and boards crumbling beneath them, hit with fragments that felt like bullets and might have been, knowing that when the automatic weapons fire died the SS would charge.

And they did, quickly. Three rushing forward with grenades. One rearing back and throwing just as he was hit, the grenade falling at his feet, and the other two letting go, one short, very short, but the other coming closer, ballooning, floating toward them as if it knew them.

Ota flashed at it and missed by half a foot. The grenade slowed and seemed to drift up over the boards, as if being laid carelessly on a shelf.

He lunged at it, moving slow, far too slow and ineffectively through a swiftly decelerating pocket of time, wondering what that bastard had meant when he said: Fuck this place.

The loft, the church, Prague, Europe, Earth?

Or had he meant life? The arc of it in time.

Ota saw time just for an instant, lighting in his mind like the bits of phosphor and gold that had been strewn across the workbench in the back of Novotny's shop.

* * *

Kral had been hit, too, but he did not know how badly and did not want to look. He had not lost consciousness when the grenade detonated because Ota had taken the brunt of the blast, absorbed it, and passed little on. At eye level at ten o'clock and stuck firmly to the beam was a whitish piece of striped cloth with meat in it.

Sergeant Kubis, you should be there by now. What's the password? Do we use our real names or our covers with God?

Kral felt overwhelmingly tired. Loss of blood, energy? Loss of hope? Had there ever been enough of either?

He could not allow the miscalculation that would deliver him to the enemy alive. So many things might go wrong. Men had been shot fifty times and survived. They had been burned to cinders, trapped inside a charred husk for years, kept alive by machines that performed every function of living.

Kral swallowed the cyanide capsule. And he put the pistol to his head.

CHAPTER 31

The three bodies recovered in the gallery were bloody and broken. One was literally a body, his eyes goggled and teeth bared in that familiar cyanide grin. The others were alive, but by so small a margin that it did not seem possible they would survive to the hospital.

Von Pannwitz forced himself to look closely at their faces. The results were disturbing. The dead man and one of the wounded did not match the descriptions of the assassins. And none of them was the man known as Ice.

One out of three. If they were all parachutists, that meant there were more than von Pannwitz knew about, plus two still at large.

"Horst."

"Yes, Commissioner."

"Where is Cyril?"

"On the way from headquarters, along with the boy."

"Have this body put outside. We'll want an identification."

"Sir, they could be brought in here."

"And have them see this?"

Horst always reacted well to the obvious. There was more blood on the walls and floors of the church than a stockyard. The windows had been blown out, the hangings and paintings were ashes, the altar smashed, and the door by which the Waffen-SS had charged so many times was a tall incinerated hole.

Three Czechs. Three hundred SS. A three-hour battle with no trophies and no honor.

Von Pannwitz watched the body being carried out the door in a carpet. Something dropped from the open end to the floor. As he bent to retrieve the object, von Pannwitz saw it was an icon. The glass had cracked, perhaps in the fall, but the brushwork was very fine. A nicely stylized Christ under duress. Von Pannwitz slipped the icon into his suit pocket as Horst appeared in the doorway again.

"Commissioner, they're here."

* * *

Cyril did not know what would be asked of him when they were taken from Bredovska Street and driven to the church on Resslova. They passed through roadblocks into a dead zone with nothing in it but screaming ambulances, and finally, around the corner to a street filled with screaming SS carrying submachine guns.

He helped Atya move from the car because the boy was weak and disoriented. They had been together since Cyril was brought to the basement where the boy had been presented with his mother's head in a fish tank. It proved too much. The Gestapo always proved too much.

Now, as they were being led across the street to the church, Atya suddenly stiffened and stopped.

"Don't stop," said Cyril. "Don't look around."

"That man," said Atya. "That one."

Cyril followed Atya's eyes to their destination, which was a short, dapper and completely evil Gestapo superintendent called Pannwitz. Cyril understood the others; they were animals. But Pannwitz was intelligent and tremendously cunning in the way he entered the feelings of the men under torture. What he did was like rape.

"This way," he said.

Cyril tried to move Atya along, but he would not budge until one of the Gestapo yanked his handcuffs and pulled them both along to the spot where Pannwitz stood in front of a carpet with several other officials.

The first was Geschke, the Gestapo chief that Cyril had seen once before briefly. The second was recognizable from all those pictures in the papers: K.H. Frank, the Czech-born German who hated all Czechs. As Deputy Protector, he wore an SS uniform, too.

"Look at this man," said von Pannwitz to Atya and Cyril. "I want an identification."

Von Pannwitz waved at an Oriental rug that stunk of smoke as another Gestapo pulled it back, revealing the bloody figure of a man that Cyril had known well. Stern and calm, his face had been the last thing Cyril saw as he dropped from the aircraft. Now, popeyed, grinning, the face seemed to mock him.

Kral had taken the capsule. It was the same that Cyril kept in his shirt when he walked into Gestapo headquarters. He had thought to let it speak for him if things did not work out, but that was one of the first things they had taken from him.

"Well?" said Pannwitz. Atya shook his head. He rocked from side to side with the movement, as if trying to dig in his heels on the paving stones. Didn't he see it was too late to hold back?

Pannwitz moved closer, centering on Cyril. "A man who once worked as a custom's official never forgets a face," he said softly. "Come, before two million marks cross the border without you."

"Opalka," said Cyril. "This is Lieutenant Adolf Opalka, otherwise known as Kral."

* * *

Cyril and the boy were sent to the hospital to identify the other two men. Von Pannwitz was almost satisfied with the way that things had gone. Opalka-Kral had been the officer in charge of the attempted Pilzn sabotage. No doubt he had directed the assassination from hiding and organized the parachutists' cell in Prague.

"Commissioner, there's something you should know."

"Yes, Horst."

"We found a fourth jacket in the choir loft," he said. "It seems to belong to none of those men."

A fourth jacket? Did that mean another parachutist was close by? Ice? Or the submachine gunner whose weapon had misfired at the Protector? Zdenek. Sergeant Josef Gabcik.

Von Pannwitz took a step back into the street for a better look at the church. It was a bottom-heavy structure. He took another step back. It seemed clear that ground level inside the church was not street level. From its lowest point, seventeen steps led up to the main church doors. Say, a foot per step. Did that mean seventeen feet underground?

"Where's the priest?"

"In his office."

Von Pannwitz turned to the block of houses adjoining the church—the presbytery—as Horst preceded him. "Has he been prepared for questioning?"

"Yes, commissioner. But he's stubborn."

"Doesn't value his life?"

Horst held open the door for von Pannwitz. "It seems."

Von Pannwitz felt the icon in his pocket; his fingers snagged along the damaged glass face. "Every man fears the end of something."

Horst nodded as he opened the next door in the hall that was guarded by two SS scharfuhrers. As it swung open, von Pannwitz saw the man sitting in a swivel chair with his trousers at his ankles. The more important parts of his body—the most private—had been wired to a field-telephone.

"What's going on here?" he asked harshly. "Why is this man being misused?"

The agent with the crank-handle between his knees looked up at von Pannwitz in shock. Horst, who caught onto change quicker, snapped to attention.

"Sir, he collaborated with the parachutists. If there are more, he knows where they are."

"But he's a priest."

"The chaplain, sir."

Von Pannwitz studied the man. With his beard and slanted eyes, he looked like a caricature of a Jew. Their martyrs often stunk strongly of urine and feces, as he did.

"We know where they are," said von Pannwitz to Horst. "We have no reason to punish this man further."

Petrek's eyes came up slowly. He said nothing, but he had understood the German. The end of pain appealed to him.

"Father," said von Pannwitz, making civilized contact with the chaplain's eyes. "Perhaps there's something you can do to help. We'd like to avoid further loss of life and the destruction of this church."

Petrek swallowed hard. "The church can't be destroyed. It's not stone and mortar."

"Well said, Father. But we know the criminals are hiding in the vaults below. I refuse to lose one more man in pursuit of them. I will be forced to use explosives. You must believe that I will bring every stone in this church down on their heads. Every icon. Every candle."

Petrek said nothing, but von Pannwitz knew the threat had touched him. His teeth ground together, as if the electrical leads attached to his scrotum and anus were still pumping pain.

"Father, those men will be taken whether you cooperate or not. You can save their lives—and this magnificent building—by doing what we ask."

"And what is that?"

He had spoken. Praise the Lord. "I want you to show us the way into the vaults—and persuade them to come out peacefully."

"Those men will never give up," he said. "Never!"

So now there were men in the vaults, which was much better than a surmise. Von Pannwitz shrugged hopelessly as he turned to Horst. "Inform Gruppenfuhrer von Treuenfeld that he should mine the building. Evacuate all personnel."

"At once, Commissioner."

As his assistant left by the door with forced rapidity, von Pannwitz moved more slowly toward the same exit. The voice that he heard behind him was plaintive but urgent. "Wait," said Petrek. "Call him back."

* * *

More than forty-five minutes after the grenades had gone off one after another and the small arms fire died and then all fire died, the stone atop the entrance hole opened.

The round light was dim for daytime. The smell of smoke was strong. The following voice sounded clear but weak.

"Boys, I want to talk to you."

Ice stepped forward half a pace. The light from above died by the time it reached the floor of the crypt. He could stand almost directly under it without much danger.

"Petrek?"

The chaplain's face appeared. He had never looked good, Ice decided. Now Petrek looked anguished and decidedly bad.

"Yes, it's me."

"I don't think so," said Ice. "You're someone else."

Petrek hesitated. His face seemed to tighten with pain. "I've been ordered to tell you that you must surrender," he said. "They say nothing will happen to you. All the parachutists will be treated like prisoners of war."

Ice turned to Zdenek. "Isn't that sporting?"

"Tell him we don't want to talk."

Ice winked his nine millimeter at Zdenek, shifted the pistol behind his back, and moved directly under the halo-hole. "I'm afraid we don't want to talk to you, Vladimir. But I'd like to hear that offer from a German."

"Ice," said Zdenek. "Get out of the light."

"It's all right," he said softly. "We're negotiating. It's a frame of mind."

Petrek's face disappeared and for a moment nothing replaced it. Ice found he was a bit spooked standing in the line of fire, but the waiting, and the knowing, had been unbearable. This was better. Much better.

A slice of white face peeked down the hole and disappeared as quickly. Ice strained for a clear view as the voice spoke from around the corner.

"The offer is good," he said in German. "Surrender, and you will be treated as prisoners of war."

"Full rations?"

The face appeared again, just a slice of fair flesh above the nose. Dark hair, dark eyes. Familiar?

"Everything will be done according to international conventions. Your friends have already been taken to the hospital."

Oh, what a dark mind. Could it belong to the Gestapo superintendent in charge of sabotage, infiltration, and the extermination of all parachutists?

"Heinz, is that you?"

The answer was slow but very sure. "Yes, old friend."

Friend? Well, they were. Pen pals. It was stimulating finally to be face to face. The trick was having it full face.

"It's good to see you're out of the basement, Heinz. Why don't you come on down. You'll feel right at home. We'll thrash this out. You'll meet Peter and Paul and all the boys."

"I didn't know there were so many of you."

"Hundreds," he said. "We've got live paras and dead monks by the score."

"I think I'd rather not meet Peter and Paul just yet."

"C'mon, Heinz. Just slip into the hole. It's like nothing you've ever experienced. Shit can't compare."

Ice saw the face edge over the rim of the halo-hole. Not evil at all. More like a cartoon. If he saw a smile, Ice could put those devious brains on the ceiling. Just a little more.

"I'll take your word for that, Sergeant Valcik."

"That's very clever, Heinz."

"Josef Valcik, parachutist," he said. "Ice, resistance leader." And he smiled.

Suddenly, so fast that he surprised himself, Ice brought the pistol up with both hands. He fired three times.

* * *

Incredible, thought von Pannwitz. He had been with the Gestapo seven years and never been fired at. Not even a stray. Yet those bullets had gone past his head by half a centimeter. He had felt the displacement of the atmosphere—the entire universe—in the roots of his hair. He had been touched, yes. His blood seemed to move in his body in completely new ways. Taking these bastards alive would be like living forever.

"Get me an SS shock team, Horst."

* * *

The loudspeaker in the street blared at maximum volume from a position near the ventilator slot: "SURRENDER AND YOU WILL NOT BE HARMED. YOU WILL BE TREATED AS PRISONERS OF WAR TAKEN IN BATTLE. SURRENDER NOW!"

Blackie was at the top of the ladder that had been placed near the ventilation slot. His voice sounded almost gleeful as he relayed what he saw.

"They've got a sound truck and propaganda unit out there. Cameras. Floodlights. This is the big time. We're going to be famous before we die."

"They'll get tired of talking soon," said Zdenek. "Keep your eyes open. Everyone hold position."

If Zdenek knew his SS, it wouldn't be long before they decided to come down the hole. But only one at a time and slowly into darkness that would blind them. Zdenek felt for those sorry assholes. Really. He was worried about the flight of stairs, too, but they had given no sign that they knew about the second entrance. It would be impossible to remove the slab without making a lot of noise.

Petrek wasn't so bad after all. He must have given them the minimum. Possibly, he was about to reappear, because there was a shadow of movement at the halo-hole. Zdenek did not see anything definite, but Ice, who had a better angle, began to laugh.

"Look," he said. "Up the chimney. It's St. Nicholas."

A pair of legs appeared in the hole and dangled. It was a long drop to the bottom, and they had probably tied a rope around him so he could be jacked out as quickly as dead weight could be moved. Dead weight. Dead meat.

Zdenek put in a round just at the knee. Ice hit higher.

* * *

They hoisted the first man back out howling and bleeding from two wounds in very bad places. The medical team got him onto a stretcher and moved him from the nave to the quarters across the hall, but his screams still carried, echoing in the high vaults like insane laughter.

The effect on morale was extraordinarily bad. Every man in the shock team was visibly frightened. They did not want to go into the hole again and their sturmfuhrer did not want to order them into it.

"Those men down there know what they're doing," he said. "They could have killed him. Instead, they took away his knee and his manhood. He'll sit in a chair and stare at the wall for the rest of his life and not even be able to come into his hand."

"Ask for volunteers," said von Pannwitz.

"Commissioner, I've seen men like this before. In Russia. Call them subhuman, but I can tell you that they've made their decision. They won't turn back."

"You seem to have made yours also, Sturmfuhrer."

"They're crack shots!" he said, pleading. "Do you know what it's like to go into a place where you can't see the enemy, but he can shoot your eyes out?"

"Reichsfuhrer Himmler will be disappointed," said von Pannwitz. "He's following these events with the closest attention."

The sturmfuhrer clenched his fists as he turned and looked around the wreckage of the church. "Volunteers!" he screamed. "I want *volunteers*!"

* * *

Scharfuhrer Steinhaus knew that he wasn't going to come through this intact, but it had been so embarrassing for the sturmfuhrer when he called for volunteers and no one stepped forward. He called again with the same result, then one last time. And Steinhaus moved his feet.

Fuck it. He knew better, but when the sturmfuhrer kept going on about Adolf Hitler, who was watching like the blackened angels in the ceiling, waiting for these criminals to be captured, how could a man resist?

He couldn't like this: two days ago Steinhaus' battalion got orders for the Russian Front. Out there they took no prisoners in SS uniform. Steinhaus would settle for a wound that got him a medal and into a hospital and out again into the arms of some horny *blitzmadel* for as long as it took to heal.

He had a plan for how to get between those tits.

Drop not with a rope. Free fall all the way to the bottom with his finger on the machine pistol, clearing the shit away, hitting on the balls of his feet, diving, rolling and firing while the next man and the next came down the chute.

It couldn't be that big a space. His real problem might be ricochets.

But the hole was narrow, hardly any clearance on either side. He would have to jump small and hope his head didn't hit the sides. He'd have to jump perfectly.

"See you in Berlin, Commissioner. I expect the German Order for this."

"Good luck, Steinhaus."

He looked down into the dark hole. No sense doing that for long because it reminded him of a lot of things, all bad. Steinhaus took one step and dropped.

Damn, but his machine pistol slapped the side of the hole and slapped back in his face. He felt his head go back and the helmet graze the hole, and he knew that he couldn't fire, but that wasn't the real problem. He was losing balance, yearning off zero, still trying to get it back when he hit.

On his heels. The jolt went up his body, compressing his spine, sending the shock all the way to the top of his head and throwing him sideways. Steinhaus tried to roll but couldn't get everything to work. He felt the machine pistol under his ribs and used it to pop with.

He came up in a three-point stance, firing in the darkness, looking for flashes, getting one, two.

Which were hits. The shoulder. The leg.

Three, four.

Bad. The last one was very bad.

* * *

Vaclav had been hit in the shoulder, probably with a ricochet. There wasn't much they could do about it but stanch the bleeding and make a sling out of his vest. It was the one they always used to make morning coffee, of which there had been none this day.

Not that it was hard to stay awake. Zdenek had been running on adrenaline for almost five hours, and on excitement for the last. For the first time in weeks, he felt warm in this frozen place. Even the tips of his fingers and toes were hot.

Is that how Ice felt all the time? Impervious to the cold, hot to the touch. Nuts.

"Look at this," he said, holding up an object that could not be seen in the darkness. "St. Nicholas came bearing gifts. Two extra clips."

Zdenek had known for a long time that it was good to have a lunatic on his side. He did not want to touch that SS man lying in blood. Ice had him undressed down to his underwear.

"Cigarettes," he said, as he threw the pack onto the iron cot. "Almost a full pack."

Christ in heaven. He had been out since early yesterday. They had all been out and now they converged on the cot, all but Blackie, who had climbed back up the ladder to keep the view of the street. That was their only window on the outside and it was more vital than ever now. The Nazis would not come down the halo-hole again unless it was with a lot more firepower.

Ice produced a lighter as he joined them around the cot. "Compliments of SS Deutschland," he said, cupping his hands around the weak flame. "These scum want for nothing."

"Is he dead?"

"And gone," said Ice. "Somebody hit him twice in the chest. I wouldn't say the heart. Nothing there."

Zdenek lit another cigarette and walked across the width of the crypt to the ladder where Blackie stood watch. He handed the butt up as Blackie took two steps down.

"Anything new?"

Blackie took a deep drag, closed his eyes, and wavered as if he would swoon off the ladder. He exhaled and took another long drag before he spoke.

"They're up to something, but I can't tell what. They've called in the fire brigade."

Firemen? To put out the fires in the church? Not likely. They had all morning to do that and didn't think it worth the trouble. There would be another reason. A strategy.

"Have they brought all their equipment?" asked Zdenek. "The trucks and pumps?"

"Yes, indeed."

* * *

A few minutes later they knocked Blackie off the ladder with a round of heavy fire. He fell ten feet, hit hard on his back, but hadn't taken a bullet.

As soon as he knew that Blackie was all right, Ice went up the ladder. He got his foot on the second rung when he heard something hit the bars that blocked the ventilation slot. Not gunfire. More like a hammer.

Three rungs and another blow. Two more and a third. Ice was at the top with his hands when the third blow hit the bars and broke them out as he got his pistol up and fired through the open space at the man—a fireman who dropped immediately against the front of the building.

Missed. Thought he did. Ice pulled himself up, leaned over the slot and blind-shot down the front of the building.

He fired three times before he caught hell. A hundred rounds—a thousand—came from every direction. They sizzled through the slot, every fiftieth one screaming into the crypt and finding new life. Ice dropped to the floor. He hit and rolled.

That ladder was no place to be.

* * *

Von Pannwitz watched the SS men drop the tear gas canisters down the hole, then move the stone back into place, sealing the crypt again.

Something nagged him. It was what Sergeant Valcik had said before he decided on murder. The near-death experience had been so profound that von Pannwitz overlooked the clue.

He said that dead monks were down there. In other words, that the crypt was catacombed. From his studies at seminary, von Pannwitz recalled the crypts of several different churches that he had seen. They all had relics buried below. The sword that had pierced the side of Christ. The robe that he had worn on His last day. Etcetera.

It was the medieval form of a tourist trade, and often, if the churches were old enough, the crypts held the remains of the saints who had built that particular house of god into thriving centers of trade—the cardinals, bishops, priests and monks.

Yes, the monks. Peter and Paul. There would be monks buried in the crypt and there must be some way to get those august bodies underground other than a small hole in the floor. Usually, the elect were interred with pomp and ceremony—a high mass, a choir, a procession.

"Commissioner von Pannwitz!"

He looked up to see a SS officer. "Yes."

"Deputy Protector Frank informs you that the criminals have thrown the tear gas canisters out the ventilation slot into the street. The Deputy Protector wishes to know what you plan to do to correct the situation."

"Tell him we should be inside the crypt in a few minutes."

"Yes, sir."

An exaggeration? Von Pannwitz did not think so. He gave orders to have all the carpets taken up, all the furniture moved, and every inch of the floor searched for the second entrance.

* * *

Ice had gone up the ladder again to eject the tear gas, but it was impossible to stay and observe or return fire for long. The SS kept up a steady stream of automatic weapons fire from the street and the windows of the buildings. The fire was inaccurate, and the rounds that came through the slot usually buried themselves in the walls, but they were a constant threat and a certain promise for anyone who climbed the ladder.

The SS tried to correct the situation by putting floodlights at the ventilation slot, but Zdenek took it out with one burst of the submachine gun. Now there were only two clips left.

Clearly, ammunition would be a problem. They had plenty the night before until it was parceled out to the men who went up into the choir loft. They still had quite a bit left—several clips apiece for each of their pistols—but that just *seemed* like a lot. If the SS breached the crypt, the expenditures would be uncontrolled and uncontrollable. Reserves would go quickly.

Zdenek lit another cigarette and threw the pack across the way to Ice. They were both forted behind the huge pillars that kept the church from falling into Resslova Street. The pillars gave good cover with deep recesses that would keep almost everything off but a severely angled ricochet.

The second cigarette was nearly as mystical as the first. Zdenek felt light-headed, good, focused, until he began to hear those distant sounds.

A thump.

Another. Another.

Now a rhythm. Someone was beating on the floor of the church upstairs. He thought he could feel fine dust descend on his head, shaken loose from the ceiling, but that was probably his imagination.

"What's going on, Blackie?"

"I'm afraid they found the way," he said from his position at the pillar near the bottom of the stairs. "They're using hammers on the stone."

Zdenek ran zigzag along the pillars until he reached the stairs, then went up half a dozen steps, stopping when Blackie stopped on the step above.

The hammers pounded in a steady rhythm almost directly above his head. Big hammers. The Prague Fire Brigade came well equipped.

"It'll take them a while," said Blackie. "Using sledgehammers on that stone is like whittling a tree."

"Unless they tire of it."

Blackie nodded. "Dynamite."

The SS had not used explosives against the crypt. It was obvious that they wanted to take Heydrich's killers alive, but that wouldn't last forever. They had done it the hard way in the choir loft until they decided that their losses were unacceptable.

"Zdenek!"

He turned toward Ice, who was invisible down the length of the crypt. "Hoses!" screamed Ice. "Hoses at the slot!"

* * *

Up the ladder again. Ice wouldn't have gone for all the pleasures of Mrs. Pannwitz's orphan twat, but when the SS put the hoses in the slot, they blocked the fire that had been coming sporadically into the crypt.

All right. He had shit for an angle on the street through the hoses, but if he leaned over the slot, the view opened up thirty degrees. Enough. Ice saw the pump team, Czechs, and three SS with rifles for a guard.

Shiny buckles on their belts and a row of silver buttons running down to the crotch. Ice got a certain hit on the first shot.

The response was immediate. The dumb bastards seemed not to care about shooting up the hoses, because they fired from everywhere, mostly high, and Ice swung back along the ladder until he was holding onto it by his fingers and jamming the muzzle of his pistol into the wall for traction.

Not a good idea, but it gave him the leverage to swing back just when he thought they would be picking that sorry prick up and carting him away.

Three. One at his legs and two on his shoulders. Ice drew down and fired half a clip. One probable hit, but they all went to the ground.

Then something struck the side of the slot and sprayed his face with debris. He fired again within the burst and his hand suddenly jumped back in his face. His pistol flew in the air, he flew, flailing his arms and reaching out for the rungs and missing, turning in mid-air for a header, waiting for the ground when something softer than stone broke his fall. Blackie. They were both on the ground but only one had a hand that was totally numb and a pistol gone to hell.

Ice began to move his good hand around him on the floor, searching for his weapon, when the pain came. He bit into his shoulder. No loud noises. Zdenek would be pissed if he heard a scream that let the Nazis know they had scored.

He thought he might have blacked out, because suddenly the light in the crypt grew dimmer. Down and down and out.

"They blocked the ventilator," said Blackie.

Ice looked up. Yes, they had.

He was staring up at the slot when with a hiss and a jerk like a gigantic muscle the hose began to gush water into the crypt.

CHAPTER 32

With their field knives they cut the hoses, and using the ladder pushed the torrent of foul water back into the street. Next, they pushed away the mattress that the Nazis had brought up to block the ventilation slot, but as soon as the aperture was clear, the SS pounded the small space with everything they had.

Then they began to pound literally. Bringing up a truck with a huge timber battened to the rear, they leveled it like a ram at the level of the crypt.

The big Adler reversed and slammed the side of the church three times. The first run bounced and crashed but did no damage to the wall. The second knocked the ram backward into the cab and nearly toppled it into the street. With the cab teetering on its mount, they made a third and feebler try that saved the driver's life but hardly raised a noise inside the crypt.

The SS had to tow the truck away with a broken axle and a dangling cab. That gave Blackie a chance for harassing fire. He was a good shot, better than Ice, who was a left-handed gun until he got his fingers back. Shouting taunts out the slot, Blackie delivered fire to effect until automatic weapons began to bracket the slot again. He bolted then and took cover behind the first pillar.

They kept their heads tight against the wall and the pillars, because ricochets were the biggest problem. Once a bullet got inside the crypt, it was free to run. Eight walls. Ten walls. Until it stopped.

Zdenek was counting, holding his breath, when he sensed a lull in the volleys, dying outside, then more slowly in. He was already moving toward the slot when the fire brigade brought a hose up and pushed it into the crypt again.

It entered the slot like a slithering prehistoric thing as Zdenek called to Blackie before the water began to roar. "Give me a hand with the ladder."

Blackie could see what was needed. He tipped the end of the ladder back toward Zdenek and jumped to the middle rungs.

With no room for miscalculation, and just a bit of luck, they got the ends of the ladder into the mouth of the severed hose as the water gushed again, this time with a stronger blast that almost knocked them down.

God, it was cold when it poured over your head through your clothing into your shoes. Stinking water pumped up from the river full of shit, bottom-sediment and chemicals. Zdenek felt like he was melting into the frigid blast, his body dissolving.

It would have been hard enough with the force of the water, but they were meeting resistance from the other side and could do nothing to discourage it. The fireman and SS stood right outside the slot, pushing back.

The only thing that Zdenek and Blackie had working was leverage with the ladder. Slowly, braced by their bodies and all the strength that they had, the hose began to move back out the slot. Counting by half-inches now. Quarters. Frigid quarters. When it was nearly gone, peeping from the slot, they heaved together on a count and threw it all the way out.

They must have stopped then, drew a breath, looked at each other for congratulations, when the end of the ladder flew up and leapt toward the window. Blackie barely got a hand on it, and suddenly he was going up, kicking air.

Zdenek grabbed for his waist, got the knees, and held on for their lives. If that ladder was lost, their only outpost on the street was gone. He felt himself going up too, rising off the ground, screaming, "Ice! Ice!"

Zdenek heard the slosh across the crypt, heard the crazy voice say, "Hang on!" and at the same time felt a superhuman drawing away from the other side. He had no idea what the SS had done—what they were using—but they were winning fast, moving Blackie toward the wall so quickly that he hit it hard, let go, dropped off, and dropped them both down into the water.

The water rose to their ankles and then to their knees when the hole opened again. They gave it respect this time, because it seemed likely that smoke or explosive grenades would follow. Instead, a familiar but hopelessly forlorn voice called to them.

"Com-m-m-m-rades!"

"No," said Ice. "It can't be."

"Com-m-rades! Can you hear m-m-me?"

Zdenek said nothing. He had known it was Cyril as soon as the man began to stutter. For hours he had wondered about who gave them up, deciding, at last, that it was irrelevant. It had happened and that was all.

But this was worse. Much worse. Cyril knew enough to wreck the resistance nationwide. Radio Libuse and all the people in Pardubice could be taken out. Auntie Moravcova, Uncle, and if either talked, the entire network, including Libena and his child. Everything they had worked for and loved might be brought down because Zdenek had refused to waste a bullet.

"I'm sorry," he said. "He's my fault. I had the chance in Pilzn to be sure of him."

"Do you think he'll show himself?"

Zdenek shook his head. Cyril was not a stupid man, just one of the most nervous. And one of the last that should have been sent on a mission behind the lines.

"Comrades, listen! I s-s-s-urendered and am being treated well. Give yourselves up. Kral took his life with his own hand. Eugen and Ota died on the way to the hospital. There's no way out."

"There's one, you son-of-a-bitch!" said Ice. "You can die like a man."

He fired twice up the hole at nothing.

* * *

Dressed in his gruppenfuhrer's uniform, Deputy Protector Frank entered the church with his entourage. He seemed distracted by the damage that lay everywhere, and his irritable voice arrived in spasms.

"A few minutes, von Pannwitz?"

"Gruppenfuhrer, these men have nowhere to go. They have no way to fight back. Patience will bring us what we want."

"What is that?"

"Justice," said von Pannwitz. "Obergruppenfuhrer Heydrich's assassins must be captured and brought to trial. That would be a fitting tomb."

"And how long will this take?"

"The water will do its work, Gruppenfuhrer."

Frank shook his hawk-like head. "The water level is rising slowly in the crypt. Why?"

"It may be a larger space than we think," said von Pannwitz. "These old churches were built over generations with great care given to the foundations."

"Yes," said Gruppenfuhrer von Treuenfeld, stepping forward from the pack. "Built like fortresses. How do you know the water won't escape through hidden passages? The criminals could find the same way out."

"I doubt that. Or they would have gone long ago."

"But if the water shows them a way—"

Von Pannwitz found that he could not answer a hypothetical question with an answer that might cost him his head. His only weapon was logic.

"Sir, we could have taken these men at any time if our object was to liquidate them. They are the last of the assassins. They must be taken alive."

"They're making fools of the SS!" Von Treuenfeld screamed as he turned to Frank. "That can't be!"

Von Pannwitz also spoke to Frank. "Sir, don't turn them into martyrs. That's a terrible mistake."

The Deputy Protector's career as a bookseller in a spa town in Bohemia had not prepared him for command. The struggle for coherence was plain in his face, as was the automatic reflex.

"We have a pitched battle in the center of Prague," he said. "A thousand men against a handful. Word will spread. We could have a major insurrection on our hands."

Von Treuenfeld clicked his heels. "Have I your order?"

Frank nodded.

* * *

For some reason, the SS shut down the water coming into the crypt. That was good, for otherwise they never would have heard it. Ice, standing guard at the stairs, tapped twice for Zdenek to join him.

"What?"

Ice put his finger to his lips and pointed upward. Zdenek listened. A distant slick sound. Whining but within a variable band.

"A drill?"

"Two drills."

That could mean several things, but the sounds seemed to come from the slab that overlay the entrance to the staircase. Zdenek moved up the stairs quietly, taking the latrine bucket that had been placed on the second step to keep it out of the water.

Third step from the top, he stopped and put his ear to the corner of the slab. Ice was right. Two drills. They were boring into the stone at high speed, which could only mean one thing.

Zdenek emptied the shit bucket on the steps and made his way back into the crypt. The staircase was wide enough for two men abreast if they were unencumbered. Troops with weapons and ammunition would be forced to descend in single file, which could not be better for concerting fire.

When he reached the bottom of the stairs, Zdenek brought the others to him in front of the second story tomb where they had placed Vaclav to protect him from the rising water. Though his shoulder was badly torn up, and he had lost a lot of blood, he had not made one sound.

"Can you still handle a pistol?"

Vaclav nodded, but he would have done that if he had been unconscious.

"Watch the hole," said Zdenek. "Make damned fine noise if they come."

"Are you sure they will?" asked Blackie.

"They're drilling the slab," said Zdenek. "They'll blow that at least. Maybe a lot more. As soon as the area is clear, they'll charge the stairs and probably drop down the hole, too."

"Let me take the stairs," said Blackie. "I'll guarantee them a thrill."

"Do it," said Zdenek, hefting the submachine gun. "I'll stand by the second pillar and moderate. Ice opposite."

Zdenek put out his hand. It was covered by three hands. "Let's give them something to remember."

* * *

Jindra was not quite to Charles Square when he saw the Czech policemen directing traffic away from the square and the streets that led to the Dietzenhofer Bridge. Something was unquestionably wrong.

Instinct told Jindra to detour and never return. For the last thirty-six hours the silence that arrived from all the usual places had been ominous. Most disturbing was the complete lack of contact with Uncle.

He pulled the hearse to the curb and left the motor running as he got out and approached one of the policemen.

"Is there any chance of getting through this way?"

"Absolutely none," said the fellow in the tall crested cap. "If you passed here, you'd still have to deal with the SS."

"Trouble?"

The question was a bit too direct, Jindra realized late. The policeman—an older man with a silver mustache—looked at him like a suspect.

"Where are you going?"

"To the church to pick up some dead bodies," said Jindra. "It's what I do."

"Which church?"

Jindra did not like the way the question was asked. It was too casual. "Over to St. Ignatius," he said. "On Jecna."

"Good thing it's not the other."

"What do you mean?"

"If you were going to Saint Cyril's, you'd need more coffins than you could fit in that ratty machine."

Jindra shrugged to disguise his dread, and quickly turned toward the hearse. He had seven coffins in there, crowded, but not nearly enough, according to that man. What had happened to the paras? Jindra's hand was on the door, swinging it open, when he heard the noise. It was distant, a sharp explosion, but muffled like a sound in a dream. He swung the wheel and the car turned out of line, but now a man in a dark suit stood in front of him by the curb, pointing one grim finger through the windshield. On the left another appeared. And on the right.

Gestapo.

* * *

The explosion seemed to blow from every direction, roaring above their heads and vibrating through the walls, but the cloud of dust came down the stairs in an orderly way, like a vanguard. If the SS had followed at once, they would have been invisible in the darkness, but they had to clear the slab from the entrance. Ice heard them chucking pieces of rock aside, and the shouted orders from their officer: "*Kurzer! Kurzer*!"

Make it snappy.

Ice could tell when they completed the work—a film of new light shone down the stairway. With that bit of glory at their backs, they'd make silhouettes.

Relax, he told himself. Relax the hand. It was the wrong one, and Ice was not ambidextrous, which made him something like an average shot. How good to be finally average. One of the boys.

Suddenly, something dropped into the water somewhere behind him. Ice turned at the ready, although he was sure the noise could not have been made by a man dropping through the halo-hole.

Again. Again.

"Gas," said Vaclav. "Three canisters."

Ice couldn't see well in the lighter darkness under the hole, but he knew that it didn't much make sense to drop tear gas into water. Slowly—seconds later—small white tendrils began to ride the surface. Little wisps of poison.

Morons. All that did was put them on a timetable. The SS would wait a minute or two for the gas to have an effect before they came in force. Nice to know.

The first sound from the stairs approximately thirty seconds later did not sound human. Clunk-clunk. Clunk-clunk. Like a peg-legged man.

Ice was still wondering what the sound was when Blackie's voice sounded loud: "Grenade!"

Ice was slow shielding his face behind the pillar. He saw the detonation a fraction of a second after the grenade hit the water. A dark bright flash. A hump in the water, a gulping roar as the surface churned and lashed out, throwing spray all the way to his position.

Ice felt the cold shitty water all over. He heard the dull clunk-clunk again.

"Number two!" called Blackie.

Ice humped back behind the pillar. The grenade detonated clear of the water, a bright flash lighting up the entire crypt, blowing hard against the walls, throwing fragments of metal and stone everywhere.

He looked around the corner. Nothing. A swirl of smoke at the entrance to the stairs, backlit by the light seeping through, but no shapes.

"The hole!"

Ice turned as Vaclav screamed and fired. A pair of legs and then a heavy form and a splash. Ice fired. A hit and a scream. A second hit and another splash, slower.

Now there was firing from the stairs. Ice left the hole to Vaclav and took the long view just as the first SS fell head first down the last step, smashing hard into the water.

Blackie fired again and Ice followed. Knowing that he had missed, Ice fired again but Zdenek did not. What the hell was he doing?

Two SS jumped the last step, vaulting over the body in the water and landing low, hip deep in the water. At least two more came directly behind them, charging down the stairs and firing with their submachine guns at their knees. Blackie was under pressure but still firing and Ice was peeking and firing and the ricochets were sawing off the walls every bad fucking way when Zdenek finally spoke.

With a long controlled burst, he took out the two crouched in the water, flipping them like coins, then very deliberately began to walk the fire up the stairs, sweeping it like a broom until the clip was exhausted.

He ejected and fired again. After that, there was nothing but smoke and silence until one of the SS on the stairs ripped off his gas mask and began to scream.

* * *

"Numbers?"

"One over here," said Blackie. "I'm hit in the hip. No problem."

"Two," said Ice. "Intact."

"Three," said Vaclav.

Two whole men and two half. That was bad, but not the end. Not yet.

The bodies of the SS almost blocked the stairs. Zdenek did not see how the rest—and there would be many more—could get into the crypt to do their work . . . unless they blasted the bodies away, the wounded along with the dead.

Would they do that? Better question: would they do it to take the men who had killed Heydrich?

"They'll clear the staircase with explosives," he said. "But when they reach the bottom, they'll have the same problem with the water. Try not to give them a long toss."

That might be harder than it seemed. Stick grenades were not much for accuracy but just fine for distance. The best thing was not to allow them the chance to toss. They would have to be stopped on the stairs again with only half a clip of rapid fire left.

The men at the bottom of the stairs—the ones in the water face down—would have ammunition. Zdenek did not want to bet his life on their weapons, but the cartridges were waterproof. And the grenades.

He moved out as fast as he could but quietly, shifting the water more than stepping, hugging the wall for cover, making his way from the deep recesses of one pillar to the next. When he reached the pillar near the bottom of the stairs, across from Blackie, he tested the light.

The weak gleam on the water did not waver when he drew the barrel of the gun across it. Nothing. Zdenek took another step, skirting the entrance and bringing him even with the dark hump in the water. He saw only one.

The dull shining thing that caught the glow would be its helmet. It lay face up, floating but not drifting in the shallow water.

Zdenek took the thing under the chin with one hand and under the shoulder with the other. He pulled gently but firmly, and again more firmly when it seemed to be stuck. Just a foot out of the weak light and he could reach the ammunition belt safely.

"Grenades!" screamed Ice. "Grenades!"

In the back down the hole.

"Grenades!" screamed Blackie.

In the front down the stairs. Zdenek heard them, too, but late.

He didn't think he had time to reach the recess behind the pillar, so he heaved on the body. It was heavy, stuck, waterlogged. He had gotten his arms under its shoulders just as two grenades detonated under the hole.

Almost no flash, little noise, but the concussion blew all the way through the crypt like a personal earthquake and the water geysered high. Zdenek had the body to his shoulders for cover but he was falling back, slipping into the water up to his chest, the thing pressing him down. If he went under completely, the force of the explosions underwater would mean his brains in his hands. The end.

He held against the wall when the first grenade blew on the stairs. The flash screamed from the opening, flooding the white walls with light and hurtling debris, some of it human.

The second grenade blew on the stairs, too, lifting a shapeless mass out into the water. A zombie. Zdenek was deafened by the concussions. He did not hear the third grenade come down the stairs or see it fall into the water, but suddenly the darkness all around him surged and leaped high, taking him by the feet and driving him back along the wall.

With the dead thing. Zdenek held on to it, held it close, while the barrage of grenades continued to drop down the stairs and through the halo-hole. The surge of water was continuous, throwing him toward the ventilation slot one way and against the wall in the other. The water climbed the walls and churned high toward the ceiling, looping and crashing.

The backlash might have been the reason that he did not lose consciousness. The water rose in his face and over his head and up his groin, cold and slimy, a shock every time. When it stopped, Zdenek felt the adrenaline that had kept him going stop, too. He felt dazed, weak.

This was the time when they would come. The shock team right behind the shock.

They're coming now, Zdenek.

* * *

When he saw Zdenek rise up, throw something aside, and try drunkenly for the pillar, Blackie stepped out from the wall and fired into the stairway.

It was weird when you couldn't hear and could only half-see and your ass was busted out your trousers, but it was worse for them because they couldn't see at all and the ricochets up that staircase made every shot like ten.

C'mon, SS Deutschland. I'm over here. Here now to the right.

And then he saw the shape come down the stairs and it was wrong. Spinning. Or: tumbling.

Blackie fired. He thought that he hit it but the shape completed the circle, lifting itself over the meat that was left at the bottom of the stairs, turning, splashing into the water. Answering with a submachine gun. He heard the rounds dig in the water to the left and some of them sheer off from the water and ricochet, rounding out of the other side of the crypt. Blackie got off another shot, hit him, hit him good, when he felt the tear in his side.

Hit from behind. The Second Coming or maybe the Fifth. He reached down and felt the wound and the hard pointed thing stuck and pushing at his belly. Hit? No, he was pierced through at the side.

And there were more coming down the stair, not tumbling but tramping hard. Blackie fired twice and got nothing on the last. He ejected and worked in another clip when he saw three flashes to the left.

Zdenek. Another shape on the stairs went headlong suddenly, tumbling, but out of control. Screaming.

Who was the best shot in the Czech Brigade?

Hell, it was still a contest.

Blackie fired and hit. Fired and hit. Fired and fired and got another hit, he thought. Fired. Fired.

Another clip. Did he even have another clip?

Blackie moved sideways, planning on a fall, as he sloshed into the water behind the pillar. He slid into the muck softly.

It was up to his neck, almost. It stunk like a sewer, and by God, if that wasn't a turd by his nose.

A turd.

He knew he should pull himself up. Sometime soon, one of those bastards would throw another grenade in the water, and with the blast his heart would stop. But why did it want to keep on beating?

* * *

"Blackie! Blackie!"

Zdenek screamed when the booming on the stairway stopped and the flashes from Blackie across the way stopped at almost the same time.

If they lost their triangulated fire on the staircase, they were finished. If Blackie was finished, they had to maintain his position at the point.

Zdenek took a slow wading step across the crypt, pulling his body like a caboose, when heavy machine-gun fire began to rattle from the top of the stairs.

Fifty caliber? The sound was distant, hollow, but the chain of fire came down the stairs and carried for long seconds. The SS were counting on ricochets off the surface of the water, and they were getting every tenth one, which was plenty.

Zdenek lurched behind the niche. Bullets walloped all around, churning the water, skittering off the walls and ceiling. He pressed hard against the stone, embracing the same cold refuge that he had found from the first day he landed. Mother Earth. Motherfucker.

Think of it. He had hurt his foot on a tombstone. He had languished in a quarry. He had come to these dank catacombs. Why hadn't he seen it?

He had seen it. The firing squad. The man from Kolin. The end that was known. By whom?

Suddenly, the machine gun ceased fire. Zdenek did not try to cross the crypt again. He counted. What was in the magazine. And one spare clip.

Here they come again.

* * *

One of them got lucky. Ice saw him raise his arm, saw the quick forward movement, the follow-through, and knew it was long and dangerous. The grenade disappeared in darkness as it flew down the crypt. If that prick was a champion it might wing all the way to the back wall, hit, and explode out of the water.

Zdenek should have seen it, he should have hugged the wall like Ice was doing, but he maintained fire. Probably killed that son-of-a-bitch, but shouldn't have taken the chance, because the grenade blew just off the surface of the water.

Ice had wrapped his hand around his head but the concussion ripped it away and threw him hard. He hit the water in a sprawl but fell softly onto the stone, aware of everything that had happened. And his deafness. A chunk of the ceiling fell on his shoulders near the base of the neck. The stench of cordite was so strong that it seemed as if he had been dropped from the sky in the middle of this thing. Hadn't he?

And what in hell was he doing now, sitting in dirty water like a baby in his filth?

Ice heaved himself up. The barrel of the CZ gushed water. Would it fire?

Blackie was down, but Zdenek still maintained fire by the flashes. Vaclav, with his shoulder torn away, still fired. What the hell were these people made of?

Clay.

There was clay all around. It had kept them from digging their way out. It meant to envelope them, of course.

Ice stepped out from behind the pillar and walked toward the stairs. Waded. He was well aware that he had lost his mind. Again. As he moved, he fired. Excellent. He took the backup pistol from his belt and got acceptable results. It was easy. Put the rounds right up the stairs like it was a chimney.

Ice saw multiple flashes from the staircase but heard the spatter far away, like pellets. Short and off to the left a grenade whomped big in the water, stopping him and twisting him sideways like a toy. Ice tottered, held, resumed firing.

Got one. A pop that drove the submachine-gun fire directly down into the water. No ricochets.

A hand in silhouette went up again to the left of the stairway but stopped, wavering, as Ice fired again. Got another.

The grenade must have dropped into the water at the feet of SS Deutschland, because the explosion underwater lifted him like a paper dummy. Swear he hit the ceiling. A piece of water struck Ice like a fist. He stopped walking. He had been stopped. The blow brought back his hearing. He was cold, deeply chilled, and the crypt was silent.

The noise had stopped completely.

Targets. Where were the targets?

Something moved in the staircase. It was big and broad-backed and beginning to move away up the stairs. It was climbing.

Ice fired and fired again until the cylinder clicked. Empty. All gone.

What about the other pistol?

* * *

Zdenek saw Ice move toward him in the dark. No one else would come like that—as quiet as death but cocky. No one else would have gone in the clear against the staircase and massed automatic weapons but Ice. And no one else could have done what he had.

"Are you all right?" he asked as he knelt in the water.

"I was hit in the arm and the neck," said Zdenek. "I don't know by what."

"Ammunition?"

"None," he said. "And you?"

"Half a clip."

Zdenek tried to push the pain out of his mind, but it would not go. He began to think of many things very fast. All of them were good things and none touched on this.

"Let's do it now."

"I'll do it," said Ice. "It's my job."

Zdenek knew that Ice had tried to tell him something that should have been known from the beginning. He meant that certain people were born to do unimaginable things. They did them because of who they were.

"See to the others first," said Zdenek. "Hurry. They'll come again."

Ice moved across the crypt to the place where Blackie lay behind the niche. Ice bent down slowly, hesitated a moment, then fired.

He moved on quickly, stopping before the man-sized tomb in the wall where Vaclav lay. Bending over, he spoke softly into the tomb, like a confessor to the dead, then straightened and pointed and the whole black length of the catacombs lit up within the flash.

Ice turned and crossed the crypt again.

Still no noise in the water. Zdenek had heard a little as he went across, but none when he returned. Could he not be heard coming? How weird was that man?

Zdenek had never gotten used to that damned black hair and black mustache. It was as if his friend had been inked and defaced, ruined by a force that was not of his own making and impossible to understand.

Now it didn't matter. Zdenek could see nothing like color in the darkness. He could pretend that Ice was his old self, Josef Valcik, bright and blond. An angel. He put his hand out and took Zdenek's in a quick hard grip.

"Goodbye, Josef."

"Goodbye, Josef."

POSTSCRIPT

Although the assassination of Reinhard Heydrich was the most successful clandestine operation of World War II, and one of the most successful in the history of warfare, the price of success was high.

The Nazis carried on the devastation of the Czechoslovak Resistance for months. Nearly all the people associated with the paratroopers, many related only by blood or circumstance, were murdered by the Gestapo with the help of Karel Curda (Cyril), and Ladislav Vanek (Jindra), who collaborated to the limit of their abilities.

The communications team Silver A vanished when Captain Alfred Bartos (Emil) and radio operator Jiri Potucek shot themselves to avoid capture. The village of Lezaky, which sheltered Radio Libuse, was destroyed. All the men, women and children were shot, except for two small girls spared for Germanization.

The Nazis condemned the churchmen of St. Cyril and Methodius to death on September 3, 1942. At the end of that month, two-hundred-and-fifty-two friends and relatives of the paratroopers were sentenced in Prague. Among them were Libena and her family, Anna, Atya, and many others mentioned casually in this narrative. At Mauthausen Concentration Camp on October 24, 1942, the men were shot, the women and children gassed.

The events symbolized by the destruction of Lidice did not have the desired effect for Hitler's Germany, however. Because the existence of mass extermination camps was not widely known, Lidice came to stand for all Nazi atrocities. The blockbusters that fell on German cities often carried the name "Lidice." Allied tanks went into battle with "Lidice" painted on their turrets. A small village in Czechoslovakia became the revenge cry of Allied victory.

Nothing could deter the grisly fates that awaited the Nazi figures that appear in this story. Major Paul Thummel (Rene) passed the war in Terezin Concentration Camp, where he was murdered in April 1945, with the Allies approaching from both directions. His superior, Wilhelm Canaris, who had taken part in the 1944 bomb plot against Hitler, was executed at Flossenburg Concentration Camp, hung from a meat hook by his ribs.

Adolf Hitler committed suicide in his Berlin bunker on April 30, 1945, crying with his last breath for "scrupulous observance of the laws of race." On May 23, 1945, Heinrich Himmler committed suicide by swallowing a cyanide capsule while in the custody of American Intelligence. Karel Curda, Hauptsturmfuhrer Max Rostock, Gruppenfuhrer Karl Frank, and Obergruppenfuhrer Kurt Daleuge were hanged in Prague after the war.

Heinz von Pannwitz surrendered to the French in Austria in May 1945. He was promptly extradited to the Soviet Union, where he spent the next eleven years in the Gulag.

President Edward Benes lived long enough to see his country disappear behind the Iron Curtain. Colonel Frantisek Moravec (Franta) followed him home before he fled to the West, where he ended his days working for the CIA.

Although the remains of the seven paratroopers who died on the morning of June 18, 1942 were scattered by the Nazis, fresh flowers can usually be found outside the church in Prague-New Town that marks the site of the battle.

In the post-war years, the village of Lidice was rebuilt and repopulated.

In December 1989, Czechoslovakia was finally freed.

Printed in the United States
86777LV00003B/58/A

9 780972 373746